THE INFECTED MAN

THE INFECTED MAN

ROBERT SPINA

To order additional copies of this book, contact:
Xlibris
1-888-795-4274
www.Xlibris.com
Orders@Xlibris.com
727681

Contents

CHAPTER 1

Gerald and Kaitlin Have a Baby Boy

The year is 1968, and Kaitlin is in the Rosewood General Hospital, getting her checkup. Kaitlin is nine months pregnant, and she is going to give birth to her first baby. She is actually due to give birth in two weeks, and she is having her last scheduled exam before childbirth. Her exam goes well, and her doctor asks that she consider one last time the offer that has been extended to her and her husband, Gerald. "Thank you, Dr. Adams, I appreciate that you are concerned about the well-being of our baby, but I feel fine and I know my baby is healthy and everyone here has told me all throughout my pregnancy that everything is normal. I don't see the need to put my baby through all kinds of unnecessary tests."

"I know you are right, Mrs. Hammond. I just want to let you know that all the doctors in the area have been instructed to tell all new parents-to-be that for some reason, in the upstate region of New York, there have been terrible outbreaks of scarlet fever, influenza, tuberculosis, pneumonia, and other diseases that have been taking the lives of young children and especially babies. We are all dedicated to solving this problem, but we need the consent of the parents in order to give two exams per month of the newborn babies. This will be two exams per month for the first six months of the baby's life for a total of twelve exams. The hospital is willing to compensate parents $500 dollars a month for six months in order to examine their baby or babies and make sure they are healthy."

"Wow, Dr. Adams, that is really a lot of money. Let me talk with Gerald, and we will give you an answer before we leave, OK?"

"That sounds good, Mrs. Hammond." Dr. Adams gets up from his chair, carrying his clipboard. "I will get your husband and tell him you are ready to see him."

"OK, thank you. I will get dressed, and we will give you an answer before we leave." Dr. Adams leaves the examining room, and Kaitlin gets dressed. Gerald enters the room and sits down next to Kaitlin, saying, "So did the doctor talk to you about having our child cared for? I think it is a good idea."

"Yeah, he talked to me about it, but I just don't think it is a good idea. I don't think it is a good idea having our baby poked and getting all kinds of vaccines when we don't know what the effects will be."

"I am very surprised to hear you say that, Kaitlin. I thought you of all people would want this. You are the one who is always talking about being healthy and getting all your shots and taking vitamins and things like that."

"Yeah, I guess it would be a good thing. It definitely can't hurt. You are going to have to bring our baby here for his or her checkup twice a month," says Kaitlin.

"That won't be a problem for $500 a month, no problem at all," says Gerald, nodding his head up and down.

Kaitlin looks down and looks up, saying, "OK, let's go tell Dr. Adams we will sign up our baby for twelve examinations for the first six months of his or her life." Gerald helps Kaitlin up, and they exit the room. They are quickly greeted by Dr. Adams and his nurse, and they are already asking if Kaitlin and Gerald have come to a decision.

"Yes, Dr. Adams, Kaitlin and I will allow our baby to have the examinations," says Gerald.

"Good, that is very good. Please come with Nurse Reisen and I. We will have you fill out the proper paperwork," says Dr. Adams. Kaitlin and Gerald go with Nurse Reisen, and she gives them way more paperwork than they had expected. There are pages of writing, and the Hammonds do not read it all. They just ask the nurse what it is and what it is for and she explains. The Hammonds say OK many times and just sign at the bottom of the pages. This process takes about thirty minutes, and when all the paperwork has been filled out, Nurse Reisen tells the Hammonds what a good decision they have made to help protect their firstborn child from all the diseases and fevers that have been taking so many newborn lives. The Hammonds are all set for their first baby to be brought into this world. There are no more scheduled examinations for Kaitlin, but her doctor is always available for her if she needs medical advice or an appointment to be made. For now, she is waiting for childbirth to begin, and the hospital is on alert as any time now, she is expecting to have her first baby. The Hammonds say good-bye and leave to go home. Gerald does not even make it to the car before he lights up a cigarette. Kaitlin does not mind; she smokes as well and is used to Gerald always having a cigarette in his hand. Kaitlin has really cut back her smoking while being pregnant, but she still smokes a few cigarettes a day. Gerald drives them home, and they have no conversation at all. It is a very quite ride home, and once home, Gerald helps Kaitlin into the house, and then he leaves to go to the bar for some beer and more cigarettes. Kaitlin and Gerald are not what you would call a close couple. They get along fine, but they spend a lot of time apart. Kaitlin stays at home a lot now that she is near the end of her pregnancy. She works at the hospital across the street from her house where she helps the mentally handicapped, but she is on leave now until after her baby is born. Gerald spends a lot of his time at the bar right at the end of the street that the Hammonds live on. Gerald works at Xerox and makes a good buck and then spends most of it at the bar and on the car and house payments. The $500 that the hospital offered the Hammonds to consent for their newborn baby to be examined lit Gerald's eyes up, and he was on board as soon as he heard the amount. This is his big topic of conversation at the bar tonight.

Gerald walks into the bar with a big smile on his face and calling to Herb the bartender. "Herb, give me a tall one and one for Harry and Joe." Herb points at Gerald, wiping off his hand on the towel slung over his shoulder, saying, "You got it, Gerald." Herb pulls three glasses and pours three beers from the tap. Gerald sits on the barstool next to Harry. Harry slaps Gerald on the shoulder, asking, "So what got into you, Gerald? You walk right in and buy the first round. I could get used to this."

"Well then, get used to it, Harry, because the hospital where Kaitlin is having our first baby is giving us $500 a month to give our firstborn baby two checkups a month. So that's going to be $3,000 over the next six months, so I will be buying a lot of rounds," Gerald says, laughing and smiling, holding up his beer.

"All right, Gerald," says Harry.

Joe lights up a cigarette and says, "Are you sure that is a good idea, Gerald. You know a lot of babies are dying in the upstate area, and all these babies have so-called doctors giving them checkups, and they are still dying."

"So are you saying that we should not have our baby checked by doctors? Are you saying that the doctors are killing babies? What are you talking about, Joe?" Gerald says with an inquisitive look on his face.

"No, no, I am just saying that a lot of babies are dying and no one knows why," says Joe.

"Joe, where do you get all this nonsense from? Shut up and drink your beer," says Gerald with a sigh, looking at Herb.

"OK, Gerald, but pay close attention to your baby because a lot of babies are dying around these parts and no one knows why," says Joe, taking a drag from his cigarette, followed by a big chug of beer.

"Joe, you just drink your beer, and you let me worry about my baby. My baby is going to have the world by the ass. He is going to be strong and healthy, and he will have everything he wants."

Herb asks Gerald, "What if you have a girl?"

"Well, if it is a girl, then she will have the world by the ass. Girl or boy, my baby will have everything she or he wants."

Gerald lights a cigarette and points at Herb, saying, "Come on, Herb, pour us all another round and pour yourself one as well."

"You got it, Gerald," says Herb, and he pours everyone another round. People start coming into the bar as happy hour is starting. Herb is becoming very busy serving patrons to his bar, and Gerald spends most of the night smoking cigarettes and drinking beer with his friends. He stays until almost midnight and goes home drunk and wobbly. Fortunately he lives very close to the bar, less than a mile away, and actually makes it home without hitting anything with his car. He goes into his house and jumps into bed, smelling of alcohol and cigarettes, and falls quickly to sleep. Kaitlin is already sleeping and barely notices Gerald get into bed. They both sleep, and the alarm goes off at 5:00 a.m., and Gerald is up and has gone to work like he does not miss a beat. Kaitlin does not even wake up. She notices Gerald get up and leave, but she stays in bed and sleeps as this is her favorite thing to do. She sleeps for another three hours and finally gets out of bed to make something to eat. She turns on the little black-and-white TV and watches *I Dream of Jeannie* as she fixes something to eat. She makes a big fat ham-and-cheese sandwich, and it is so good. She watches TV, and her attention is stolen by the TV as a special news bulletin is broadcast. The TV anchorman is reading a report on the heartbreaking deaths of four more babies in the Upstate New York region.

"These four babies have all died of scarlet fever in the past three weeks," says the anchorman.

Kaitlin rubs her belly, watching very closely the bulletin. The anchorman goes on to say how more than a dozen babies have died this past month alone due to scarlet fever, influenza, tuberculosis, and pneumonia. This is an unusually high number of deaths, and doctors in the region are baffled as to why so many babies are dying. Parents are cautioned to pay close attention to any unusual behavior by their young children. Parents of very young children and especially babies are being advised to pay very close attention to the health of their children and any illness should be taken very seriously. The first sign of fever or cold should be treated very seriously, and a doctor visit is highly advised. The hospitals are staffing to maximum capacity because of this very serious situation that is developing across the upstate region of New York. The hospitals in the upstate area are having doctors from all over the country come to help examine and look at children. They are trying to figure out what is going on and why so many young children have died in the past ten months. There have been over sixty-five fatalities of very young children less than four years of age. This epidemic has caused the federal government to act. They have funded all the hospitals in the area to staff and seek out medical knowledge on how they can figure out what is going on with the children.

Kaitlin has no idea that what her doctors and the nurses at the hospital were telling her and Gerald about is so serious. She is now glad that she is allowing her baby to be examined by the doctors because this is very serious. She has no idea over sixty-five babies have died over the past year, and she rubs her belly very concerned as the bulletin ends, and *Bewitched* begins on TV. Kaitlin turns the TV off and rubs her belly, eating her sandwich and talking to her belly like her baby can hear her. "Well, you have nothing to worry about, you are going to be fine. We have doctors and nurses already waiting to check you out and make sure everything will be fine with you." Kaitlin rubs her belly, smiling and eating her sandwich.

Gerald takes his first break at 9:00 a.m., and the only thing he has been thinking about all morning is getting to break so he can smoke more cigarettes with his coworkers. He walks out to the break area with cigarette already in hand because in 1968, you can smoke at work. Gerald gets to the picnic table and sits on it with his friends, and Gerald is very popular these days. Everyone is very interested in how he and Kaitlin are doing and how they are handling the news about so many babies being sick with flu and fever. Gerald really does not watch much TV, and he is not up to date with the news. He gets updated by all the people he talks with at work and at the bar. Gerald's friends ask him if he is not worried about all the babies that are getting sick. Gerald tells them no. He is not worried; his baby will be fine, he tells them all. He tells them how Rosewood General Hospital has already set up two checkups a month for his baby so he can make sure everything is just fine with his baby. All his friends are relieved to hear this and wish Gerald all the best as they have been doing for a long time already now. Break ends, and Gerald hates the fact that he has to get back to that line and inspect all the parts coming out of the machine to make sure they are good. Gerald hates his job; if he has his way, he will sit in the bar all day long every day just drinking beer and smoking cigarettes. That is his perfect day. Gerald makes it through the day and gets home to see Kaitlin sitting on the couch all sweaty and breathing heavily. He rushes over to her, and she grasps his arm tight. "Gerald, I feel like at any minute, I could go into labor."

"Well, come on, let's get you to the hospital."

"No, not yet. Let's wait, it is not time yet, but it is close."

"Are you sure, honey. I don't want to wait too long and then you are having a baby in the car on the way to the hospital."

Kaitlin laughs, telling Gerald not to worry because she will let him know when the time to go is, and then she tells Gerald, "Let's go, the time is now." Gerald helps her off the couch, and they head right out to the car. He helps her into the front seat and gets in himself, starts the car, and they are off to the hospital. They live about twenty-five minutes away from the hospital, but Gerald makes it there in fifteen minutes even though Kaitlin keeps telling him to slow down. Once in the parking lot, Gerald helps her into the hospital, and she is quickly put on a wheelchair and wheeled away. Gerald is told to wait in the lobby, and someone will be with him shortly to let him know what is happening. Gerald waits for two hours before he finally makes a scene and gets some answers. Yes, his wife is having a baby, and everyone forgets about Gerald who is waiting in the lobby. His anger is quickly taken over by excitement as he realizes he is going to be a father soon. He paces back and forth for hours, smoking cigarettes, walking in and out of the hospital, just waiting. Gerald patiently waits until midnight and asks one of the girls at the front desk what is going on. They tell him to hold on, and they will find out for him. A few minutes later, the receptionist gets back to Gerald and tells him that everything is fine, just some labors take longer than others, and Kaitlin is taking a very long time, but everything is OK. Gerald says OK and continues to pace back and forth in the waiting area. Finally at 2:00 a.m., Gerald asks again at the front desk, and again, they tell him everything is fine; he is just going to have to wait. He can go home and come back in the morning, if he would like to. Gerald says no and waits in the waiting room. He falls asleep on the chairs and sleeps until seven in the morning. He wakes to see all new receptionists and immediately asks how his wife is. They get back to Gerald, telling him she is still in labor. Gerald is starting to get mad, saying, "It has been over twelve hours, it should not be taking this long." The receptionist tries to calm Gerald down, but he is getting all worked up and demands to see his wife right now. The receptionist tells Gerald to calm down and hold on as she is calling a doctor that will come and take Gerald to see his wife. He says OK and paces back and forth until a doctor comes and escorts Gerald to a washroom, where he has Gerald wash his arms and face very good. Then he has Gerald put on blue clothes that cover his body completely, and he even has a blue cap to put over his head and a face mask to cover his face. "OK, are you ready to go see your wife?" asks the doctor who is covered head to toe in the same blue clothing. "Yes, I am doctor. Why is it taking so long anyway? It has been over half a day now," asks Gerald.

"Well, it is not all that uncommon for labor to take over twelve hours. Especially when the child is turned in the womb like this one is," says the doctor.

"Turned in the womb, is that dangerous? Will our baby be all right?" Gerald asks following behind the doctor as they pass through a bunch of doors that swing open when they walk through them, and they come to the room where Kaitlin is giving birth. She is heavily sedated but still conscious. There is a nurse by her, holding her hand and talking to her, and a doctor working on getting the baby facing the right way so Kaitlin can give birth. The doctor Gerald followed into the room whispers to Gerald explaining what is going on.

"You see, Gerald, the doctor here is actually turning the baby in the womb. He has his hand inside the womb, and he is gently and slowly turning the baby by hand so when it is coming out of the birth canal, it will be facing the right way. If it is not facing the right way, then very bad things can happen. This is a very slow process, and time is not on our side, but we are still OK. As soon as the doctor can get the baby lined up correctly, then he will help Kaitlin push the baby out of the birth canal with the least chance of injury to the baby."

Gerald can hear the doctor talking to Kaitlin. "Kaitlin, how are you doing? You are doing great, Kaitlin. How do you feel?"

"I feel fine, doctor. Is that my husband over there against the wall? Gerald, is that you, honey?"

"Yes, Kaitlin, it is me." Gerald walks up to Kaitlin and holds her hand.

"Gerald, that is you. How do you feel, honey, because I feel great. They got me on this no-pain drippy stuff coming from this tube into my arm, and it feels great. Hey, doc, where is my baby?" Gerald squeezes Kaitlin's hand and can tell by the smile on her face and the slurring in her words that she is on some kind of pain medication. She ends each sentence with a happy laugh, and Gerald wipes the sweat from her forehead as the doctor speaks to them. The doctor is actually very close to having the baby ready for delivery. He has actually reached his hand in Kaitlin's birth canal and very gently caressed and moved the baby into position for delivery, and he tells Kaitlin to push as he gently presses on her belly to help the baby move out. Kaitlin tries to push, and the baby, which has not moved at all in the past twelve hours, is now finally starting to move, and it moves all at once. Gerald and Kaitlin hear the doctor saying, "Here it comes, here comes your baby," and very quickly, the baby births, and he catches the baby and raises it up for the Hammonds to see. The doctor is holding the baby upside down by its feet with its back flush to his hand, and he rests the baby on his hand for the Hammonds to see. They look to see their first child crying as the doctor puts some kind of clamp on the umbilical cord; he then cuts it and places the baby on Kaitlin's chest. Kaitlin starts to cry as she cradles her newborn baby.

"Gerald, we did it, we did it. It's a boy, we made a boy."

"We sure did, Kaitlin, we made a boy."

Dr. Kaplin stands and shakes Gerald's hand, saying, "Well, Mr. Hammond, you are now a father."

"Thank you so much, doctor. I can't believe it, I am a father," says Gerald, smiling, and he kisses Kaitlin on the forehead. Dr. Kaplin waves one of the nurses over to him and asks her to clean the newborn baby. "Kaitlin, Nurse Saunders is going to clean off your baby and cover him up for you, OK? She will be right back just give her a minute," says Dr. Kaplin. Nurse Saunders takes the baby to a small bath and cleans and clothes the baby while the doctor talks with the Hammonds. Dr. Kaplin takes Kaitlin's legs out of the stirrups and lays them on the bed, which is much more comfortable for her. All of a sudden, she looks exhausted. Gerald kisses her on the forehead again, asking, "How are you doing, honey? You look more beautiful to me now than you ever have before." Kaitlin smiles and closes her eyes like she is very close to sleep. "I am so tired, but I want to see my baby. Where is my baby?"

"Here he is. Here is your baby," says Nurse Saunders, and she puts the baby on Kaitlin's chest. The baby is wrapped in what looks like a big sock with another big sock on his head. He is absolutely adorable and already sound asleep on his mother's shoulder. Kaitlin holds him and smiles to Gerald, saying, "Well, here he is on his birthday. What is the date anyway?" she asks Gerald. "It is September 13, 1968, and it is about ten in the morning," he says as he looks at his watch. Kaitlin smiles and holds her baby, looking at Gerald as her eyes are getting heavy and she is falling asleep. "I am so tired. I need to sleep now," says Kaitlin. Gerald picks up the baby and cradles his new son in his arms. Kaitlin looks at her husband with all the love she has ever felt in all her life and says, "What are we going to name him, Gerald? Of all the names we talked about, I just thought of one which I really like. I like the name Drake. What do you think?"

"Drake? What made you think of the name Drake?" asks Gerald.

"I was thinking it's his birthday and no birthday comes without cake and Drake rhymes with cake. Why I thought of that I have no idea, but I really like the name, and I would love to call him Drake. He looks and feels like Drake Hammond," says Kaitlin with very heavy eyes.

"You know, Kaitlin, I like it. I like it a lot. That is it, we will name him Drake Hammond. How about Drake Raymond Hammond?" says Gerald.

"Yes, Drake Raymond Hammond. That is our first son," says Kaitlin, smiling and holding her hand out to hold the blue clothing over her husband. Gerald is holding Drake with both hands and looking over his new boy. The nurses and doctor have been cleaning up and getting ready to move Kaitlin to a room where she can rest, and they are now asking Gerald if they can take the baby to a room where he can rest as well. Gerald hands his baby to a nurse, saying, "This is my first boy, Drake Raymond Hammond."

"He is adorable, Mr. Hammond. I am going to take him to a bed where he can rest. You can come with me if you like. You can watch, and you will know exactly where he is. We are going to take Kaitlin to a room where she can get some much-needed sleep as well," says the nurse.

"That sounds great. I want to watch you put Drake in a bed, and then I will go see Kaitlin, OK?"

"That is fine, Mr. Hammond, follow me," replies the nurse. Gerald follows the nurse, and she tells him to walk down a hallway with windows in the wall, and he can watch as the nurse goes into the nursery and puts Drake into a bed where there are already many babies already sleeping and some are crying. Gerald watches as the nurse walks into the room, and she lays Drake down. He watches as Drake lies there and sleeps so peacefully. He watches until the nurse comes around and escorts him to the room where Kaitlin will rest and regain her strength. Kaitlin is so tired and already sleeping when Gerald and the nurse get to the room where she is. They leave Kaitlin to rest, and the nurse talks to Gerald outside her room in the hall, and then she escorts him to the front of the hospital. He will come back later this evening after Kaitlin and the baby have rested and the hospital has all the paperwork and things in order. The benefits of having their child signed up for the monthly checkups is that all the vaccinations and immunizations are all taken care of with the doctor checkups at no cost to the Hammonds. The nurse informs Gerald that the first checkup will happen today before he gets back to the hospital so already the first checkup will be complete. There will be a checkup every two weeks from today until March of next year. Gerald says that is great and he will be back later this evening to check on his wife and baby. The day goes great, and Gerald can't get any sleep because he is so excited. He makes all kinds of phone calls and drives around seeing everyone he can to share his good news. The next few days go great. The Hammonds have a great experience with their first child, and all goes very well with the hospital and everything. Two weeks later, and they are getting situated and used to having a baby, which is a trying experience for everyone but one of the joys of life.

The Hammonds are getting ready to bring Drake to the hospital for his second checkup. Actually, Gerald will be off doing whatever it is he does, and it will be Kaitlin taking Drake to the hospital on the coming Saturday. Kaitlin has come to realize in her marriage to Gerald that he is not too reliable. He says a lot of things but seems to forget them immediately and is off doing whatever it is he wants to do. He has already left the responsibility of taking Drake to the hospital on Kaitlin and she does not argue with Gerald; she takes Drake to the hospital and gets him in for his second checkup.

The next day, Kaitlin wakes up to the crying of Drake. He is crying very loudly, and Kaitlin rushes to his crib that is in her room. Drake is kicking his legs and moving his arms, crying very loudly like he is in great pain. Kaitlin picks him up and cradles him in her arms, but nothing she does will calm him down. She looks him over to see that his left arm is swollen very badly, and there are red lines very visible all up and down his arm. She gets very scared and calls the hospital immediately. She tells the hospital she has no idea what is going on and describes what she sees wrong with Drake. The personnel at the hospital tell her to bring in Drake immediately and they will check him out. Kaitlin barely even puts on any clothes and rushes Drake to the hospital. Times were very different in the sixties. There are no car seats, at least none that are mandatory, and Kaitlin puts Drake on the seat next to her, wrapped in a blanket, and she herself is still in her pajamas, slippers, and a robe. She gets to the hospital and rushes right to emergency with Drake. She shows the people there Drake and his arm that looks like it is very badly infected. The doctors and nurses take Drake and tell Kaitlin to wait in the waiting room while they check Drake. Kaitlin is almost in tears, scared to death that something bad will happen to Drake. This is just like all the bad reports of all the babies dying in the upstate area, and it looks like some sort of deadly disease has Drake. Kaitlin has not even called Gerald yet and calls him from the emergency room and tells him what is going on. He tells Kaitlin he is on his way and he will be at the hospital shortly. Kaitlin hangs up and waits, pacing back and forth, crying, not knowing what is going on with her baby. Gerald gets to the hospital about forty minutes later and meets with Kaitlin in the lobby.

"Kaitlin, what is it? What has happened?" asks Gerald.

"I don't know. I woke up to Drake crying, and he had infection all in his left arm. I could see it very clearly, so I rushed him right here. This is just like all the babies that have been dying. I am scared, Gerald," says Kaitlin who hugs Gerald and cries on his shoulder.

"Well, where is Drake now? What are they doing to him?" asks Gerald.

"I don't know," says Kaitlin.

"Come with me. We need to know what is going on," says Gerald, walking with Kaitlin behind him to the front desk and demanding to know what is going on with his baby. The girl at the front desk is very intimidated by Gerald's very aggressive tone and strong language. She understands that the Hammonds are very concerned about the welfare of their baby, but there is nothing she can do except call a doctor to come help them. The Hammonds wait a few minutes, and then they are greeted by Dr. Adams who is their personal physician. He tells the Hammonds that Drake has come down with a very serious case of scarlet fever and has been put in a sterile bubble to help protect him from all outside bacteria and help him fight the virus that is in him, but he is in very bad shape.

"He was just here yesterday, and everything was fine with him. My wife brought him home last night after one of your great doctors said everything was not only good with our son but that our boy was as healthy as any baby could be. So what the hell is this? Why is Drake all of a sudden in a sterile bubble fighting for his life from what a fever?" asks Gerald in a very loud and concerned voice.

"Mr. Hammond, I understand you are very concerned and for good reason, but we have the best doctors in the country looking at Drake right now and doing everything they can do to make sure Drake will be all right. As a matter of fact, Dr. Rieval is looking at Drake right now. Dr. Rieval is the leading doctor in the nation on viral and contagious disease. Drake could not be in better hands than he is in right now," says Dr. Adams.

"Where is our baby? You take us to see Drake right now," demands Gerald.

"OK, follow me, but I advise that you be prepared because Drake is in an oxygen tent right now," says Dr. Adams, who is very intimidated by Gerald. The Hammonds follow Dr. Adams to a window where they can see Drake in a clear plastic bubble. Drake has an IV tube in his arm and in his leg, and he is crying while kicking his arms and legs. There is a doctor standing by the oxygen tent, and a doctor and nurse walk in.

"Dr. Adams, what are they doing?" asks Kaitlin.

"They are doing everything they can, Mrs. Hammond. If anyone can help and heal Drake, it is Dr. Rieval and Dr. Kevnick," says Dr. Adams.

"Which one is Dr. Rieval?" asks Gerald.

"The doctor on the right, that is Dr. Rieval. He is the best doctor in the country, and he will find out what is wrong with Drake," says Dr. Adams.

"He damn well better since it was him that just yesterday told us everything was fine with Drake, and now less than twenty-four hours later, here we are," says Gerald, looking at Dr. Adams, and Dr. Adams takes a deep breath, feeling the anger in Gerald's voice. Dr. Adams says, "Well, actually, it was Dr. Kevnick who looked at Drake yesterday, but he is also one of the best doctors in the country. They will fix Drake up," says Dr. Adams, loosening his collar with his left hand. Kaitlin and Gerald watch as the nurse unzips the oxygen tent and picks up Drake. She then follows the two doctors out of the room and out of sight.

CHAPTER 2

Dr. Rieval Gets Noticed

Going back a year and a half to early 1967. Earl Rieval has just gained his master's degree from the University of Atlanta. Earl Rieval is considered to be one step away from genius. He is twenty-five years old and breezed through college with a near-perfect grade average. He is very ambitious, but his only goal in life for now is to master the human genome. This has consumed his life since he was a teenager, and he loves chemistry and biology. He is considered by his peers to be the brightest and smartest young doctor in the country. There is one huge setback for Earl that is holding him back and preventing any hospitals and/or agencies in the country from giving him even the chance for an interview. Earl has published three papers over the past three years stating very clearly his views and his vision of how to proceed in mapping the human genome and how people should fight against disease and virus in the future. Earl has stated very openly that he is not a religious man. The decisions he makes in life are based solely on work that has been proven scientifically in the past. Earl believes that cloning of people is essential in order to study and further evolve science and knowledge of the human body. Earl has stated in his papers that by cloning people, he can now introduce all kinds of methods in which to learn from without harming actual people. The clone can be kept sedated and worked on in real time, giving doctors real data and precise answers to what is happening inside the human body when disease and/or virus is introduced. The obvious argument to Earl's position is that someone will have to be the person to be cloned, and then the clone will be killed. This process is murder, and the argument continues. Earl clearly states in one of his papers that people should have the right to volunteer, and Earl himself would gladly volunteer himself to be cloned to further the study of the human body. Earl desperately wants to study disease and sickness in the human body, and with the use of clones, he can do this without harming actual people. He would be working on the clones. This point of view is making Earl an untouchable. He cannot find work, and no one will give him audience to hear his point of view. Earl has no agenda, nor does he have a sinister plot to try and hurt people. He wants to study people, and by using clones, he can introduce different viruses directly into the bloodstream of a living being and study it. Earl has proven in the papers that he has written how this method of study will speed up mankind's knowledge on diseases and viruses by decades and maybe even hundreds of years opposed to not using clones. Earl had not really thought that the consequences to the papers he has written would be so controversial. He really did not even know there was so much interest in him. He has been viewed by all the top government agencies and most of the top hospitals in the country. Earl is, without question, one of the top minds coming up in the medical world, but his views have turned away every hospital and agency that has looked at him so far without even one interview for a job opportunity. Earl really wants to be a part of the Centers for Disease Control and Prevention. He wants to be in the field, studying Ebola and all the other deadly flu and viruses that are in the world. He has put in many resumes and applications but has not had any response to them. This is very surprising to him. Earl has always had people or agencies or schools contacting him, asking him for his knowledge, his opinion or his participation. All of this has stopped, except for schools that constantly are asking him to go to their school, which makes no sense now that Earl is one of the top medical minds in the country with a master's degree from the University of Atlanta. Earl never thought about how controversial the cloning issue is, and the arguments just seem to never end.

It has been almost a year, and Earl cannot believe he has had no job opportunities at all come his way. He is starting to realize how controversial his views are, and the use of clones is just not going to happen. Earl is getting very discouraged that he cannot find work and is ready to go work at fast food just to occupy his time. Frustrated and demoralized, Earl is getting ready to go apply at a fast food restaurant. He opens the door of his home to head out, and there are two men standing at the door, just about ready to knock.

"Earl Rieval?" asks one of the men at the door.

"Yes, I am Earl Rival."

"Earl, I am Roger Stergis, and this here is my partner Richard Yarlow. We have come to speak with you. May we come in?"

"Sure, come on in." Earl opens the door fully and walks to the living room where he and the two men can sit down and talk. "So what is it you would like to talk to me about?" asks Earl as he sits down.

Roger addresses Earl. "Earl, Richard and I are with the Centers for Disease Control and Prevention, and we would like to talk to you about the possibility of maybe you coming and working for us."

"Oh, that would be great. I have wanted to work for the CDCP for as long as I can remember. I have come to realize that the papers I have written expressing my views on how the human genome should be mapped and how we, as a people, should proceed in the fight against disease and viruses using clones is very controversial. I was starting to think that it does not matter if I am the top mind in the medical field because no one will give me a chance," states Earl.

Roger addresses Earl again. "Well, Earl, we are here to see if you will be a good fit for us. We would like to take you to Atlanta where we can interview you further and see if you would be interested in working for the Centers for Disease Control and Prevention."

"Oh my god, would I. I would love to go and you won't be disappointed. I will be a great fit for you," says Earl, very excited and slapping his hands together.

"Well, Earl, that is why we are here. We want to see if you want to come back with us to Atlanta, interview, and possibly work for the CDCP. Is there anything you have to take care of here? You know, any loose ends? Because we are ready to take you with us right now if you are ready," says Roger.

"All I have to do is call my mother. She is at work. Let me call her and get some clothes and things together, and we are out of here," says Earl.

"Well, that sounds good, Earl. We will wait for you at the car outside, and when you are ready, you will ride to Atlanta with us," says Roger, and he and Richard head out of Earl's house.

"OK, thank you, guys. Give me thirty minutes, and I will be in the car ready to go," says Earl.

Roger and Richard leave the house and go wait in the car while Earl calls his mother and gets his necessities ready to go. The next thing Earls knows, he is off to the city of Atlanta to interview for the Centers for Disease Control and Prevention. Earl lives about two and a half hours outside of Atlanta, but he notices on the drive that they are not headed toward the city of Atlanta. Earls asks the men, "Where are we going? This is not the way to Atlanta. I thought we were going to the CDCP in Atlanta?"

Roger explains to Earl. "Well, Earl, yes and no. You are being interviewed to work for the CDCP but not in the traditional sense. You have been personally selected because of your outspoken views and your brilliant study in college. You have come highly recommended from our sources as the man with the highest potential to fit our needs."

"What do you mean to fit your needs?" asks Earl.

"Well, Earl, there are those of us who recognize the need to stay one step ahead of disease, and there are those in the world that would use biology as a form of warfare. We work for a secret and unknown branch of the CDCP. We are known by the acronym ASAFEW, pronounced "as a few." That stands for A Safe and Free Educated World. You see, Earl, we need highly intelligent, dedicated, and devoted personnel like yourself to work outside of the normal boundaries. We need people who are willing to take the risk no one else will take in order to make sure we live in a safe and secure world. We need people like you who understand that doing what is right does not always fall into the mainstream thought process and requires handling of, well, let's say, a discrete nature. You have expressed views in your papers that go against the norm and fall way out of line with mainstream views. We here at ASAFEW find your views very refreshing, and we share your views. We are trying to find and incorporate the smartest minds to work as a separate entity of the CDCP. What we mean is this. We do not use clones, we do not have bodies or people for you to work on with consent. You will have the ability to study and research on real human blood samples along with real viruses and diseases from the vault of the CDCP. No one will know what you are doing except those of us in ASAFEW, and this is the only way to get done the work we all know needs to be done. We know how important this work is, and we here at ASAFEW have been waiting for a leader, someone with your high standards and your goals, to come along and take a lead position, running a state-of-the-art modern laboratory dedicated to the study and understanding of deadly viruses. You will have to be your own leader. You will have to be your own discoverer and learner of virus. We will be funded by the CDCP, but we will be a separate and secret entity, we will be ASAFEW. You will work for yourself to discover, to learn, and to make medical breakthroughs. The world is full of bad people who would use biology as a form of evil, and we need people like you to study disease and virus so that we can use this study to further our knowledge on sickness and finding cures for sicknesses. We are taking you to a secret facility where we have probably the brightest mind in all of the world working on the study of disease in the human body. You may have heard of him. His name is Dr. Alexander Kevnick. He has asked us to locate you and ask you if you would meet with him. He has read the papers you have written in college, and he wanted very much to meet with you. Have you heard of Alex Kevnick?" asks Roger.

"Of course, I have heard of him, and what an honor it would be to meet and work with him," says Earl.

"Well, Earl, we are just about there," says Roger as he pulls into a garage of a single house. The house is on a long unpopulated road. There are people in the house, and they are associates of ASAFEW. Once the car pulls into the garage, the door closes behind them, and the floor sinks with the car on it. The floor sinks one story below the ground to what is a fantastic laboratory. Rick and Roger get out of the car and open the backseat door, and Earl gets out to be greeted by none other than Alex Kevnick.

"Wow, Alex Kevnick, what an honor. I cannot believe I am here with you," says Earl.

"You are Earl Rieval. I have heard a lot about you, and I am a big fan of yours," says Alex as he reaches out his hand to shake with Earl, and they shake. "Come with me, Earl, let me show you around. Oh, Roger and Richard, you may be dismissed," says Alex who is walking toward a beautiful laboratory with Earl following him. Roger and Richard get back into the car, and it ascends back to the surface, and the laboratory is closed to the outside world. Earl follows Alex around this beautiful laboratory with all the latest in state-of-the-art equipment. Earl is blown away as he listens to Alex, but he is most impressed with all the space and equipment that is here. Everything needed to start working and discovering is here. "So, Earl, what do you think of the facility here?" asks Alex.

"It is fantastic. All you could ask for is here," replies Earl.

"Yes, it is. Now let me tell you why I have asked for you personally to be my assistant. Let me tell you exactly what I am doing. What my goals are, and you will be free to choose whether you want to work with me or not, first of all, I am trying to make man immune to disease. I know that is impossible, right? Or is it? There are people in the world who inject themselves with poisons from snakes to make themselves more and more immune to the effects of the poison until they can be bitten by a snake with a deadly venom and they can survive the attack. I believe we can do the same with Ebola, pneumonia, influenza, and forms of swine and avian flu. The point is this. All of these forms of virus and disease are absolutely deadly in minute amounts but not to everyone. There are those in the population that have the right coding in their DNA to make them immune to the deadliest of sickness. We have to find these people and what it is in them that makes them special and exploit their very special traits. We have to examine them and share their immunities with everyone else, making the threat of disease less and less until it is no more threat at all—" Alex is interrupted by Earl.

"Dr. Kevnick, hold on a minute. This is nothing new. Doctors have been working on this since the beginning of time. What you are talking about is great, but all the great doctors in the world are working on this every day right now. This is why I have argued so strongly for the use of clones. The fact is we cannot work with these deadly diseases on people because they will die. The reason I want to use clones is because they will die, but is it not acceptable to clone someone—and that clone will never be awake, will never even know it is alive—and use this clone to work with deadly disease and virus, and should this clone die, is that not acceptable for the greater good of learning? This is how I believe we eliminate disease and virus deadly to the human species. To me it is a clear-cut and an easy decision, but my views have been swept under the rug, and no one apparently agrees with me,"

"Well, Earl, I do agree with you, but there is no cloning allowed anywhere in the world, and it is something we cannot do. What I have been working on is a way to use newborn babies by taking samples of their blood and working with these blood samples to see how different babies' blood responds to different disease and viruses. If you decide to help me, you and I can sample the blood of many different babies of different nationalities and races. We can study them and coordinate them and see how they are the same and how they differ. We can combine blood, virus, and antibiotics. We can study them in real time to see what the results will be. You and I, Earl, we can learn to eradicate disease by combining the strengths of different human blood samples. We can use these samples to fight the diseases, but we will have to work hard, and we will have to be hidden in plain sight," says Alex.

"I don't think I am following you, Alex. Are you saying we will be doing illegal work? I mean, to experiment on blood samples is one thing, but that is still just blood. Blood in the body is a whole different animal," says Earl.

"Earl, you yourself have said in your writings that if cloning is not going to be accepted in the mainstream and become a viable source of learning for the professional doctors in the world, then the only alternative is going to be working on the living. You are right, Earl, and the fact is this, only the bad people will be doing this work, and they already are. It is not pretty, and yes, innocent people around the world are dying. If no one does this work except bad people with bad intent, then we are all going to be doomed, and I know you know this by reading your papers. I need you to be by my side to take on this challenge with me. I need you and your professionalism to work this process and make it successful like I know it can be. I know that you and I together can wipe out viruses and diseases that kill millions and millions of people every year. Not only that but you watch, it won't be long until some crazy doctor or doctors somewhere in the world have created man-made viruses and who will be there to fight against them?" asks Alex.

"The CDCP will, that's who. Listen, Alex, you are a fantastic doctor and chemist. I know whatever you do you will be successful at. I can work on blood samples, no problem, but I cannot work on babies, putting lethal disease into them. That is something I cannot do," says Earl.

"I understand, Earl. You have good morals and high living standards. I just wish others around the world had your same ideals," says Alex.

"What do you mean?" asks Earl.

"I mean other doctors all around the world have been doing this kind of experimentation for years already. Even if you and I were to start today, we would be years behind the competition. It may already be too late for us. Other doctors around the world may be so far ahead of us by now that we may not be able to catch up to their knowledge before it is too late and I mean too late to prevent a biological catastrophe. Come here and take a look at this, let me show you what I am talking about," says Alex.

Earl follows Alex to a TV screen, and Alex puts in some tapes and explains to Earl what the doctors are doing. Sure enough, the tape shows doctors working on babies and small children. The images are horrible. The children and babies are dying from disease, and doctors are injecting patients that are tied down to beds. The patients are crying and screaming. There are before and after shots, and you can clearly see very healthy babies and young children, and then in later scenes, you see the same babies and children, in a very short time, have been infected and are dying very quickly from horrible diseases.

"OK, enough, enough. Turn it off," Earl says. "I will work with you, Alex, but we are not going to do this to people. I will work with blood samples to cure disease and study it, but I will not infect children or adults with this horror," says Earl.

"We will do what we need to do to make sure this kind of sickness and death does not happen. We will be the healers," says Alex.

"OK, Alex. So how does this work? I mean, do we live right here? Do we eat, sleep, and work right here?" asks Earl.

"We sure do, come on and follow me. I will give you the full tour," says Alex.

Earl follows Alex around the room, and all the equipment here is state of the art. Earl follows Alex up a spiral staircase, and he looks down on the laboratory as they ascend the stairs. Looking at all the equipment in the room, Earl dreams of what he can learn and accomplish here. The stairs lead right up into the house. Earl is shown to a bedroom that will be his and a kitchen, bathroom, even a living room, which is now his home. The house is a great front for the laboratory below them. There are two men sitting in the living room reading the paper, and they are here for what Alex calls protection. Earl is just blown away; it's like a dream come true for him. His whole life has been spent studying and learning biology and science, and now he gets to explore science with the best equipment money can buy, and to be able to work with Alex Kevnick is something he never thought possible.

CHAPTER 3

Why Did All Those Babies and Young Children Die in 1968

Earl spends all his time working in the laboratory, but he eats, showers, and sleeps upstairs. Earl is woken from his sleep at 3:00 a.m. by one of the men who are always in the house. "Dr. Rieval, wake up. Wake up, Dr. Rieval. There is another emergency, and Dr. Kevnick needs you to go see him at Rosewood General Hospital. He told me to tell you to bring the H vials. He said you would know what he meant by that," says Larry.

"What time is it?" Earl asks, rubbing his eyes.

"It is 3:00 a.m., Dr. Rieval, and Dr. Kevnick says we better hurry," says Larry, shaking Earl and pulling him from his bed. "Come on, Earl, get up and get the H vials. John and I have the car ready, and we are going to take you to the hospital."

"OK, Larry, OK, I am getting them," says Earl, realizing there is another emergency, and he is becoming extremely stressed to his breaking point. Earl has been working with different viruses, mixing them with blood samples and antibiotics given to him by Dr. Kevnick. Dr. Kevnick has taken blood samples of babies from over twelve different hospitals in the Upstate New York region. Earl has been given the samples from over one hundred babies of all different races and nationalities in the past year and four months. He has been using all these different samples and mixing them to study the results in real time. Dr. Kevnick has obtained the deadly virus and disease samples along with antibiotics from the CDCP in Atlanta. Earl has been mixing and combining all the blood samples from the babies with all the samples of virus that Dr. Kevnick has obtained from the CDCP and Earl has been watching the virus, blood and antibiotic mixtures under the microscope. He has been watching the effects of what is happening on a molecular level as it happens. Earl is trying to make people immune to these viruses by mixing the blood samples with them and studying them in real time. Earl has been mixing different amounts of virus and antibiotic with different blood samples in all kinds of ways. He has even been mixing different concoctions of blood with one another to see what happens when they are mixed together. He is trying to make the immune system of people resistant to all diseases and viruses by introducing a little of the diseased blood and/or virus at a time and making the immune system stronger and stronger to them until the disease and sickness is completely killed creating a serum that can be safely injected into people. Earl has been making serums all day every day to combat viruses in the blood samples, and he has been sending samples of his serums to Dr. Kevnick for study. Dr. Kevnick had all of this process in place before he recruited Earl so that Earl would have a constant supply of blood, virus, and antibiotic samples to work with. Once Earl joined, he was immediately put to work, and he has not stopped since. Earl was under the assumption that Alex worked inside the CDCP, and all of Earl's serums were going to Alex at the CDCP for further analysis, but that is not the case. Earl's working in the laboratory in the house is a front for ASAFEW. This study and research is maintained by Dr. Kevnick, traveling to many hospitals in the Upstate New York region and obtaining blood samples from many different babies to keep Earl supplied with enough fresh human blood to work on a continual basis. Earl has hundreds of strains of viruses already growing in the laboratory along with antibiotics in the house that Earl believes have been supplied by Dr. Kevnick directly from the CDCP, making this operation the highest of secret operations in the nation, and Earl is somewhat correct in his assumptions. This makes Earl very proud, and he works extremely hard to make everyone proud of him. Dr. Kevnick is very good at being discrete about getting the blood samples to Earl in his laboratory. Dr. Kevnick used the CDCP as a smokescreen, gaining him access to the hospitals in the Upstate New York region along with recommendations from very influential people, where he is granted access to babies where the parents have given consent for their babies to be examined twice a month for six months. Dr. Kevnick was getting all the blood samples from these babies and sending them to Dr. Rieval, and then he was injecting the babies with the serums that Dr. Rieval was making after he had injected the babies with deadly viruses and diseases. Alex is illegally injecting babies with lethal viruses and then injecting serums that Dr. Rieval is making in his laboratory looking for cures to the diseased babies. Dr. Kevnick has not told Earl of his actions. Dr.

Kevnick was given access to about a dozen hospitals in the Upstate New York region where he was allowed to check the health of newborn babies. He was not given authority to do anything other than give physical checkups. He was given authority to take blood samples from babies whose parents gave consent, and this was so he could study the health of newborn babies on a molecular level, and this is why ASAFEW provided Dr. Kevnick with the house and the laboratory that he and Earl are now working in. Earl was so excited to be working with real blood, virus, and antibiotic samples that he worked tirelessly, never taking time to stop and think about what he was doing. Earl had only one thought process, and he believed he was going to cure people from all viruses. He thought that would make all his hard work worthwhile and a good thing. This morning, it really starts to hit home with Earl as John and Larry are rushing Earl to a private jet to fly him to Upstate New York. Earl has been working in the lab for almost a year and a half now and has not kept up on current events at all. He picks the paper from John on the flight to Rochester, New York, and the front page headline reads: EPIDEMIC KILLING BABIES IN UPSTATE NEW YORK CONTINUES. Earl reads the article and realizes for the first time that the research he has been doing in the lab has been making its way to the hospitals that Dr. Kevnick has been visiting. Dr. Kevnick has been injecting babies with the serums that Earl has been working on in the lab after injecting the babies with lethal doses of disease and/or virus. This in turn has been killing babies. Earl is beside himself in disbelief as he pieces together the situation in his mind. He cannot believe that Dr. Kevnick is doing this. Earl knows he has to

turn himself in, but first, he has to get to the hospital and see
what the immediate emergency is. Earl has brought the H
vials with him, and he has communicated to Dr. Kevnick that
this serum has the potential to eradicate the Ebola disease.
Earl is shaky and nervous; he can't believe Dr. Kevnick has
been actually injecting babies with deadly viruses. Earl does
not know how to confront Dr. Kevnick with his intent to turn
himself in. After so many deaths of babies, how is it possible
that Dr. Kevnick has not been discovered? All the deaths have
been attributed to scarlet fever, influenza, tuberculosis, and
pneumonia. How has Dr. Kevnick been able to hide the true
reason for the deaths of the babies? Earl has a lot to figure
out, but he knows that the reason for all the deaths of the
babies here has to be the work he and Dr. Kevnick have been
doing. Earl sweats and rubs his face, all jittery on the flight,
and John and Larry take notice asking, "What is wrong?" and
Earl tells them he is just tired and needs to rest. "Well, there
is no time to rest now, Dr. Rieval. We are approaching
Rochester right now, and we will be on our way to the hospital
as soon as we land," Larry says, looking out the small window.
Dr. Rieval picks a case in the seat next to him and opens it
up. Inside there are lots of vials containing different serums
he has worked on. He has made hundreds of serums over the
past months, and now he realizes that Dr. Kevnick was
injecting babies with his serums. This, in turn, was killing
the babies. Dr. Rieval stares at the seat in front of him while
the plane lands. He looks at the vials, knowing, believing that
one of these serums here will be the cure. One of these serums
will make humans immune to Ebola virus. Dr. Rieval forgets
the torment of babies dying as the scientist in him takes over.

He has this struggle within himself about right and wrong, and yes, he is deeply distraught, thinking that people are being hurt or worse killed by his actions. These feelings do not last long as the scientist in him takes over his mind and justifies the good, which far outweighs the bad. Again the scientist in him drives his actions as the plane lands, and Larry and John are now rushing Dr. Rieval to a car and taking him to Rosewood General Hospital. On the way to the hospital, the shy nonscientific part of Earl gets the best of him, and he looks at the vials one more time. Earl thinks to himself, *This is it. This is the last time I will allow my work to be used this way. I will use these serums here, and if this baby dies, that is it. If this baby dies, I will turn myself in.* Earl bites his fingernails and is all jittery on the hour-long ride to the hospital. Once at the hospital, Larry and John escort Earl all the way to the baby ward where they are greeted by Nurse Reisen, and she escorts Earl alone from this point on. Nurse Reisen can tell that Earl is very nervous, and he is hugging his case like a million dollars is in it. "Is everything OK, Dr. Rieval?" asks Nurse Reisen. "You look very hot," she says.

"I am fine," Earl says, staring at the floor. "Where are we going?" Earl asks.

Nurse Reisen pushes open a swinging door, exposing a cleansing room where they can wash up. "Here we are, Dr. Rieval. We can get cleaned up and go see Dr. Kevnick after we wash. Here let me take that for you." Nurse Reisen tries to take the case from Earl, and he pulls away from her quickly startling her.

"No, no, I will handle this case," says Earl, setting the case next to the sink, and he begins to wash. Nurse Reisen senses great tension in Earl and keeps a little distance between herself and him from now on. After they have washed up, Nurse Reisen leads Earl into a room where Dr. Kevnick is. The two doctors and Nurse Reisen are all covered head to toe in sterilized clothing, and Dr. Kevnick addresses Earl. "Earl, you have brought the H vials?"

"Yes, Dr. Kevnick, I have brought them."

"Good, good. Come with us. Nurse Reisen, bring the baby, we must go to the other room now." Dr. Kevnick says this with his hands held up in front of him and backing through the swinging doors. Nurse Reisen picks the baby from a sterile oxygen bubble and follows Dr. Kevnick. Earl looks through the window in the wall to see a doctor and two adults watching. Earl can see that the man is clearly angry and giving the doctor quite a mouthful. Earl wonders if these two adults are the parents to Baby Drake who was just taken out of this room by Nurse Reisen. Earl follows through the swinging doors and walks out of sight of Kaitlin, Gerald, and Dr. Adams. Nurse Reisen brings the baby to another room, following Dr. Kevnick, where there are two other babies and no windows for their actions to be seen by spectators. There are two other nurses in this room, and Dr. Kevnick motions them to leave the room, and they do. There are three babies lying on a table here, and all three of them are clearly very sick. They have swollen arms and legs. Their eyes are swollen, and there are red lines throughout their bodies, making the veins in their bodies clearly visible. Earl almost starts to cry when he sees the naked babies. His eyes water, and he snaps at Dr. Kevnick. "Dr. Kevnick, what have you done? You have actually been injecting my serums into live babies? How could you do this? You are putting the lives of these babies at risk. We are supposed to be studying the effects of my serums with contaminated blood samples in real time to make educated proposals for the use of my serums, not injecting babies with deadly disease and then injecting my untested serums into babies. This is murder." Earl lets his emotions out completely forgetting that Nurse Reisen is still in the room.

"What do you mean you are injecting babies with viruses and untested serums? What are you doctors doing here?" asks Nurse Reisen, very concerned.

Dr. Kevnick gets very loud, shouting at Earl, "Are you serious, Earl? Are you going to do this right now? We have three very sick babies right here on this table, and you have the cure right there in that case. Now let's stop this arguing and get these babies cured." Dr. Kevnick looks at Earl, shaking his head and raising his hands after shouting at him, waiting for Earl to make the next move.

Earl says, "Yes, yes, we must cure them." Earl sets the case down and opens it. There is a flap in the top half of the case that Earl opens, and there are lots of syringes here. The bottom half of the case has lots of vials resting in soft foam, and they all contain different serums that Earl has called the H vials. Earl touches the vials and picks a syringe, saying to Dr. Kevnick, "I need to know what you have done to each baby. I need to know what and how much of what you injected into each baby."

Dr. Kevnick replies, "They all have the same injections. Each baby has 3 milligrams of A46294AB avian flu, 14 milligrams of PGRU7853STU swine flu, and 0.002 milligrams of Ebola QR78PGRE65. All three babies have been injected with 80 milligrams of your Q serum and 40 milligrams of your T-rone serum. So far your serums have been ineffective."

Earl looks at Dr. Kevnick in disbelief, saying, "You can't be serious. You have been conducting these kinds of experiments over the past year with my serums?"

Dr. Kevnick snaps at Earl. "Earl, cure them. It is time for the H vials to do their work. We can argue later, right now, let's get to work." Earl turns and concentrates on his H vials. He pulls many vials and fills three syringes with very specific concoctions of his serums. He measures the serums in very specific and accurate amounts. He uses different combinations until he has three different serums one for each baby. While he works on the serums, he tells Nurse Reisen to take blood samples from each baby. This is the point where Nurse Reisen speaks up. "What are you two doing? You are killing babies. This is the epidemic sweeping the region. It is not natural, it is you two. You are purposefully injection viruses into babies and killing them. You cannot get away with this." Nurse Reisen starts to run out of the room when Dr. Kevnick catches her by the arm and grabs her other arm and faces her. "Nurse Reisen, it is true we have been injecting babies with viruses, but what is done is done. If we do not act now, these babies will die. If you must turn us in, then you must, but if you do not help us now, then these three babies here will die for sure. You can help us save them. Please help us, or they are doomed." Nurse Reisen looks at the babies and looks at Dr. Kevnick, saying, "What can we do?" Dr. Kevnick responds by saying, "Right now, do what Dr. Rieval says." Nurse Reisen shakes her head, saying, "OK, OK, let's help these babies." Earl tells Nurse Reisen again to take blood samples from all three of the babies, and she does. Earl gives the first serum to Dr. Kevnick, and he administers it to the first baby. They follow through with the second and third baby. Earl takes the blood samples from Nurse Reisen and, after marking them, puts them in his case for study. Nurse Reisen starts to cry looking at the babies who are crying, and she thinks they are going to die. "Nurse Reisen, you need to stay calm. We need you to monitor the babies and keep a close watch on them. Keep them apart from one another and help put them in their own antibacterial bubble. You get that baby and I will get this one and Earl will get that one," says Dr. Kevnick as he points out the baby for each of them to move to its bacteria-free bed, and the three of them move the babies. Nurse Reisen is trying so hard to keep her emotions in check. Her heart is breaking, knowing these babies are in pain, but keeps focused on trying to keep them alive. "Dr. Rieval, do you think they will make it?" Nurse Reisen asks as she inserts an IV into the baby she is working on. Dr. Rieval and Dr. Kevnick are doing the same to the babies in front of them, and Dr. Rieval says, "These serums here are the most promising serums I have worked on so far. I think the babies have a good chance of surviving, but we need to be vigilant. We need to be right here with them monitoring them every step of the way. We have to pay very close attention to the serum being introduced into the babies through the IV. I need you two to stay here with the babies while I examine the blood samples in the next room. You two need to let me know immediately if their situation gets any worse, OK?" Nurse Reisen and Dr. Kevnick says OK in unison, and Earl heads into the next room to examine the blood samples that Nurse Reisen has just taken from the babies.

Earl has very good equipment here to work with. He has powerful microscopes, and of course, he has a lot of serum in his case. Dr. Rieval has told Dr. Kevnick that these serums are the cure-all serums, his H vials as he calls them. H is short for Herculean. Earl is working in real time with the samples of blood that Nurse Reisen has recently taken from the babies. He is taking very small samples of blood and serum and watching the results as he mixes them in all kinds of ways. This is a very time-consuming process, and before Earl knows it, time just slips away from him just like the past year did. He is so consumed in his work that he forgets about time and just works tirelessly on his task.

In the next room, Nurse Reisen is noticing that Baby Phillip is getting weaker and quieter. His cries are becoming faint whimpers, and his kicks are becoming slight movements, and she calls for Dr. Kevnick. "Dr. Kevnick, Phillip is getting weaker, you better come and check on him." Dr. Kevnick comes over and looks Baby Phillip over. He puts a stethoscope to the baby and says, "This is not good. His pulse is very weak. Keep an eye on him, OK? I am going to get Dr. Rieval," Dr. Kevnick says as he leaves the room to get Earl. A moment later, the two doctors return. Dr. Rieval looks the baby over and picks him up. He notices how weak the baby has become and tells Dr. Kevnick to take a blood sample from the baby. Earl goes into the other room and returns with a new serum that he puts into the IV. Dr. Kevnick gets the blood sample and gives it to Dr. Rieval who returns to the other room to study the sample. Nurse Reisen and Dr. Kevnick monitor the babies, and an hour later, Baby Phillip expires and Nurse Reisen can't hold back her tears anymore. She cries and calls the doctors murderers. She runs for the door, but again, she is stopped by Dr. Kevnick, who grabs her by the arm. "Nurse Reisen, Ryan is in bad shape, please help me with him. We need to get Dr. Rieval back here immediately." Nurse Reisen has her thoughts sidetracked, and she says, "I will get Dr. Rieval. Watch Baby Ryan while I get Dr. Rieval," and she rushes to the other room. "Dr. Rieval, we are losing Ryan, he is showing the same signs as the other baby, please hurry." Nurse Reisen turns and heads back to the room with the babies after calling for Dr. Rieval, and he follows her. Dr. Rieval has a serum that he has been working on and tells the two to hold Baby Ryan still while he injects the new serum directly into the baby. Baby Ryan cries and cries, kicking his legs as the doctors work on him and take more blood from his tiny body. Dr. Rieval looks Baby Ryan over and sighs. He walks over to Baby Drake and says to the others. "We cannot wait. Hold Baby Drake still. I have to try something with him. I will be right back." Dr. Rieval goes into the other room, and in a few seconds, he returns. He holds up a syringe, saying, "This is my last effort. What I have in this syringe is the most powerful combination of blood and antivirus I have been able to come up with. I think we need to inject Baby Drake with this now. I cannot lie, this is my last hope. One of these two babies may survive, but if neither of them survives, then I cannot go on with this anymore. I cannot pretend to be saving people while we are killing babies. Do you understand, Dr. Kevnick. This is wrong, and I cannot be a part of this any longer. I pray this will save this baby." Dr. Rieval injects Baby

Drake with the last serum he has just made. Nurse Reisen looks at Dr. Rieval, saying, "What was that? What did you inject Baby Drake with?" Dr. Rieval looks at Nurse Reisen emotionless, saying, "This is a combination of blood, virus, and antibiotic. This will either kill him very quickly or the combination can possibly fuse together, making his immune system impervious to all diseases and viruses. We will know very quickly." Nurse Reisen looks at Dr. Kevnick who looks back and then at Dr. Rieval who looks at the floor with his eyes still open in silent prayer. Dr. Rieval walks toward the room where he can study the blood samples. "Wait," says Nurse Reisen, "before you go back in there, let me make sure I understand what is going on here. You two have been injecting babies and very young children with lethal viruses and diseases? So this is why all the babies in the upstate region have been dying? What in the world are you two thinking? You are two of the top medical minds in the country and you are murdering children, why?"

"Let me answer you," says Dr. Kevnick. "Listen, first of all, Dr. Rieval had no idea what I was doing. This is all my doing. Let me explain. I recruited Dr. Rieval over a year ago and told him he would be working with real blood samples in real time with real viruses and antibiotics. He had no idea I was injecting babies and young children from the Upstate New York area with viruses and then trying to cure them with the serums that he was working on. Anyway, Nurse Reisen, I assure you Dr. Rieval was told over and over by me that he was working for the CDCP and under their guidance." Dr. Rieval raises his hand to stop Dr. Kevnick from speaking any further. "Let me stop you right there, Dr. Kevnick. It is true I did figure out long ago that obviously we were using illegal means to do illegal things, and I ignorantly ignored all the signs. It was not until the trip here that it really hit me what we are actually doing. We may have the best intentions in the world—the eradication of disease and/or virus in humans—but what we are doing is murdering babies and young children. This has to stop right now. I am turning myself in to the authorities and telling them everything." Dr. Kevnick runs his hands through his hair, stunned, and says, "Earl, what are you saying? You can't be serious, Earl, we are so close. We have possibly the solution to all virus right here in these two babies right here. You can't stop now, we are so close." Earl shakes his head in disgust, responding to Dr. Kevnick, "So close, are you kidding me, Alex? Look around you, these babies are dying, and what did you expect? We have killed nearly one hundred babies in the past year. Do you not have a conscience? How can this not make you crazy? We are doctors, for christ's sake. We took an oath to help people, and we are killing babies by injecting them with lethal viruses, this ends now, right now." Earl heads out of the room, and Nurse Reisen follows close behind Earl. Dr. Kevnick yells behind them as they are leaving, "Wait, wait, don't go. Don't go, we are so close." Earl and Nurse Reisen make their way for the exit of the hospital. Walking hurriedly down the hallway, Nurse Reisen asks Dr. Rieval, "Where are you going? How are you going to get there? What about the two babies we left behind? Dr. Rieval, where are we going?" Dr. Rieval turns to Nurse Reisen and stops. "We, what is this, we? Are we suddenly a team?"

"Yes, yes, we need to help each other. We need to tell all the people what has been going on. I know it will be hard, but you have to do it. Think about all the people who have lost babies, think about that and what if it was you in their shoes. You have to do the right thing and get the truth out in the open."

"Yes, Nurse Reisen, you are right," says Dr. Rieval, covering his face in his hands, disgusted that he has been a part of this terrible crime that has taken the lives of so many babies and young children. Nurse, can I ride with you? Can you take me to the local authorities? We have to go now before I lose my nerve."

"Yes, Dr. Rieval. I can take you, follow me." Nurse Reisen leads the way to her car, and Earl follows her.

Dr. Kevnick is still in the room with the two babies, and it is now nearly 3:00 a.m., and Dr. Kevnick watches and holds Baby Ryan as he expires. The only baby now alive is Baby Drake, and amazingly, he is sound asleep inside his oxygen tent. Dr. Kevnick looks Baby Drake over. He listens to his heartbeat, which is fairly strong. There is redness and swelling all over Baby Drake's body, but he is still alive. Dr. Kevnick rubs his eyes with a less than confident look on his face and closes the oxygen tent. Dr. Kevnick then picks up the phone on the wall and dials a number.

Larry is in the lobby of the hospital, leaning against the wall, and he is talking with someone on the phone. Larry snaps his fingers at John who is reading a paper, sitting in the lounge area. John gets up and walks over to Larry. John hears Larry say, "Don't worry, no problem. We will take care of it." Larry hangs up the phone and turns to John who says,

"Take care of what?" Larry points to the exit, and John turns to see as Dr. Rieval and Nurse Reisen are exiting the hospital.

It is now 3:00 a.m., and the night sky is full of hard-falling rain. "Shoot," says Nurse Reisen, "it's pouring out," and she grabs the keys to her car from one of her oversized pockets. Dr. Rieval shakes his head and raises his hands, saying, "So we are going to get a little wet. Let's go." Nurse Reisen runs toward her car, and Earl follows her. It is raining very hard, and they get soaked before they finally get to her car. Nurse Reisen tries to hurry and unlock her car and ends up dropping her keys on the ground, so they get extra wet before she finally opens her door, gets in, and opens the passenger side door for Earl. Earl gets in, saying, "OK, let's go, take me to the authorities right now." Nurse Reisen puts the car in reverse and backs out, and they leave the hospital.

It is raining very hard, and the windshield wipers are on high. They are still very wet from walking to the car, and visibility is very bad in Nurse Reisen's Camaro. It is pitch-black outside, and all they can see are the car headlights, which are on high, and they can hear nothing but the heavy rain pounding on the car. "Earl, do you mind if I call you Earl? I heard Dr. Kevnick call you by your name so that is how I know your name."

"That is fine, you can call me Earl as long as you tell me your name." Nurse Reisen says, "My name is Betty. So is it true you really did not know that Dr. Kevnick was injecting babies with these terrible viruses?" Betty looks to Earl for his response to her question. Earl tells her. "I was, for the most part, always in a laboratory until this past day. I was working with viruses, antibiotics, and human blood. I was engineering serums using all the samples that Dr. Kevnick had provided me with. I was mixing and combining them and trying to make human blood immune to the deadliest of viruses. I was not aware that Dr. Kevnick was injecting my serums directly into babies and young children. I should have known something was not right, but I was so focused on my work. I really thought I was going to create a serum for human blood that would make us immune to all the known viruses in the world today. I worked hard to achieve this. I should have known this was just a misguided dream on my part. I know this for sure. I have to go to the authorities and confess to all the wrong that has been done. I must make known what has happened here, and everyone should know that I and Dr. Kevnick are responsible." Right after saying that, the Camaro they are in is hit from behind. Betty looks in the rearview mirror to see headlights light up behind them, and a much bigger car is speeding up to hit them again. "Earl, someone is behind us. They are coming again," Betty says, getting very scared. Earl looks behind and out the rear window, yelling, "Speed up, Betty, go faster. They are coming again." The car behind them rams them again, and the small Camaro spins almost out of control, but Betty regains control of the car after swerving all over the road. Betty steps on the gas and takes a turn very fast and almost loses control but manages to keep the car on the road. She knows these back roads very well, and she knows that if she can get past the bridge crossing the canal, they can make it to the main road, and she can outrun the car behind them. Betty steps on the gas and tells Earl to hold on, but they are hit from behind, and this impact sends the Camaro swerving back and forth. Betty tries to maintain control but loses control, and the Camaro swerves off the road just before entering the bridge. The land to the sides of the bridge is all overgrown with brush, heavy grass, and small trees. The Camaro hits a small tree, which turns the car sideways, and it tumbles down about twenty-five feet into the canal below. A large black town car stops just before it gets onto the bridge, and Larry and John get out of the car and look into the canal to see the Camaro on its top side sinking into the canal. John and Larry look at each other as the heavy rain soaks them. They watch as the Camaro sinks into the canal.

CHAPTER 4

How Did Drake Survive Childhood

Kaitlin starts to cry as she and Gerald watch the two doctors and the nurse take Baby Drake from the oxygen tent, and then they walk out of the room through the swinging doors. "Where are they taking him, Dr. Adams?" Kaitlin says, crying, and Gerald hugs his wife. "Yes, where are they taking our baby?" Gerald says. Dr. Adams responds by asking that the Hammonds please wait in the waiting area while he goes to find out what is happening with their baby. The Hammonds go to the waiting area and wait. Two hours go by, and the Hammonds hear nothing; no one comes to check or update them on anything that is happening, and Gerald cannot take it anymore. It is getting late now, and there are already very few people around. Gerald has a heck of a time just trying to find someone he can talk to at the front desk. Finally, he finds a receptionist and asks to be informed on the status of his child, Drake. Gerald is quite upset at this point, and he makes this clear. The receptionist says she will get right on it for Gerald. Gerald goes back to the waiting area and sits by Kaitlin. A few minutes go by, and a doctor who they are not

familiar with comes to update them. He is very quick and
not very informative. The Hammonds are left in the waiting
area, and all they know is that Drake is in a very serious fight
for his life. Right now, he is stable, and the best doctors in
the country are working with Drake to make him better. The
Hammonds cannot believe this at all, and before they can
get any questions in, the doctor tells them that it is best that
they go home and come back to the hospital tomorrow, but
there is no way that is happening. The Hammonds wait right
there, and before they can get to ask any more questions, the
doctor tells them that he must return, and for now, he has no
answers for them. The Hammonds sit there in the waiting
room for two more hours, and Kaitlin is getting more and
more nervous as time goes by. Gerald is really getting steamed
himself. It is almost three in the morning, and Kaitlin is just
about crying, scared out of her mind, and Gerald can take no
more. Gerald stands up and grabs Kaitlin by the hand, telling
her, "Come on, Kaitlin, enough of this, we are going to get
our baby, and that is that. Something is not right here, and I
am not going to allow this to go on anymore." Gerald leads
Kaitlin to the receptionist's desk, and there is no one there.
They look around, and there is no one to be seen anywhere.
Gerald leads the way, holding Kaitlin's hand, telling her,
"Come on, Kaitlin, we will go find our baby." Gerald lets
his instincts lead the way, and he walks down the hallways
with Kaitlin behind him; they walk up stairs and down more
hallways. They head back downstairs, and they see baby
pictures and painting on the walls hinting that they may be
on the right floor. They see a nurse, and Gerald recognizes
the man as Dr. Rieval. Gerald steps in front of the doctor

and puts his hand on his chest, saying, "Dr. Rieval, you are Dr. Rieval."

"Yes, may I help you?" says Dr. Rieval, looking at Gerald's hand on his chest. "Yes, my wife and I are looking for our baby. His name is Drake Hammond, and we saw you were with him a few hours ago. We would like to see him right now," Gerald tells this to Dr. Rieval in a very intimidating tone, and Dr. Rieval responds immediately without hesitation. Dr. Rieval points down the hall, saying, "He is through the second door down on the right. There is a doctor in there with him." Dr. Rieval and Nurse Reisen hurry away from the Hammonds on their way out of the hospital. Gerald and Kaitlin curiously watch as the doctor and nurse hurry down the hallway away from them. Gerald and Kaitlin then head down the hallway and into the room where their baby is and what they find stops both of them dead in their tracks.

They walk into the room to see Dr. Kevnick on the phone, and their baby is sleeping with IV tubes in his arm and leg. He is sleeping but is very red with noticeable swelling all throughout his body. Not only do they see their baby not looking very healthy, but they see the two babies that have expired, and Gerald loses his cool and grabs Dr. Kevnick by the collar with both of his hands and pulls his face close to him. "What is going on here?" Gerald says this to the doctor in a very deep voice and tightens his grip. "I said, what is going on here?" Dr. Kevnick trembles a little, saying, "We are trying to save this baby from a new virus that is killing many babies in the region. We do not know where this disease has come from or how it is being spread to the children, but that is what we are trying to solve. These two babies here have not survived, but this baby here is still fighting. We believe he will make it, but we must maintain our constant watch on him." Gerald slams Dr. Kevnick against the wall, shouting at him, "You are full of shit. I don't know what is going on here, but I can tell you this, it is over right now. Kaitlin get our baby out of that bubble, we are getting out of here." Dr. Kevnick raises his hands to Gerald, yelling, "No, no, you can't take the baby out of the hospital, he will surely not survive without our care." Gerald slams his right hand into the chest of the doctor, slamming him back into the wall and pointing his finger right in Dr. Kevnick's face. "You are not ever going to touch my son again, do you understand me? If I so much as even see you in a room with my son ever again, I will knock you out." Kaitlin is crying, seeing the tubes in her baby's arm and leg, and she calls for Gerald. "Gerald, I don't know what to do about these tubes in Drake. I don't know how to get them out." Gerald walks over the Kaitlin, saying, "Just be gentle and careful, Kaitlin. We are going to need some bandages." Gerald looks to the counter and finds some bandages in the cabinets, and then he grabs them and slowly removes the IV tubes from Drake. He then bandages the two wounds where the needles were in Drake, and he and Kaitlin head out of the room with their baby. Dr. Kevnick yells, "Wait, wait. You do not know what you are doing. Drake will not survive the night if you take him." Gerald steps right back into the face of Dr. Kevnick, saying, "Drake obviously will not survive the night with you, at least with us, he is with family, and he is our son. If he is to die, then he will die with us. I am not going to read about his death in some paper like all the other babies that have been dying and wonder where my son is.

He is coming with us." Gerald and Kaitlin leave the hospital with their baby, and Dr. Kevnick knows better than to get in their way.

Soon after the Hammonds have left and Dr. Kevnick has caught his breath, he begins to work on the babies that did not survive. He pulls syringes from a carrying pouch that he has hidden in a separate room. He proceeds to give the babies injections, and this is how he has masked the deaths of the babies so far. He has been injecting the babies with enough of scarlet fever or pneumonia or other types of illness that have masked the true reason for the deaths of the babies. Dr. Kevnick has learned how to administer these shots in such a way to be very effective in hiding the true reason for the death of the babies. He knows this is not going to be sufficient because the government has called upon the CDCP to begin investigating the deaths taking place in the Upstate New York region. The babies that die from now on will be taken into the care of the CDCP for very thorough examinations and blood screenings. Dr. Kevnick will not be able to hide his activities any longer, but he still tries. There is no way he can just get rid of the babies that have not survived; he has to report the deaths, and the babies will be taken by the CDCP. Dr. Kevnick for the first time starts to sweat; he knows it is all coming to an end for him. Before he gets too caught up in his hysteria, the phone rings, and it is Larry calling him, telling him that Nurse Reisen has been killed. She drowned in the canal because she could not get out of the car, which submerged in the canal. Dr. Rieval did survive, and John and Larry have him secured in their car. Dr. Kevnick tells Larry to take Dr. Rieval back to the house in Atlanta and wait. They are not to let Dr. Rieval out of their sight, and he is not to leave the house for any reason. Dr. Kevnick has things he has to take care of at the hospital today, and then he will head back to the house in Atlanta. Dr. Kevnick paces around, confused and scared. He has not even contemplated that already the CDCP and doctors around the area have been taking notice of his actions. They have not been able to pinpoint any of the deaths to him yet, but the suspicions are high, and Dr. Kevnick is top on the radar. The morning comes and so does top personnel from the CDCP along with doctors and authorities from the area. The deceased babies are taken away, and Dr. Kevnick is read his rights and arrested by the authorities. His charge is suspicion in the deaths of over fifty babies and young children in the Upstate New York region that have been worked on by Dr. Kevnick personally in the past nine months. There are more children that Dr. Kevnick has worked on personally, but in some cases, Dr. Kevnick has been able to destroy all paperwork linking him to the babies. So far, all babies that have been experimented on by Dr. Kevnick have died all except for Drake. There are lots of authorities from many different agencies that fill the Rosewood General Hospital this morning. Dr. Kevnick has been taken away, and the hospital is abuzz with suspicious excitement. The authorities come dressed in suits representing the CDCP, and the White House has sent their chief spokesman Tom Treau to the hospital to take and answer questions on this horrifying situation. This story has made its way to the top. The Rochester Police Department has sent teams of law enforcement personnel to watch over the hospital and help keep tensions and emotions under control. There are parents from all over, coming to the hospital, asking all kinds of questions, because the early morning news stations have been broadcasting every little bit of information that they get wind of, and very quickly, the hospital here in Rosewood, along with a dozen other hospitals in the upstate region, are being deluged with concerned people. By the end of the day, Upstate New York has become a national sensation. The authorities are putting the pieces together, and slowly information is slipping out onto the airwaves. Of course, all kinds of propaganda and speculation are broadcast along with bits of the truth. The nation is instantly consumed with this story. Almost seventy babies and very young children have been murdered in the past eight to twelve months, and all the clues are pointing to Dr. Kevnick. The local police are tested as a lot of the parents are enraged and emotionally devastated. Many parents are not able to control their anger and are arrested all over the upstate region for disorderly conduct. The day ends with more unanswered questions than anyone could have ever believed possible before this day started. The big question is why. Why would Dr. Kevnick poison and kill innocent babies? What could be his reasons and motivations? How and why could anyone, especially a brilliant doctor who works for the CDCP, do this? None of the hospitals in the upstate region are ready for what has happened today. The government agencies have moved in so fast on Dr. Kevnick and took him away that no one was able to question him at all. The local news stations are somehow tipped off to what is going on, and they are on the ball. They get the word out so fast that by noon, all the hospitals are inundated with people, and the hospitals are overwhelmed in just trying to handle all the people coming in their hospitals and asking questions, not to mention handling the normal daily functions. To say the least, the day is complete chaos for the Upstate New York hospitals. More questions arise than are answered, and doctors and nurses everywhere are left scratching their heads, feeling that somehow they are to blame. Somehow they should have known better, and this should not have happened. In all the chaos and confusion on this day, there is one very important link. There is one very important piece of the puzzle that is lost and forgotten about. That puzzle piece is Drake Hammond. What has happened to Drake goes unnoticed. The paperwork linking Drake to the work of Dr. Kevnick has been destroyed. Not only that but somehow the file on Kaitlin Hammond has disappeared as well as the file on Drake Hammond. There is no file on the Hammonds in the hospital anymore. It is not until late afternoon when Nurse Reisen's car is noticed, and it is not until just before dark that there is actually someone in the canal and notices that her body is still in the Camaro. Even with all of this going on, you would not think that Dr. Adams would forget about Baby Drake Hammond, but he does. With all the commotion going on at the hospital and with him being pulled in a different direction to answer this question and fix this problem and so on, with never having a moment to just reflect on the past for one moment, Dr. Adams completely forgets about the Hammonds and Baby Drake. He never mentions them all day, not a once. He really is torn and a little scared himself at all the activity going on at the hospital, and the loss of Nurse Reisen really shakes him up as well. He is actually a little scared because babies have died here at his hospital, and the raging parents have made very threatening comments that Dr. Adams cannot help but take very seriously. The thought that angry parents have killed Nurse Reisen has passed his mind. Dr. Adams is pulled into one conversation after another all day long. One conversation about security, then one about competence, then one about procedure, and the day just never ends for him.

After Gerald gets home from work the next day, the Hammonds watch the events of the day on their black-and-white TV. Kaitlin is sitting in a comfortable La-Z-Boy chair, and Gerald is on the couch, smoking a cigarette. Gerald looks to Kaitlin, saying, "We are never going to that hospital again. In fact, from now on, I don't trust any hospital. I trust nothing and no one but you with Drake. In fact, I think this is a sign that you should breast-feed Drake from now on." Kaitlin looks at Drake who is sleeping on her left arm. He is red all over his body. He is sleeping, but Kaitlin can tell he is not sleeping well. He moves and shakes a lot, and even though the swelling in his body has gone down from the night before, he still looks like he is sick. Kaitlin knows Gerald has always wanted her to breast-feed their baby, but Kaitlin has always been against it. It is just very embarrassing for her. Kaitlin says to Gerald, "You know I do not want to breast-feed. I do not want to walk around with my boob hanging out. Not even around our own home, but what has happened over the past few days has even me a little crazy, so I tell you what. You go and you find me one of those breast pumps, and I will make breast milk for our baby to drink. Gerald grins and nods his head, saying, "Fair enough." Gerald gets up and heads out to find a breast pump for Kaitlin. Before Gerald gets out the door, Kaitlin starts to cry, saying, "Gerald, our baby is going to die, isn't he?" Gerald rushes back to Kaitlin, hugging her and kissing her on the forehead, saying, "He is not going to die, because he has his mother's love and strength to protect him. No more of those phony doctors and hospitals that made him sick in the first place. He was born from you, and your milk will make him healthy. Your milk will make him strong. Mark my words." Gerald heads out of the house confidently after saying that, and Kaitlin waits quietly, holding Drake until Gerald returns.

It takes Gerald four and a half hours before he returns with the breast pumps. He walks in the door, saying, "You know what I had to go through to find these." He goes on to tell the story to Kaitlin about how hard they were to find and how many people he had to ask before he finally found the breast pump and accessories. Kaitlin starts pumping her milk for Drake this night, and this is all he drinks for the next few months. The Hammonds notice that Drake begins to get healthier over the next few days. The swelling in his body goes down, and he seems to be gaining strength and weight like a normal baby should. They watch the news over the next few weeks as this story consumes the nation, and somehow, the Hammonds have been completely forgotten about, and that is just fine with them. They don't want any attention, and they certainly don't want to be involved in this circus at all. They learn that it was Dr. Kevnick who was experimenting on the babies in twelve different hospitals. He was illegally injecting viruses into babies to study the effects, and he says he was trying to make humans immune to viruses and cure all diseases. Dr. Kevnick was an employee of the CDCP and one of their top researchers, but for some reason, he went rogue. He had it in his mind that he was going to cure people of all disease and virus. The representatives talking on TV say that Dr. Kevnick worked too hard. They say for some reason, he lost his sense of right and wrong and just went off the deep end. Everyone in the nation is consumed with Dr. Kevnick, and he takes all the spotlight in this story. Dr. Rieval is completely unheard from and is never even mentioned. Dr. Kevnick is sentenced to life in prison. It takes less than a year for him to stand trial and be sentenced.

Soon after Dr. Kevnick is sent to prison, the Hammonds have their first serious problem with Drake since he was last in the hospital. Kaitlin has stopped working to take care of Drake, and Gerald still works at Xerox. Gerald gets up very early and is off to work at 5:00 a.m. Kaitlin sleeps in until Drake wakes her. Drake is such a good baby. The Hammonds have truly been blessed. Drake is put to sleep at around 8:00 p.m., and he sleeps until about nine the next morning, and he is very constant. Drake does not cry a lot. Drake is very content in his bed just playing with his toes, which he grabs with his hands. He looks around and tries to stand and crawl around in his crib. He does not make a lot of noise unless Mommy sleeps too long and he gets hungry, and even then he just kind of makes happy moans and cries, which gets the attention of Kaitlin. On this morning, Kaitlin wakes up on her own, and this is a little strange to her because she usually waits until she hears Drake cry for her, and he always has this big smile waiting for her. She loves her little Drake. Well, on this morning, she does not hear Drake, and she has rolled around in bed for a while and gets up to go see her little man. What she sees sends her into panic. His whole body is flush red. His left arm is held stiff in front of him bent at his elbow with his left hand facing to the right side. His right arm is similarly positioned facing the same direction. His feet are sticking up with his knees bent to his tummy and they are shaking. In fact, his whole body is shaking. Kaitlin goes to feel him, and she can absolutely feel that he is burning up. She panics and calls Gerald's work. She gets Gerald on the phone and tells him what is happening with Drake. The Hammonds did have two cars, but Gerald sold one of the cars to help pay the bills, which includes his drinking at the bar. Anyway Kaitlin is panicking, and Gerald knows it. She tells him they have to take Drake to the hospital, and they have discussed this a lot, and it was agreed they would not take Drake to the hospital ever again, but Kaitlin is insistent, and Gerald tells her he will come home. Gerald gets home a half hour later, and Kaitlin is waiting in the driveway for him. She gets into the car and says, "We have to get to the emergency room now. Feel him, he is burning up." Gerald feels Drake's forehead and burns rubber toward the hospital. They get to the hospital, and they rush Drake right to the emergency room. Gerald makes quite a scene to get the attention of a doctor, and it works. A young man comes to investigate, and with one look and feel of Drake's forehead, he sees what the scene is all about. The doctor tries to take the baby, but Gerald says, "Drake is going nowhere without me." Gerald will be with Drake the whole time, and there will be no needles. There will be no blood drawn, and there will be no injections. This causes quite an argument between Gerald and the young doctor, and finally, the doctor concedes and allows Gerald to carry Drake to the examining room. Kaitlin comes along as well. They get Drake to a room, and the doctor immediately takes Drake's temperature and can't believe what he sees. "This can't be right," the doctor says, scratching his forehead. "What can't be right?" replies Gerald. Dr. Carson is looking at the thermometer and says, "We have to try this again." He puts the thermometer in Drake's mouth, and he gets another one to put in Drake's rectum. Surprisingly, Drake is not crying at all, and he has not cried at all this morning. It is like he is unconscious, but he is still twitching and shaking. The doctor takes the thermometers, both of them, and says again, "This just can't be right." Gerald gets the doctor's attention, saying, "What is not right, doctor?" Dr. Carson looks at the Hammonds, very confused, saying, "Drake's temperature is 112 degrees. He should not be alive. Nurse get a bath ready now and fill it with water and ice, we need to cool this baby down immediately." The nurse and Dr. Carson quickly get a bath, fill it with water and ice, and Dr. Carson looks at Gerald, shrugging his shoulders and hands silently, saying, "May I?" because Gerald has been very protective of Drake, not letting him out of his reach. Gerald nods and steps back, and the doctor picks up Drake and sets him in the bath. The doctor holds Drake completely submerged except for his face. He holds him there for a minute and picks him up. "Nurse, feel his forehead, would you?" says the doctor. She does and says, "Put him back in." They repeat this for almost eight minutes, and Drake's temperature starts to come down. It comes down enough to where they put him on the examining table and take his temperature, which somehow has stabilized at a good 96 degrees. Dr. Carson looks to Gerald and Kaitlin, saying, "We need to take a blood sample." Gerald steps right up to the table, saying, "There will be no needles and no blood samples." Dr. Carson says, "This baby most likely has scarlet fever, but we won't know for sure unless we can examine his blood to find out that is what we are dealing with." Gerald looks to the doctor, saying, "Let's assume he has scarlet fever, how would we treat him?" Dr. Carson says, "Well, we could give him paracetamol for the fever. We could prescribe a ten-day amount of antibiotics for the fever itself."

"Well then, let's do that," says Gerald. Dr. Carson rubs his forehead, saying to Gerald, "If we give you antibiotics for scarlet fever and your baby has something else, then we could be doing more harm than good. We really need to take a blood sample to be sure." Gerald shakes his head no, saying, "Listen, doctor. Kaitlin and I have had very bad experience with hospitals, and we will never allow another doctor to put another needle in our baby ever again. I beg you, please give us the prescription we need, and we will pay you for your best educated guess. Not only that, we will sign a waiver for you, if you like, saying you are in no way responsible for any possible bad things that may happen to our baby as a result." Gerald and the doctor go round and round while the nurse and Kaitlin patiently and quietly watch. Somehow, an hour later, Gerald and Kaitlin leave the hospital with a prescription and some medicines that they can buy at any drugstore. Drake has had no blood taken, and the Hammonds go right to the drugstore to get their prescription and some paracetamol. The paracetamol is simply in case Drake gets a high fever again, and this will help lower his temperature. The antibiotics are to be taken twice daily, once in the morning after he eats and once in the evening after he eats for ten days. They are to give the entire prescription to Drake until it is gone. By afternoon the next day, when Gerald gets home from work, Drake is fine like nothing has happened at all. They don't have to give him any of the paracetamol because his fever never comes back, but they give him his antibiotics as they are supposed to for the next ten days.

This is the best time of Kaitlin's life. She has stopped working and spends all her time taking care of Drake. Things are great for Kaitlin. Gerald works full-time at Xerox, and when he gets home from work, he goes off to the bar, and Kaitlin really does not mind at all. She is very happy staying at home, watching Drake, and she has friends that come over and visit now and then, and she has her Tupperware to sell, and this brings a lot of women and their young ones over to the house every weekend. This drives Gerald crazy, and he is very bitchy about all these women at their house on the weekends, but that does not matter much since he just leaves and goes hunting or camping on the weekends. Kaitlin has been noticing that Gerald has been more and more irritable as time goes by, and they are starting to argue more and more, so she is kind of grateful when he leaves. She does love him very much but wishes they did not argue so much. Gerald has his vacation coming up and has been asking Kaitlin to come to the mountains with him camping, but Kaitlin says Drake is too young, and they should wait until next year to take him to the wilderness. Kaitlin wins the argument, and Gerald gets ready to go camping the next day without her and Drake. Gerald gets all the gear that he is going to take and packs it all. He is going to leave very early in the morning, and before he goes, he heads off to the bar to say good-bye to all his friends for the week. Gerald gets home three hours later drunk as can be and in a very playful mood. He is all over Kaitlin, and she hates the way he smells of booze and cigarettes, but she loves the attention and lets him have his way with her. Before long, he is asleep and so is Kaitlin. Early in the morning, Kaitlin wakes up, and Gerald is already gone. She could never figure out how he could be so drunk and so under the weather and still would be up out of bed and gone before she had even woke. She gets out of bed and goes to see Drake who is awake and already standing holding himself up by the bars in his crib. Drake is a little over a year old now, and he is starting to make sounds with his voice. He cannot say words, but Kaitlin and Gerald know he is trying to speak. He is trying, and he will be speaking soon but for now just a lot of grunts and indistinguishable words. Kaitlin loves the way Drake rarely cries; he is not a needy baby at all. He can be content in his crib for hours and only cries if left unattended for too long with his diaper needing to be changed or if he is really hungry. Drake has only been drinking his mother's milk, which she pumps for him, and now he is eating baby food, and of course, he drinks water as well. Today something really catches Kaitlin's eyes as she picks up Drake. She notices that his eyes are shining. They are shining like they are diamonds. They fade back to the shade of light blue that they are most likely going to permanently be. Kaitlin looks again and shakes her head, saying, *I must be imaging things.* Then she notices the veins in his body becoming visible in his neck, and she undoes his pajamas.

She takes his pajamas off and is horrified at what she sees. "Drake, what is happening to you?" she says. Drake is smiling and kicking his legs and grasping with his tiny hands like nothing is wrong. What Kaitlin sees is the veins in Drake's body become visible not all at once but a little at a time and in motion; for example, the veins in his shoulder come visible all the way down to his elbow; then they are not visible. Then she sees the veins from his elbow all the way down to his hands, and then they are not visible, and then the process goes back up his arm throughout his chest, down to his stomach, and across his belly. Then the veins are visible from his hip down to his knees and then down to his feet, and then they go back up his body. This goes on for ten minutes, and Kaitlin can tell even with this going on that Drake is OK. She does not know what is going on, and then she gets a real shock. All the veins in Drake's head become visible through his skin, and she is horrified. Drake, on the other hand, is smiling big and laughing like he is being tickled. This lasts only about two minutes, and Drake is still smiling and laughing, holding out his hands for his mother's touch, and she picks him up, saying, "Drake, what did they do to you?"

The next year goes by, and Drake has no medical issues at all, and the Hammonds do not take him to the hospital or to see a doctor at all. Kaitlin becomes pregnant and has just had her second boy, and his name is Lance. It is now the early summer of 1970, and the Hammonds do go to the hospital. Kaitlin is not about to have a baby without the care of a hospital, and the Hammonds notice how there is much more paperwork now than there was in 1968. They are at a different hospital this time. She has her second child at

Norwood General Hospital. The Hammonds are practically forced into signing on with a new physician for their two boys. A month after Lance was born, Kaitlin is glad she has a physician because Drake really gives her and Gerald a scare, and they almost rush him to Norwood hospital. It is early Saturday morning and Gerald and Kaitlin are woken up to Drake crying loudly in his crib. Gerald is up and out of bed and goes to check on Drake. He is very surprised to see that Drake has a very high temperature and he has dark red blotches all over his body. He is crying and, quite clearly, in a lot of discomfort. Gerald picks Drake up and can't believe that Drake is actually hot to the touch, way hotter than he should be. Gerald calls to Kaitlin, "Kaitlin, get up and get Lance. We are taking Drake to the hospital."

"What is it? What is wrong?" asks Kaitlin, getting out of bed. "It is Drake, he has a very high fever," says Gerald, and Kaitlin responds by saying, "We have that medicine we got at the drugstore, don't we? You remember the medicine for bringing down fever, what was it called? It was called like proactamol or something." Gerald scratches his head, saying, "Oh yeah, do we still have that?" Kaitlin responds, "I can't remember what we did with it." They search the bathroom vanity, the kitchen, and all the cupboards they can think of but cannot find it anywhere. Gerald says, "Come on, Kaitlin, we cannot wait any longer. We have to get him to the hospital now." Kaitlin has seen the condition that Drake has a couple of times now where his veins become visible throughout his body, and she knows that the doctors had done something to Drake when he was at Rosewood hospital. She has not even told Gerald of this, and she knows she cannot take Drake to the hospital. She has been protecting him his whole life so far, and her maternal instincts are to keep him safe by making sure no one knows of his condition even though she has no idea what his condition is. She looks to Gerald with a great idea, saying, "Gerald, remember the last time we were at the hospital and Drake had a fever. Remember what they did? They put him in an ice bath, and it brought his temperature down. We can do that. We can fill the sink with water and put ice in it and bring his temperature down. I don't trust the hospitals, do you?" Gerald replies, "No, I don't trust the hospitals, but I am not going to just let our son die, Kaitlin." Kaitlin says, "I know," as she fills the sink with water and gets all the ice out of the refrigerator. She says to Gerald, "Let's try this, Gerald. We can do this right now, and this may work."

"OK," says Gerald. They fill the sink, and Kaitlin notices that they will need more ice and tells Gerald to go the gas station and get more ice. He hurries and is gone to get some ice. The sink is nearly full of water and two trays of ice, and Drake has been and is still crying out of control like he never has in his whole life. Kaitlin strips him of his diaper and puts him in the bath of water and ice. Drake kicks and cries horribly, and Kaitlin cannot keep a good hold of him. He sinks in the water and is gagging and choking, breathing in huge mouthfuls of water. Kaitlin picks him out of the water only to lose her grip again, and this happens over and over. It seems like Drake is constantly gagging and choking on water, and Kaitlin starts to cry, knowing she is doing a terrible job, and her two-year-old child is suffering. She can't get a good hold of Drake because he is kicking and screaming, and Kaitlin is getting more and more scared that this is not working. Gerald gets back with a bag of ice and rips it open, dumping the ice into the water, saying, "Here, let me get a hold of him." Kaitlin steps back, and Gerald has much bigger hands, and he can hold Drake much more securely. Drake is still crying out of control, and Gerald says to Kaitlin who has her hand over her mouth, crying, "Kaitlin, go check on Lance and make sure he is OK." Kaitlin goes to check on Lance, who is still in his crib. Gerald holds Drake in the ice water for a while and lifts him out, inspecting his temperature. Gerald is very concerned about the swollen red blotches all over Drake's body but amazingly they are seemingly getting smaller and less red in color. Gerald holds Drake in and out of the bath for nearly two hours until the fever has been reduced and the red blotches are still there but seemingly going away. Gerald wraps Drake in a towel and holds him while he sits on a kitchen chair. He looks at the clock to see it is not even 6:00 a.m. yet, so there is no drugstore even open yet to go and get fever-reducing medication for Drake. Drake has finally calmed down and has stopped crying, but now, he is shivering. Gerald notices something powerful about his son. Drake is shivering all wrapped in the towel and just looking at his father without crying. He is somehow very calm. Gerald admires his son and the inner strength that he knows Drake has.

Over the next two years, things go very smoothly for Drake and Lance. That is not true for Kaitlin and Gerald. Gerald has grown more and more unappreciative of his job and spends more time at the bar than at home. Gerald has been falling behind on paying the bills, and his marriage to Kaitlin is growing weak. Gerald leaves almost every weekend for the whole weekend, leaving Kaitlin alone with Drake and Lance. On one particular weekend, Gerald does not come home. Kaitlin gets a call from Gerald late Sunday night saying he has quit his job and he is moving and Kaitlin is to pack all her things and the boys because they will be moving this weekend. Kaitlin cannot believe what she is hearing and says she is not packing and she is not moving, and she hangs up on Gerald. Gerald finally comes home on Wednesday, and he and Kaitlin have the worst argument ever. It actually turns into a shouting match between them, and they yell and scream at each other. Drake sits on the couch, holding his younger brother by the hand as Gerald and Kaitlin argue and fight. Gerald punches Kaitlin in the side of the head, knocking her to floor, and he storms out of the house, slamming the front door, breaking all the glass in the door. He comes back in the house a few minutes later, saying, "Kaitlin, I am so sorry, but I can't do this anymore." Gerald approaches Drake and Lance, saying, "Drake, who do you want to live with, your mother or me?" Drake does not say a word. His mother crawls to the couch, crying and saying, "Gerald, I love you, why can't you stay here? Why can't we be a family? I don't want to split up." Gerald again asks Drake who is only four years old, "Drake, do you want to live with your mother or me?" Drake says, "I want to stay with whoever will not live with lance. In that way, none of us will live alone." Gerald walks out of the house, and that is the last time Drake sees his father for a very long time.

CHAPTER 5

The Smartest Thing Kaitlin Ever Did

Kaitlin has a very difficult time over the next two years. Gerald has gone; he just left her with nothing. The house goes into foreclosure, and Kaitlin has to move in with her parents. This is a very small house, and Kaitlin shares the room she grew up in with Drake and Lance. Kaitlin's parents buy Kaitlin a used car, and you would think it is actually a boat because the cars built in the late '60s and early '70s were huge. Kaitlin spends a lot of time down at the welfare office, trying to get help with food stamps and trying to find a place for her and her two sons to live. Drake is going to be five in September, and he is going to be enrolled in school this year. Kaitlin is desperately trying to find a new place for her and her children to live but has had no luck so far. Kaitlin's mother, Brenda, is not very good with small children. She does not have the energy to keep up with them and is always swatting the boys, telling them to sit still and stop running around the house. Drake is at the age where he is starting to learn about his body and rubbing against the furniture in provocative ways, and Grandma has Drake on a constant leash, telling him to stop that. Brenda cannot deal well with the boys and is always telling her husband Jack to calm the boys and make them sit still. Jack has a calm nature about himself and a great sense of humor and tells Brenda to leave the boys alone, that they are fine, and they are doing what boys do. The second Grandma takes her eyes off Drake who is sitting on the couch, he runs up the stairs with Lance right behind him. The boys are laughing and giggling and on a constant run like they have a never-ending supply of energy. Grandma Richardson puts her hands on her hips, yelling to the boys who have just run up the stairs, "Boys, you stop that running, and you come down here right now. Jack, tell the boys to get down here and sit down." Jack is sitting on his favorite recliner chair and tells Brenda, "You leave the boys alone honey. They will be fine, and if you make them sit down now, they will be up all night. It is better to let them run around now, and then, they will sleep tonight." Jack rolls his head over to the side and closes his eyes for a nap. Brenda goes right back to chasing the boys around.

Kaitlin gets back from the welfare office, and her mother is all over her, saying, "Kaitlin, you have to find a place for you and your boys. I cannot take care of these kids." Kaitlin responds by saying, "I know, Mom. I am searching, but it is very hard to find a place to live. I have found an option today that might be able to help me. It is called the Greenwide housing project in Macksville. That is about two hours from here to the east, but they may be able to help me. I am going to go there tomorrow and meet with the landlord. The government will help me pay for rent and food so I may be able to move in there." Kaitlin's mother is relieved, saying, "I hope so because these boys are driving me crazy. Your father is no help either." The girls look to Jack, and he is sound asleep in his favorite chair and did not hear a word they have said. Early the next morning, Kaitlin gets up early and is off to the Greenwide housing project to meet with the landlord about an apartment for her and her boys. Not too long after she has gone, Drake gets out of bed, and he is already running around the house, and Lance is right behind him. The boys are laughing and giggling and running everywhere, and Grandma gets out of bed, yelling, "Boys, stop that running right now!" She walks out of her room just as the boys are running right toward her, and she points her finger at the boys, yelling, "Stop!" Drake stops with a smile on his face, and Lance runs right into his back and falls backward onto the floor. Lance gets up quickly and grabs his bigger brother by his arm. Drake is looking right at his grandmother and loses the smile on his face and starts to choke. Drake puts his left hand to his throat and is turning red. Grandma Richardson looks at Drake, saying, "Drake, what is wrong? Stop playing around, Drake." Grandma starts to smack Drake on the back, and she can hear he is gagging and choking. Drake is turning sickly red and almost blue, and he is trying as hard as he can to get air, but for some reason, he is choking. Brenda yells, "Jack, Jack, get out her. Drake is choking. He is choking to death. Jack, get out here." Jack rushes out of the bedroom to see Drake has fallen to the floor and he is choking. Jack bends down to Drake, saying, "What has happened?"

"I don't know," replies Brenda. "He was fine, and all of a sudden, he started choking." Jack looks into Drake's mouth, and he can see that his throat is swollen shut. Jack picks Drake up and heads toward the car. "Where are you going?" asks Brenda. "Come on, get Lance, we are taking Drake to the hospital," says Jack. They get in the car and are off to the hospital. It is very fortunate that the Richardsons live less than two miles from the hospital. Jack has not driven this fast in over thirty years, but he makes haste right to the emergency room and carries Drake into the hospital. Once in the hospital emergency room, a doctor looks at Drake and takes him immediately away. The Richardsons are told to wait in the waiting area and they will be updated as to what is going on with Drake as soon as the doctors know. The Richardsons sit in the waiting area for almost four hours, doing their best to keep Lance still and within their sight. Finally, someone comes to tell them that Drake had swollen tonsils, and they had to be removed. "Mr. and Mrs. Richardson, Dr. Pearl will come meet with you very shortly and tell you what has happened with Drake and why he had to have his tonsils removed, OK?" says the receptionist. Jack says OK to the nice young lady, who leaves them, and shortly, Dr. Pearl comes and introduces himself to the Richardsons.

"Mr. and Mrs. Richardson."

"Yes, that is us," says Jack. "We are Drake's grandparents. His mother is out looking for a home for them right now."

"Well, Mr. and Mrs. Richardson, Drake had very swollen tonsils. They were so swollen that his throat was blocked, and he could not breathe. We could not bring down the swelling and had to perform a tonsillectomy. We had to remove his tonsils, and this is not at all uncommon. It was a very simple procedure, but I must admit to you. I have never seen tonsils that look like Drake's tonsils. I would like to have them sent to our laboratory to have them examined if you don't mind. I really need the consent of his mother, but since you brought Drake in and you are his legal grandparents, then you can sign for this. Would that be all right with you?" asks Dr. Pearl.

Jack says, "Sure, that won't be a problem at all. Will Drake be able to come home with us?"

Dr. Pearl says, "Drake cannot go home right now. He is still sedated, and we had a lot of trouble trying to stop the bleeding. Although a tonsillectomy is a very simple procedure, it is still a surgical procedure, and everyone is different. We had a hard time stopping the bleeding even after the wound had been sewn up. We would like to keep him here overnight to keep an eye on him and make sure he heals all right."

"OK, so we should come back in the morning," says Jack.

"Yes, that would be great," says Dr. Pearl. The Richardsons sign some paperwork and head home with Lance. The Richardsons get home with Lance before Kaitlin gets back, and they get dinner started. Kaitlin gets home about an hour later and notices that Drake is nowhere to be seen. Kaitlin asks, "Where is Drake?"

"Oh, he is at the hospital," says her mother, putting mashed potatoes on the kitchen table, and Jack comes out of the kitchen with a pot roast. Lance is sitting at the table, and he has the biggest smile on his face, watching Grandma and Grandpa bring out all this food to the table. "At the hospital? What do you mean Drake is at the hospital?" says Kaitlin. "Honey, sit down with us and have dinner, we will explain everything," says Jack as he pushes Lance in his high chair to his plate, which he just put potatoes and carrots and pot roast on. Jack sits down and prepares his plate, and Brenda sits down as well, saying, "Sit down, Kaitlin. Drake is fine. This morning, he was having trouble breathing, so we had to take him to the hospital. He had an emergency tonsillectomy. The doctor said they wanted to watch Drake overnight. He was still bleeding after his tonsillectomy, so they wanted to keep him overnight and make sure his throat heals."

"Mom, you know how I feel about taking Drake to the hospital. After dinner, I am going there to check on Drake, and if I can, I am going to bring him home." Brenda replies, "I remember the doctor saying Drake's tonsils did not look right, and he had them sent to a lab for analysis."

"Oh no. Mom, this is very bad," says Kaitlin. "What is bad, Kaitlin? Drake could not be in better hands. Now be quiet and eat your dinner," says Brenda, taking a bite of her pot roast. Kaitlin gets noticeably scared, saying, "Mom, Dad, I never told you this before, but do you remember when all the babies were dying right when Drake was born? Do you remember almost a hundred babies had died, and the news said it was pneumonia or scarlet fever or whatever, do you remember that?"

"Oh yes," says Brenda. "Terrible, that was just terrible. All those poor families"

"Well, Mom, Dad, Drake was a part of that. The babies were dying because doctors were experimenting on them. Drake was one of the babies, but he lived, and they did something to him Mom. We have to go get him now. Trust me. We have to go and get him." Jack pays most of his attention to his plate and eats very contently. Lance is the same, only he kind of picks a little bit of food here and there and eats it humming happily to himself. Brenda replies to Kaitlin, saying, "Your father and I are not going anywhere at this time of the night." (It is only 6:00 p.m.) "If you think you need to go see Drake in the hospital, then you go. Your father and I will go in the morning but not sooner." Kaitlin gets up from the dinner table and heads for the hospital.

Kaitlin gets to the hospital at a little after six and heads right to the receptionist. "Hi, my name is Kaitlin Hammond, and my son Drake Hammond was brought her by his grandparents. They said it was an emergency that he could not breathe. I am scared to death, and I need to see my son. I need to know he is all right," says Kaitlin in a trembling voice. "Hold on, Mrs. Hammond, let me check for you. I will be back, one moment please," says the receptionist. Kaitlin watches as the receptionist walks down a walkway full of folders on both sides of the walk, and she picks a folder that must be Drake's and walks back to Kaitlin at the desk, saying, "Oh yes, Mrs. Hammond, Drake is fine, and he is resting now. Visiting hours have ended, so you will have to come back in the morning to see him."

"Please, please," says Kaitlin, pleading with the receptionist. "I must see him now. Please, please, can I see him now?" The receptionist breathes deeply, saying, "It is not really allowed, but I guess, just this one time and only for a short while, OK, Mrs. Hammond?"

"Oh thank you," says Kaitlin.

The receptionist walks around and through a door from the inside area she is in to see Mrs. Hammond and waves to Kaitlin. Kaitlin follows her down the hall. They walk down the hall and up one flight of stairs, and the receptionist shows Kaitlin into a room and says "Just be very quiet, OK? There is a chair next to the bed, and you can sit there. I am sure you will be fine." Kaitlin shakes her hand and says, "Thank you, thank you."

"You are very welcome, Mrs. Hammond," says the receptionist as she heads back to her station. Kaitlin sits in the chair next to Drake, and he is sound asleep. She rubs his forehead and kisses her son, but he sleeps soundly and looks so comfortable. Kaitlin looks Drake over and notices he has a band around his wrist with his name on it. She looks to the bed next to Drake, and there is another boy lying there, and he is sound asleep also. Kaitlin is as docile a person as you will ever meet, and adventure is something completely foreign to her, but right now, for the first time in her life, she has an instinctual impulse, and she has to follow it. She walks into the hall and can see no one around. She walks down the hall a little, and there is a dresser with long wide drawers, and Kaitlin pulls one of the drawers open. There are coloring books and crayons and stuffed animals in this drawer. She opens the next drawer, and there are different toys in this drawer, and she opens the drawer on the bottom, and she pulls out a small pair of scissors made out of plastic, but they will work. She finds a roll of scotch tape on a tape holder, and she takes the tape and scissors back to the room Drake is in. Kaitlin can't believe she is doing this, but she cuts the band from the wrist of the boy sleeping in the bed next to Drake, and she cuts the band from Drake's wrist as well. She then swaps the bands and tapes them back on the wrists of the boys. Kaitlin puts the tape and scissors back in the drawer where she found them and heads back into the room with Drake. She sits next to Drake quietly for over an hour and falls asleep. She sleeps soundly until midnight, and she is awoken by two men making noise in the room. Kaitlin wakes to see two men wearing suits, and they do not look like doctors. "What are you doing?" asks Kaitlin. She can see one man look at the wristband on the boys' hands, and he looks at the other man, saying, "This is Drake." The other man says to Kaitlin, "Oh, we are so sorry to bother you, ma'am. We had no idea that you were here, that is why we are wearing our suits tonight and not our white coats. This boy here, Drake, has had complications, and we were called from home to come in and take him to an examining room for further tests. You can never be too sure, you know?"

"Oh, I know what you mean. I hope you find what you are looking for, and I sure hope Drake comes out of this just fine," says Kaitlin. "Oh, he will be just fine. He is in the best care right here at Sprencer hospital," says one of the gentlemen, and he follows the other man who is carrying the boy out of the room. Kaitlin waits a few minutes until the men have left, and then she sighs, getting very nervous. She rubs her face and shakes Drake a little, whispering, "Drake, Drake, wake up, Drake." Drake is well sedated, and he is still sound asleep. Kaitlin cannot believe what she just saw, and she really can't believe her instincts were right. Someone has come to take Drake. Kaitlin picks up Drake and rests him on her right shoulder, and as calmly as she can, she walks to the stairs and heads down them, carrying Drake. She gets hold of the band on Drake's wrist and takes it off him, putting it in her pocket. She exits the bottom level of the stairs and is in a hallway that leads right to the receptionist and the front door. Kaitlin dressed Drake in his pajamas that he was wearing this morning when his grandparents brought him to the hospital. They were in the locker right next to the doorway leading in and out of the room Drake was sleeping in. Kaitlin knows she can't just walk out of the hospital without the receptionist noticing her, but she has to get by the receptionist somehow. Kaitlin has the best idea of her life and does what she thinks is the smartest thing she has ever done. She rushes toward the receptionist and starts to cry, yelling, "Help, help me." The receptionist who is a different girl from the one who was there earlier says, "Ma'am, where did you come from?" Kaitlin is hysterical crying and saying, "Help me, get a doctor, my son won't wake up. I don't know what is wrong with him. Get a doctor, hurry, please get a doctor." The receptionist can see Kaitlin is scared for her son and says, "Hold on, ma'am, hold on. I will get a doctor, hold on." The receptionist hurries out of sight, and as soon as she is gone, Kaitlin runs out of the hospital with Drake on her shoulder. Kaitlin is scared and is not sure what to do. She decides to go to the police station and make a report. She gets to the police station, and there is one man there. She enters the door, and there is a second door on the inside that is locked, and a voice talks to her on an intercom. "Hi, how can I help you?" Kaitlin says, "Hi, my name is Kaitlin Hammond, and I would like to make a report for my son."

"Sure, come on in," a voice says, and Kaitlin can hear that the door has been unlocked. She opens the door and is greeted by a very young man. "Hi, my name is Jerry. How may I help you?"

"Hi, Jerry, my name is Kaitlin, and I have a very strange story, but I am so scared, and I did not know what else to do other than come here."

Jerry can see that Kaitlin is very worried and has her son on her right shoulder. "Come over here and have a seat, and we can talk about what is bothering you," Jerry says as he helps Kaitlin to a chair, and she sits down with Drake still on her shoulder, and she moves him to a more comfortable position on her lap. Jerry sits behind a desk, and he listens to Kaitlin talk for over an hour, telling him the incredible story of how Drake was worked on by the doctors that had killed so many babies and young children five years ago. Jerry remembers that because it was a huge story all over New York State. Somehow, Drake survived, and now Kaitlin is worried that those same doctors, even though they were all sent to prison and are supposed to be locked up, somehow are still after Drake because he survived. Kaitlin tells Jerry the story of what had happened at the hospital tonight and how she came to be in the police station with her son on her shoulder. It just so happens that tonight is Jerry's first night on the job, and the first night he has been left alone in the station. He takes very good notes and fills out a report, but there is nothing he can do, and Kaitlin understands. She asks Jerry for his advice and what she can do. Jerry tells her that she has to be aware and pay attention to everything going on around her; other than that, there is nothing they can do. Kaitlin feels somewhat relieved because at least she has filled out a report, and that is better than nothing. She gets Jerry's personal phone number, and he gives it to her, telling her that if she ever needs Jerry for anything, she can call him. It is very late, almost four in the morning, and Kaitlin leaves the police station with Drake. She gets home to a dark and quiet home and puts Drake to bed, and he never woke once. This really did not surprise Kaitlin much because Drake, for all his life, has been a deep sleeper. He can sleep through thunderstorms and anything, and being that he is sedated, nothing will wake him. Kaitlin walks around in the kitchen, nervous and scared. She is unsure of what to do and feels like she is on the run when she should not be on the run from anything. *Those doctors, what did they do to Drake, and why are they still after him now,* she thinks to herself. She walks around for a little while and then goes to bed. It is going to be a long day today. She had a great visit at the Greenwide housing project yesterday, and she can move into a two-bedroom apartment with her two sons. This is great because she will be able to keep an eye on her boys, except when they are at school, and Drake has to be enrolled very soon so he can attend school this September, which is something that was discussed yesterday at the meeting at the housing project. Kaitlin plans to get up in a few hours and take the boys to see their new home and get Drake enrolled in school.

Kaitlin gets up very early and has no problem getting the boys up. They wake up, and they eat breakfast, and Kaitlin says good-bye to her parents, and they are off to the Greenwide housing project. The day goes very well, and the project already has an apartment ready for the Hammonds to move into. It is mostly paid in full by government programs, which include rent and food stamps and help with the electric bill as well. Within the week, the Hammonds are all moved in, and Drake is enrolled in the Greenville Elementary School. The project they live in is only three blocks from the school, and Drake can walk to school. Kaitlin and Lance walk to school with Drake for the first week, and then he walks there on his own. The next two years go very well for the boys and Kaitlin, but Kaitlin always has this funny feeling like someone is always watching them, but this feeling fades in time. She has met a man named Thomas Durguss, and they have fallen in love. Thomas courts Kaitlin for a year, and they get married. The four of them live in the project until Drake is ten and Lance is eight, and then they move into a house in the small town of Dunshes. Drake takes a great liking to Thomas because Drake loves football and has played on the team in Greenville since he was six years old. Thomas thinks Drake is a very good football player especially being as young as he is and has looked specifically for a house in the town of Dunshes, which is known for having a very good football program. Drake has told Thomas over and over that he is going to be in the NFL when he grows up, and he is going to be the best wide receiver there ever was. Thomas is a fan of the New York Giants, and Drake is a fan of the Oakland Raiders, and every Sunday they watch football on TV and bet each other five cents on which team will win the game they are watching on TV. This is a Sunday ritual, and really the only time the boys spend with Thomas because Thomas works night as a CNC machinist.

The years go by, and Drake is becoming a superstar in the small town of Dunshes. By the time Drake starts his sophomore year in high school, he is already just under six feet tall, weighing 180 pounds. In ninth grade, Drake makes a name for himself in Dunshes by making the varsity football team as their premier first-round wide receiver. Drake has become the go-to guy and catches almost anything thrown his way. He is fast and strong, and you will think his hands are made out of glue. Drake has become the talk of the county, and he almost led the Dunshes Spikers to the title game in his freshman year. The Spikers make the sectional final game again in Drake's sophomore year, and this is a barn buster, to say the least. The guy defending against Drake is a senior, and Drake is facing him for the sixth time. Last year, the Tilleage Tramplers beat the Spikers to make the state title game, but this year, Drake and the Spikers will not be denied. Brandon Scotts is the boy defending against Drake, and Drake remembers him well. Brandon made an interception last year against the Spikers and ran it back for a touchdown, and ultimately, this play won the game for the Tramplers. Drake and Brandon fight hard all game, and they are really working each other hard. Brandon is hitting Drake as hard as he can off the line and knocking him down a lot. Drake is hitting back as hard as he can, but Brandon is winning this battle because he is occupying Drake and preventing him from getting down field and getting big plays. Drake is aware of Brandon's strategy, but Brandon is bigger and faster, and the Tramplers know they have to take Drake out of play because he is one of the biggest threats the Spikers have. Drake is guarded by Brandon, and he is also double-teamed by another player from the defense in almost every play. Now the Tramplers have to worry about the Spikers' number one running back K. R. Simmons. KR is one of the best running backs in the county, and with two of the best defenders always on Drake now, they concentrate two to four defenders on KR. This is the first game where Drake has been shut down. It is now the fourth quarter, and Drake has not made a catch yet, and he is getting very frustrated and angry. The third quarter has just ended, and the Spikers are on the sideline, getting ready to come in for the beginning of the fourth quarter, and Drake makes a big speech, telling all his team mates to watch for him and protect their quarterback. Drake tells his team mates, "You watch for me. I will get open, and you pass me the ball. I will catch it and score." The Spikers are down 14–0, and now in the last quarter, time is running out on them. They get back to the game, and Drake fights hard with Brandon, trying to get by him and open. So far, Brandon has been stronger and knocking Drake to the ground a lot. Drake summons all his strength, and these two battle, and the crowd can see it. They are pushing and running into each other, and finally, Drake gets by Brandon. The ball is thrown high, and Drake runs with lightning speed under the ball, catches it, and runs right over the guy double-teaming him. He then runs right over the deep safety and scores. The Spikers get the ball back a few minutes later, and the battle Drake is in with Brandon starts all over again. Brandon taunts Drake, and Drake shouts right back at him. The two get into a tussle after every play, pulling and pushing on each other. Drake gets free three plays in a row and makes great catches and gains a lot of yards. The Spikers are now down to the eight-yard line, looking like they are going to score again. Brandon gets right in Drake's face as the Spikers come up to the line, and as soon as the ball is hiked, Brandon knocks Drake down, and Drake gets up very heated, and the two go at it. Brandon throws an uppercut, catching Drake right on the left side of his mouth, splitting his lip and cutting Brandon's hand. The referee blows his whistle and flags Brandon, and he has to leave the game for one play. That is enough for Drake to get free in the end zone and score again on the next play, and Brandon has to watch from the sideline. Fortunately for Brandon, the referee did not see the punch; he only saw what happened after the punch, so he can return to the game. The extra point is good, and the game is tied. On the next series, the Tramplers go four and out and have to punt the ball right back to the Spikers. The Spikers return the ball to the fifty-yard line, and Brandon and Drake are facing each other once again. The ball is hiked, and Drake hits Brandon as hard as he can, and Brandon falls backward. Drake looks to his quarterback with his hand held high, and here comes the ball. Drake outruns the double-team, catches the ball and makes a great move to the right, and then runs back left and down the sideline, faking out the safety, and scores. Drake spikes the ball and raises his hands high, looking at the cheering crowd. Drake then notices people running onto the field, and Brandon is still lying where he fell. Drake runs to see what has happened, and when he gets to Brandon, he sees that his helmet has been removed, and his whole body is shaking, and he is vomiting. He is not responding to any commands, and a stretcher is brought out, and he is put on it. His head is strapped securely to the stretcher as is his whole body, and an ambulance is rushed out onto the field, and he is taken away.

This vision has haunted Drake many times during his life and has been more important to him than the fact that the Spikers won the sectional title and went to the state title game. In the state title game, Drake broke his right knee and was never able to play football ever again. There are many things that have happened to Drake in his younger life that are now haunting him. He has dreams and visions of people that he was very close to, and then they were just gone. All these events that he thought were just a part of growing up are turning out to be something terrible. Something happened to him when he was young. He was so young that he cannot remember it now. Something that was not his fault. Something has been done to him, and he is going to find out what it was and by whom before they find him. Drake knows if they find him before he finds the truth, then he will never be heard from again. The vision of Brandon, in particular, is one that he can see clearly in his mind. Even though it has been nine years now since the incident with Brandon. Drake can remember this like it was yesterday. This event happened so fast, and Drake was there to see it happen, and he will never forget it because the next day, Brandon died. What happened and why? He remembers that Brandon died, and other people he had been close to just vanished without a word when he was younger. Drake never thought about it until very recently, but something is not right with him, and he knows people from very high up in society are after him. He was lucky to get away this time, but he knows he will not be so lucky in the future. He has to think and be very smart, or he will disappear. Drake thinks to himself, sitting with his knees up to his chest, his arms wrapped around his legs, and his head resting on his knees. Here on the fenced-off beach in Pompano Beach, Florida, where he is all alone late at night and watching the hatching turtles emerge from the sand and head to the sea. Drake thinks to himself, *So what happened to me and how do I figure this all out?*

CHAPTER 6

ASAFEW

Alex Kevnick is called to a very secret and privileged meeting with the head of the CDCP Harry Klaushoven. Harry addresses Alex as soon as he enters the small boardroom. "Alex, please be seated." Harry is already seated at the head of the table with a folder lying in front of him, and he is looking it over. Alex sits to Harry's left, and Harry begins speaking. "Alex, everything is in place. We have a secret location equipped with all the latest in state-of-the-art modern equipment. It is in a house outside Atlanta, and we have secured a half dozen hospitals in the upstate region of New York to begin our experiments. We have been following one Earl Rieval who is at the top of all the graduate students in college this year (1967). We want him to work in the house and you to work in the hospitals. We need you to recruit him, and we believe he will be more than willing to work with you because of the nature of your work and because of the most interesting writings he has published." Harry drops some of the writings that Earl Rieval has published in front of Alex. "Remember, Alex, no one outside of us and the men working directly under me know of our experiments. This is the beginning of ASAFEW, and you are our leadman in the field. You know our goals now make them a reality. Larry and John are waiting for you in the lobby, and they will take you to our house, which is our front for our medical laboratory. Roger and Richard have been sent to retrieve Earl, and he will be taken to the house where you will tell him of the work that must be done in the house. Just inform him of the work he will be doing. He needs to know nothing else. I believe he will be very excited to find a cure for viruses in the human bloodstream. He will not be in the field with you, so he will not know what you are doing. He will only know what he is working on and that is what we want. Are you ready, Alex? Are you ready to be a founding father of ASAFEW?" Alex stands up, saying, "I am ready, Harry. It is time to begin." Alex walks out of the room.

Alex meets with Earl in the specially designed house the next day, and Earl accepts the challenge of working with viruses, antibiotics, and fresh blood samples in real time. Earl is instructed that what he is working on is obviously the deadliest of biological materials, and no one, not even his family, is to know what he is working on or where he is working. Earl accepts after Alex shows him a very disturbing video where innocent people are being experimented on with deadly viruses. Earl asks Alex where the healthy blood samples will be coming from. He also asks where the virus and antibiotic samples will be coming from. Alex tells Earl the blood samples will come from babies whose parents have allowed for blood samples to be studied. Alex is also granted top-security admittance to the CDCP stock of deadly virus strains and antibiotic samples, so he will provide Earl with new samples as needed. Earl finds this hard to believe but does not question it much. In the lower level of this specially modified house is the laboratory where Earl will be working on the deadliest of biological materials with fresh blood and antibiotics to create and make serum to eradicate disease and virus. Earl is so excited for this opportunity, and the laboratory is his to organize however he wishes all this wealth of equipment blinds Earl to the danger and obvious illegality of what is taking place here. From the moment Earl accepted this arrangement, he has worked day and night, and before he knows it, almost a year has gone by, and he is suddenly woken up in the middle of the night and swept away to Upstate New York. Earl has had absolute freedom to work with viruses of the worst kind like Ebola, pneumonia, swine flu, avian flu, and more. He has had fresh human blood samples provided to him every week, and Earl has been mixing all the samples with one another in different ways, and he has been studying the effects of all his concoctions under the microscope in real time as he injects the deadly mixtures into human blood. Earl also has access to all the antibiotics available as well, and he has been mixing these into serums that he has been preparing and injecting into infected blood to watch what happens. Not only has Earl been mixing all the deadly biological material with all different mixes of antibiotics and blood, but he has been mixing different blood samples with one another as well. Earl is absolutely fascinated by the work he is doing, and there is not enough time in a year for him. He makes serums every week, and every new serum could be the one to rid human blood from all forms of disease and virus. Earl gives the serums to Alex every week, and Alex tells Earl that the serums are going directly to the CDCP for examination. On the flight to New York, Earl reads the paper, and the headline and story start to bring him into the light. Of course, at the hospital, when he and Nurse Reisen confront Dr. Kevnick, that is when Earl realizes what Dr. Kevnick has been doing illegally with all his serums. Earl tries to save the three babies there with his newest serums, which he has called the H vials or Herculean serum. When the first baby dies, Earl believes there is no chance for the second and third baby, and he and Nurse Reisen leave, heading for the authorities only to be run off the road and into the canal.

It is pouring outside, and Betty (Nurse Reisen) can barely see the road in front of her. While Earl is having a conversation with Betty, the car they are in is hit from behind, and Earl hits his head on the dashboard and passenger window, not knocking him out cold, but he is dazed, and his body for the most part is limp. The Camaro slides off the road and tumbles down the steep embankment into the canal. Earl and Betty are submerged, and the car lands with the passenger widow to the top, and it has shattered, so he can fit through it and swim to the surface. Earl has no sense, no thought process; he just swims to the surface and to shore where he is scooped up by two men in suits and taken away. Betty is left to drown in the car at the bottom of the canal. Earl is bleeding from a deep gash on the right side of his forehead, where his head smashed into the passenger window, breaking it and further dazing him. The men in the car help him stop the bleeding and take him on a very long car ride back to Atlanta.

Dr. Kevnick watches as Gerald and Kaitlin leave with Baby Drake, and in a panic, he calls a secret number. "Harry, this is Alex. I know you don't want to be called on this line, but we have a problem. The Baby Drake, Drake Hammond, has been taken by his parents. They are leaving the hospital now. He is the only surviving baby, and he may be our last chance. This whole experiment is getting out of control. It may be too late already to salvage our goals. Yes, Dr. Rieval has been secured. He is being taken back to the house in Atlanta right now. Yes, I will destroy all evidence here, and then I will head back to the house myself. OK, I will talk to you more then, bye." Dr. Kevnick has keys that allow him access to secure areas of the hospital, and he heads to the file room and starts to pick files from babies that he has had ties with. He takes all the files and begins to run them through the shredder machine. He gets the file of Drake Hammond, but he does not shred this file. As fate would have it, he keeps this file intact and puts it in his briefcase. Dr. Kevnick is heading out of the hospital with all his belongings when at the front door, he is greeted by two men in suits, and unbelievably, there are camera crews behind them. The two men grab Dr. Kevnick by his arms and take his briefcase from him. They put handcuffs on him and walk him out of the hospital. The reporter asks him, "Why, Dr. Kevnick? Why have you been infecting all these babies and killing them? We all just want to know why." Dr. Kevnick looks at the reporter, knowing he is being set up as the fall guy. He says not a word, and the two men rush him into the backseat of a black car, and he is driven away.

Harry Klaushoven is on the phone in his office, saying, "It is being taken care of as we speak. I understand. Dr.

Kevnick will be fine. We have contacted the local media, and his apprehension will be all over the news today. This should relieve the CDCP from all suspicion. Dr. Kevnick will take full blame for the whole operation. We have secured a dummy to take his place, and we are making the switch. Yes, sir, it will happen very shortly. I understand. There is one surviving baby. His name is Drake Hammond. He could be the catalyst we have been waiting for. Yes, sir, we will keep him under close surveillance. Yes, sir, the file on Drake Hammond is being delivered to me as we speak. No, we will not get too close. No one will know we even exist. I understand, sir. Dr. Kevnick and Dr. Rieval will be brought to the house, and there, we will instruct them. Sir, what if they are getting soft on us. I understand, sir, they are with us, or they are no more. Yes, sir. It will be done." Harry hangs up the phone, rubbing his forehead with his right hand, very concerned, saying to himself, *I knew this would get messy.*

Alex is put in the back seat of the car, and a man gets in behind him and sits alongside him. "Just relax, doctor," says Larry. Dr. Kevnick is well aware of who Larry and John are, and he asks them, "So I am being set up to take the fall?" Larry responds, "Don't worry, Alex, we are not going to let anything happen to you although everyone will think you are going to prison for the rest of your life." A few miles down the road, John pulls the car over to the side of the road. This is a back road with no houses, and another car approaches and pulls off the side of the road as well. The men take the handcuffs off Alex and tell him to get into the other car. Alex heads to the other car, asking, "How do we make this work?"

Larry motions Alex to the back of the car where he opens the trunk, and inside is a man with his hands tied behind his back, and he is unconscious. Larry and John remove the man from the trunk and put him in the backseat of the car where Alex just was. The man looks remarkably similar to Alex. Larry says to Alex, "You are going with Richard and Roger back to the house in Atlanta. For the time being, you have to remain unseen and unheard. This man here will be going to prison for you. The world will think Alex Kevnick is going away for life, and this man here from now on is Alex Kevnick." Alex looks to Larry and John, saying, "I understand." Larry gives Dr. Kevnick his briefcase back, and he gets into the other car, and it takes off. Larry and John get into the car and drive away. Larry is in the backseat with the man, and he breaks a capsule and runs it under the nose of the man. He shakes his head and awakens. Larry looks to the man, saying, "It has begun. Your family will be set for the rest of their life as long as you keep your word." The man shakes his head up and down, silently saying yes. Alex has been condemned to the house in Atlanta, and Earl has been as well. The news the next day after the crash of Nurse Reisen's Camaro in the canal actually had said that Dr. Rieval was in the car, and he had died along with Nurse Reisen. The thing that blew Dr. Rieval away is that a body was put in place of his own, and the world thinks Dr. Rieval is dead. Dr. Rieval went back to work on his serums, and this keeps his mind off of what has happened. His H vials, which is short for Herculean serum, has been his most successful series of serums. These serums have actually eradicated diseases from blood samples, but again, this is very different from being in a human body. The two doctors are aware that Drake has survived, and they know Drake is a walking virus, but they have been instructed to wait and watch Drake. They are to study the blood and organs of possible victims that may be contaminated by Drake, and this too may help them create a cure that will be needed worldwide someday. For now the doctors are to work on people who have been exposed to Drake and wait for the day they get to meet Drake in person, and hopefully, on that day, Drake will still be alive. That day almost came nearly four years later. Harry Klaushoven has had very close surveillance on Drake his whole life, and it is an odd situation Drake's mother, Kaitlin, always had this feeling that she was being watched, so did Drake, and they did make mention of this feeling to people from time to time, but what do you do and how do you prove just a hunch? When Drake's grandparents took Drake to the hospital, and he had his tonsils removed, the tonsils themselves were sent to the lab for analysis. Harry Klaushoven had the tonsils intercepted and taken to the house in Atlanta where Dr. Rieval was able to study them. Harry had sent Roger Stergis and Richard Yarlow to pick up Drake at the hospital, and they were going to take him to the house in Atlanta. The fact that Kaitlin always had this funny suspicion that she and her sons were being watched saved Drake from the two men on this night. The two men get to the house in Atlanta with the wrong boy, making them look very incompetent. The hospital had a full-blown investigation going on the next day when the two men get back with the boy, and Harry Klaushoven has this incident covered up without it becoming a major story. The men are told by Harry to leave Drake be for now. Everyone knows Drake is not going to be hard to find because even if he were to disappear, his condition would someday bring him right back into the spotlight. Earl had received the tonsils removed from Drake and studied them. Earl and Alex study the tonsils and realize they have created something incredible with Drake, something they never had thought possible. Alex immediately called Harry to tell him of the situation they have with Drake. This is what Alex and Harry have been hoping for, and it is time to bring Earl into the fold and tell him of the ultimate goal and what they have been planning all along. Earl is brought to the CDCP with Alex, Larry and John. They head into a boardroom where Harry is sitting with Roger and Richard. Harry addresses the men as they enter the room. "Ah, gentlemen, please be seated." Harry stands up and walks over behind Earl, putting his hands on Earl's shoulders, saying, "Gentlemen, this is the man who has made it all possible. This is the man who has created our catalyst. Gentlemen, I give you, Earl Rieval, the bringer of ultimate power." The men in the room applaud. Earl looks around, confused, saying, "What are you talking about and who are you?"

"I, Dr. Rieval, am Harry Klaushoven, head of the CDCP, and you, Earl, are the creator of Drake Hammond. You have created Drake Hammond and made him what he is today. You see, Earl, what you have done is created the most lethal disease ever in the history of man. You have created a walking, breathing, talking man that is 100 percent lethal to everyone on the planet. Oh sure, there may be one or two or hell maybe up to ten people in the whole world that could live after being exposed to his saliva or his blood. You, Dr. Rieval, probably know better than any of us just how lethal this man is." Earl takes a deep breath, saying, "Yes, you are right. Drake has somehow become a carrier. His blood is the most lethal disease ever created. His saliva, the same. But I am a little confused here. We are trying to create the cure for all disease and virus, and Drake is the cure, we need to get him here now. We need to get Drake here and away from the public. He is a walking disaster." Harry smiles, saying, "Yes, Dr. Rieval, he is, and that is exactly what we have been waiting for. He is now the disaster we have been waiting for. The best part is that you have his tonsils. You have tissue from his body along with his blood. You need to make a cure from this, a cure so that anyone that was to be, let's say, infected by either his blood or his saliva could be cured from certain death. So, Dr. Rieval, you are going to be the doctor remembered for curing the human bloodstream from all disease and virus. As far as taking Drake out of the public, well, that is out of the question, at least, it is for now. He is right where we want him to be. We have him under tight surveillance, and anyone coming into contact with his blood or saliva will be studied by you at your lab. Drake is our salvation. Drake Hammond is our source of total power. The hope is that all will be so afraid of this new form of disease known as, oh, the Drake Hammond virus, that everyone will want to have the cure, and we will be the owners of this cure, making us the wealthiest men in the world. Total power will be ours." Earl stands up, saying, "You are mad. You can't do this. I cannot believe I am really a part of this madness. Thousands could die, maybe millions. We have to warn people. We cannot let Drake live free with the masses, we have to warn people and tell Drake what he is. We owe it to Drake to tell him what we have done to him, and what if somehow the virus in Drake was to become airborne? That could very possibly be the end of humanity."

The men in the room look at Earl in silence while Harry addresses Earl. "Earl, let me be clear to you. Alex is very capable of working on the cure to the walking disease that Drake is, but we all would like you as a member of ASAFEW to take the lead and make the cure to Drake Hammond and make it quick because Drake is a disease, he is a virus that at anytime can infect untold numbers of people. After all, you are the doctor who created Drake Hammond and the disease that he now is. Not only that, but you cannot go in public. As a matter of fact, the public thinks you are already dead. If you are not going to stand with us, if you are not going to rise with us as people need the cure and we are the sole owners of the cure, then let us know now. We will not force you to work with us, but be assured we are going to be the supreme power very soon. Very soon, governments will call to us for our service, for our cure, and we will be in total control. This is total power, Earl. This is the ultimate goal of ASAFEW. Are you with us or are you against us? So what is it going to be, Dr. Rieval? Are you a part of ASAFEW or not?"

Dr. Rieval looks around the room, wondering how he ever got into the position he is in now, but now that he is here, he sees no other option for him other than to commit fully to ASAFEW. "I am with you," he says and sits down.

"Very good, Dr. Rieval," says Harry. "This is what we are going to do from now on. We are going to keep a close eye on Drake, and anyone who comes in lethal contact with him will be brought to the house for Dr. Rieval and Dr. Kevnick to study just like we have been doing all these years. We will watch Drake, we will be his shadow. Now, doctors, work on the cure. The faster you create the cure, the quicker Drake Hammond will be exposed to the masses for what he is. Let us hope he does not become exposed before you have created the cure. Go now, doctors, and work on the cure, and you four make sure the house is secure at all times. I will keep Drake in check. Soon, men, our time will be very soon. That is all, you may be dismissed. Larry and John, take Dr. Rieval and Dr. Kevnick to the laboratory, and, Richard and Roger, head out to continue surveillance on Drake."

When all the men have left the room, Harry makes a phone call. "Yes, this is Harry. It is all set. Drake Hammond has become the catalyst we have been waiting for. Yes, sir. He is walking death. Dr. Rieval and Dr. Kevnick are going back to the laboratory to work on the cure. I must say, sir, this is very serious. If Drake becomes infectious by way of air, he has the potential to wipe out entire populations. I mean, our doctors had better come up with a cure to his blood and fast or true catastrophe is bound to happen. You are sure you do not want to let Drake know what has happened to him. No, sir, I am not going soft on you. It is just that we could see an awful lot of people die here. A lot of innocent people can die, sir. Is it really worth it? Yes, sir. They are working on it, sir. Yes, sir." Harry hangs up the phone.

CHAPTER 7

Drake Pieces Together His Past

There are bubbles exiting from Drake's mouth as he cries. He is a baby, and for some reason, he is submerged in cold water. He is kicking his legs and thrashing his arms in the water, but he cannot get air. He can hear himself screaming. He can feel the cold, and he thinks he is going to drown. Drake opens his eyes and sits up. He looks around the beach, and it is still dark, but the rising sun will show its bright light very soon. Drake sits up, and he can see all the little footprints of the baby turtles that have made their way to the ocean. He sits up with his knees pulled into his chest, and he rubs his face with both hands. He just woke up from a recurring dream that he has a lot, and he does not know why. He is a baby, and he feels cold. He feels like he is drowning in freezing water. His dream is always the same. He feels like he is going to drown, and then he wakes up. Drake sits there on the beach with his head resting on his knees, wondering about how he got to be where he is. Now that he is where he is, what is he going to do?

Drake has just turned twenty-five less than a week ago, and life is good for him. It is what he has made it, and he is

proud, confident, and well-to-do. He is not wealthy; he has
no family within 1,600 miles of him, and he is, for the most
part, alone. After Drake had broken his knee in the title
game way back in 1985, he and his mother had a falling out
with each other. Drake wanted to get surgery to fix his knee
so he could play football again, but his mother said no; she
did not want him to play football anymore, and she would
not OK the reconstructive surgery on his knee. Drake did
have surgery, so his knee was well enough to walk on but
not the surgery that would repair and strengthen his knee
to be able to play football again. This led to Drake disliking
his mother and avoiding her always. Drake did not talk to
her anymore about anything. He did not argue with her
or fight with her; he just stayed away from her with a deep
resentment that is still with him today. This led to fighting
between Kaitlin and Thomas as well. Lance stayed out of
the whole mess, and basically, the family grew apart. Drake
jumped at the first option that came along to get him out
of the house, and three days after he had graduated high
school, he took a flight to Orlando, Florida, to take a course
in hotel management. Drake did very well in his studies and
was hired at the Radisson Inn on Pompano Beach in South
Florida. He went right from his home in Dunshes to school
in Orlando to being hired at the Radisson Inn. Drake never
even went back home; he went right to work and stayed here
in Pompano Beach. Drake makes minimum wage, so he has
to live with many roommates, which has been very difficult
for him. Drake has always been well organized, and with so
many roommates now, organization is out of the question.
Drake had dreams of being in the NFL, and after his injury,

this is out of the question. He has decided he wanted to be a guitarist in a band.

He went to Florida simply to get him out of the house where he felt nothing but loneliness. He wanted to work and start playing guitar and get into a band so he could tour around the country meet people and play music. He actually was doing well for himself. He had to quit his job at the hotel because he started to grow his hair long, and this was unacceptable. Drake now worked as a night manager at a Subway sub shop, and he took guitar lessons during the day.

He has moved into a warehouse where he has set up a stage and put together a drummer and bass player, and they practice all the time. Drake has become quite a good guitar player, and like a lot of young adults, he has become all too familiar with the use of illegal substances, but Drake has never let this get in the way of his dreams. Drake lives his life the way he wants, doing what he wants, and he is very attractive, very independent, and very alone as he is realizing now. He decides he better go see Mom and try to piece together what is going on.

It was less than two weeks ago when a friend of Drake's had asked him for help moving. Drake said he would help, and in the process, Drake cut his finger on some furniture. It was a bad cut, and Drake washed his finger out good with soap and water and put a Band-Aid on the cut, not giving it another thought. Well, a week later, Drake's finger had swollen up very bad, and the pain was unbearable. Drake had no health insurance, but he had to go to the hospital. It was after work, and he worked the night shift at Subway, which was until 2:00 a.m. Drake went right to the hospital, and it was very quiet there. The only person he found was the receptionist, and he showed her his finger, and she noticed immediately that Drake's eyes were shining. They were like flashing, and she had never seen anything like this. She told Drake to have a seat in the waiting area, and she would be back with a doctor. A little while later, Drake was led to a room where a doctor had Drake sit on a cushioned table, and the doctor sat on a chair in front of Drake.

"Hi, Drake. I am Dr. Avante," says the doctor. Drake replies, "Nice to meet you, Dr. Avante." The doctor says to Drake, "Let me see your finger so we can see what is going on here." Drake holds out his left hand, and immediately, the doctor sees what the problem is. The middle finger on Drake's hand is swollen from the second joint all the way to the tip of his finger. It is swollen so bad that Drake cannot bend either of the first two joints on his finger. There are red spots dotting his finger that look like blood blisters. It looks like the blood in his finger is trying to force its way out through his skin. There is a red line that is clearly visible going from the middle knuckle on Drake's left hand, and it is following a vein that goes all the way up his forearm to his elbow. The red line then curves under his left bicep and travels to his armpit. You can see the line then head toward the center of Drake's chest. The doctor asks Drake to remove his shirt, and he inspects his whole arm and chest. "Well, Drake, you clearly have a very bad infection. You see this line going up your arm from your finger." Drake replies, "Yes."

"Well, Drake, this is a very bad infection. I have to tell you, if this is left unattended, this will kill you. You have to have this taken care of immediately. Unfortunately, you do not have any health insurance, so there is nothing we can do for you here." Drake is obviously concerned and replies, "You mean I am going to die, and there is nothing you can do to help me?" The doctor shakes his head with a blank look on his face and says, "Well, what we can do, Drake, is we can lance your finger for you to relieve the pressure. This must be very painful." Drake shakes his head up and down, saying, "It is excruciating." The doctor gets up, saying to Drake, "Wait here, I will be right back." A few moments later, the doctor returns with a nurse. They set up like they are preparing for surgery, and they are in the simplest sense. They have Drake lie on the table, and they lay his left arm over to a tray and lay white cloths over his hand and arm except where they are going to lance his finger. The doctor and nurse sit to either side of the table Drake's hand is on. They prepare his finger and have the tools they need to lance Drake's finger. The doctor looks to Drake, saying, "Are you ready, Drake? This is going to hurt." Drake asks, "Aren't you going to give me any kind of painkiller?" The doctor replies, "Sorry, Drake, all we can do is lance this for you, and then first thing tomorrow morning, you better get right to the clinic. I am going to give you a list of two different antibiotics. You need to get both of these and take them exactly as they are prescribed. This is all we can do for you." Sarcastically with a hint of seriousness, Drake asks, "Well, am I going to die?" The doctor replies very seriously, "If you do not get the antibiotics immediately, then you will die. OK, are you ready? This is going to hurt." Drake takes a deep breath and turns his head, saying, "Go ahead." The doctor proceeds to lance the blood blisters on Drake's finger, and there are five of them. This is the most painful thing Drake has ever felt. He does not cry, but he cannot help the tears that fall from his burning eyes and roll down his face. Drake tries to be very strong and watches as the doctor lances his finger. It feels like his skin is burning where the doctor cuts it with the scalpel. It hurts even worse when the doctor squeezes his finger trying to drain out as much of the infection as he can. Suddenly, the doctor and the nurse sigh loudly. They move back a little, and the doctor removes the bandage lying over Drake's arm. Drake can see what the doctor and nurse can see. The veins all throughout Drake's arm become visible like the blood in his arm is visible through his skin. It is not visible continuously; it starts in his fingertips and moves up his arm, but it fades a few seconds after it has been visible. It continues to his chest. Drake lifts his shirt, exposing his stomach, and they all can see the veins in his stomach for a few seconds, and they move down his legs. Drake cannot see, but the nurse and doctor can see the veins in Drake's head for a few seconds as well. This goes on for a few minutes and then goes away. Drake is very concerned and asks the doctor, "What is wrong with me? What is happening? Have you ever seen this before?" The doctor looks to the nurse, saying, "I don't know. I have never seen anything like this before." The nurse responds by saying, "I have never seen anything like this either." The doctor looks to Drake, saying, "Hold on, Drake, we have three more incisions to make here, OK?" Drake says, "OK." The doctor starts to make another incision, and the veins start be become visible in Drake again. This startles the doctor a little, and he cuts his finger with the scalpel. The nurse sees this and says, "Doctor, you have cut yourself. You had better wash that very thoroughly." Dr.

Avante responds, "Yes, Nurse, I will." The nurse and doctor finish lancing Drake's finger and bandage him up. Dr. Avante wants very much to take a blood sample from Drake, but he is not a patient here, and he has no insurance, so he does not ask; instead he tells Drake to make sure he gets to the clinic in the morning and gets his antibiotics.

The next morning comes very quick, and Drake has not slept at all. He cannot play the guitar using his middle finger because his finger hurts so bad, but he still plays for a while just using his other three fingers. He mostly paces around his warehouse on his stage and walks around outside in the warm salty night air. All Drake has is a simple landline phone in his warehouse. He has just bought a car a little over a year ago, and any spare money he has, which is not much at all, is spent at the music store on whatever he can afford. Drake makes his way to the clinic, and each antibiotic prescription costs a little over one hundred dollars each. Well, Drake can only afford one of them, and this puts his rent in jeopardy of not being paid this month. He gets one of them and goes back to his warehouse where there is one small air conditioner in the very small front office, which has a door that walks into the main warehouse and a door to the outside. Drake sleeps the heat of the days away on a couch in this small office. He is very tired and falls asleep very quickly after taking his antibiotic. Drake wakes up and goes to work where on this night he will get the surprise of a lifetime.

At work, Drake has his finger bandaged heavily, and it hurts so bad that he cannot touch anything, or it stops him dead in his tracks. The night goes pretty smooth, and it is crazy, busy like always. Drake has a steady stream of people who come to this Subway because it is on a major highway intersection that is always busy, and Drake can make forty to fifty subs in an hour no problem for ten hours straight; that is why he makes the big bucks like nine dollars an hour, which is not so bad in 1994, especially when the tips he makes is more than his hourly rate. Drake has just turned twenty-five, and he is full of life, big smiles and happy conversation all night, every night as he makes subs. Well, tonight is a little different. Drake is wearing his Subway baseball cap, and he always has his hair wrapped in about seventy multicolored hair ties making his four-foot-long hair look like a whip. Drake is in very good shape; he goes to the gym a lot, and a lot of girls are very attracted to him. It is very odd that Drake does not have a girlfriend, but he shies away from attention, especially the kind of attention that is very close. At about ten this fine evening, a very tall man walks into the store. Drake has never seen him before. Drake says, "Hi, what can I get for you tonight?"

The man says, "Drake. Are you Drake Hammond?"

"That is me," says Drake with a smile on his face.

"Hi, Drake, my name is Harry Klaushoven, and I am with the CDCP."

Drake says, "That's great! What kind of sub would you like tonight?"

Harry smiles and looks at the menu and says "You know what, I will take a BMT." Drake starts to ask Harry more questions, and Harry interrupts Drake, saying, "Please just give me a foot long on white bread with everything on it, and please take your time making it." Drake starts to make the sub, and Harry says, "Drake, do you know why I am here?"

Drake says, "You are here to get a sub."

Harry says, "No, I am here for you, Drake. You went to the Pompano hospital late last night or early this morning, depending on how you look at it, and you were helped by a doctor and a nurse."

Drake looks at Harry seriously, saying, "Yeah, that's right."

Harry says, "Well, Drake, Dr. Avante and Nurse Weller, who helped you this morning, are both dead now. Do you have any idea why or how this could have happened?"

Drake looks at the unfamiliar man, stunned; a moment passes, and Drake says, "Dead? The nurse and doctor that lanced my finger this morning are dead? How? What happened to them?"

Harry says, "Well, Drake, that is why I am here. I was hoping you could help me with that question."

Drake says, "Well, I have no idea why they are dead. They were fine when I left this morning, and Dr. Avante had given me a prescription to get some antibiotics at the clinic. I was only able to afford one of the prescriptions."

Harry says, "Well, Drake, will you do me a favor? Will you come down to the hospital after work tonight? I would like to ask you some questions, and the authorities will be there as well. We are not blaming you, but we just need to cover all the possibilities."

Drake says, "Yeah sure, I will come down after work. I get done at 2:00 a.m. tonight, and I will come to the hospital afterward."

Harry says, "Thank you, Drake," and after paying for his sub and soda, he heads out of the store. Drake rubs his face, remembering when he was a little boy.

When Drake was in first grade and went to Greenville Elementary School, he would walk three blocks to school. Well, there was a girl whose name was Lilly Branson, and she used to walk the last block to school with Drake. Lilly was such a cutie, and she had such a crush on Drake. She would always hold Drake's hand. She would make Drake carry her square tin Bobby Vinton lunch pail to school for her, and she would hold Drake's hand. It was like she was ten years ahead of Drake. Lilly would say, "Drake, carry this for me." The next thing you know, Drake would be carrying her lunch pail to school for her. Lilly would grab hold of Drake's hand, and now, they were walking hand in hand. Lilly would kiss Drake on the cheek, and Drake was never worse for wear; he did not mind Lilly at all. One day, Lilly went to kiss Drake on the cheek, and Drake looked at her, wanting to say something to Lilly, and she kissed him right on the mouth. Drake did not think much of it, but Lilly said, "Drake, will you be my boyfriend?" Drake said, "Of course, I will, Lilly." They walked hand in hand to school, and Drake never saw Lilly again after that day.

A few more people walk into the store, and Drake takes care of them, but he is totally daydreaming. He remembers when he was in junior high school at Dunshes, and he and a lot of his friends were at a swimming party. Drake went into the cellar of the house, and the kids were playing spin the bottle, and some girls asked Drake to play, and he did. The first girl to spin the bottle (and it landed on Drake) was Sally, and when she went to kiss Drake, he moved in too fast, and they smacked teeth and lips together, causing a little cut on Sally's lip. Sally got real mad and yelled at Drake, and he left very embarrassed. The next day at school, a lot of the kids gave Drake a hard time because Sally had died the night before, and no one knew why. A lot of the kids teased Drake, saying he gave her the kiss of death. There was one other incident where Drake met a girl from another town when he was a senior in high school, and her name was Lisa. Lisa asked Drake out one weekend, and Drake said yes, and Lisa came to his house and picked him up. They went for a ride in Lisa's car, and Lisa parked on the side of the road. Drake said, "What are you doing?" Lisa said, "I think we should park right here, don't you?" Drake looked at Lisa and said yes. This was Drake's first and last sexual encounter. They kissed, and one thing led to another, and the two had intercourse in her tiny little Gremlin way back in 1987. Everything was great, and the two of them had a really good time together. Lisa took Drake home, and Drake thought he had his first real girlfriend. The next day, Drake tried to call Lisa over and over. Finally later that night, Lisa's mother answered the phone, and Drake was informed that Lisa had died today, and her body was taken away. Drake never put things together until right now, right here in this Subway store.

Drake thinks, *There is no way I am going to that hospital tonight. What am I going to do?* Drake closes the store and heads to a secretive place that he knows about. The fenced-off beach where the turtles come to lay their eggs. Drake starts to think how stupid he is for never seeing, never understanding that it was him that was responsible for the people in his past who died or disappeared. How could he have made it to this point in life without anyone or any agency pinpointing him as the source of death for the people who had been close to him in his life and died? How is it that only some people, actually very few people, have died that have been close to him? How is it that no one in his family was ever harmed by him? As Drake thinks back, it becomes clear to him why his mother was the way she was. They were a close family until Drake broke his leg, but his mother was insistent that they never share silverware. They never drink out of the same glass. She never let Drake and Lance roughhouse together, and if they did, their mother threw a fit. Fighting was absolutely forbidden, and the few fights they had were met with severe punishment from their mother. Drake thinks how the people who either kissed him or cut themselves around him were the ones who came up dead or missing. Drake sits in the sand late at night, thinking about what to do now, and falls asleep. He wakes up from his recurring dream about drowning just before dawn and thinks to himself, *It is time to ask Mom what happened to me and why.*

It is 1994, and Drake has just turned twenty-five. He has a steady job at Subway but lives check to check. Drake has no cellular phone, and he does not even have a computer. All the free money he has, he spends on guitars and accessories. He does not spend money on clothes or even food, so outside of his car payment every two weeks, rent, phone and electric bills, he has very little money left, and that is spent at the music store. Drake really only goes to work and practices at his warehouse. Well, Drake is about to do something very unusual for him. Drake is very responsible; he never misses work or practice with his band, but he is now leaving. He is just leaving without even a letter or a phone call. The previous night has shaken him up so much that he is scared out of

Florida. He gets in his white six-cylinder Firebird and heads back home to the house in Dunshes where he grew up. It is time to see if his mother has any answers for him. It just so happens that Drake had cashed his paycheck before he went to work tonight. He was going to go home to his warehouse try to get to sleep early so he could go to the music store the next day and get an acoustic guitar and strings. Drake has $500 in his pocket, and he takes this as a sign to head home to New York. Drake always keeps extra shorts and shirts in the hatchback of his car, and this is good since he does not want to go back to his warehouse. He is already kind of paranoid that people are out to get him, and he takes no chances. He is on I-95, heading north before the sun even hits the horizon. On the drive, Drake concentrates on remembering his past and all the things that his mother did that he did not like or that he thought was just silly and very eccentric. He remembers how his mother would sit him and his brother Lance down and scold them if they wrestled in the house; then she would cry and make the two of them sit there and listen to her give very heartbreaking speeches about health and how important it is to stay clean. Drake remembers one time his brother Lance spit on him and he thought his mother was going to die. She lost her mind, and the boys never saw their mother so mad. She made them promise never ever to spit on anyone or anything ever, and the boys promised never to spit on anything. One time, Drake punched his brother Lance in the stomach, and again their mother sat the two of them down, and for hours, she scolded the two of them, making them promise they would never fight. Drake is remembering how often this actually happened when he was young, and maybe this was the real reason that Drake drew away from his mother. Drake's breaking his knee was just the straw that broke the camel's back, and Drake pulled completely away from his mother at that point until he was out of the house. Drake realizes there has to be something deeper, something more that his mother did not tell him. He is on his way home to find out why his mother who never cleaned the house once was so animate about her boys being so cleanly and so damn courteous to others. Drake drives and drives for twenty hours. He is in Pennsylvania now, and he can't keep his eyes open any longer. He finds a place to park and reclines the seat in his car back and tries to fall asleep. He tosses and turns more than anything but gets a couple of hours of sleep and then is back on the road again. Drake makes his way back up through New York, and the night air is noticeably colder here than in Florida. All he has is shorts, and he has to roll the windows in his car up because he is quite chilly. He makes his way back Dunshes, the town he grew up in, but it is only about three in the morning. He knows no one is up at his house, and being back home gives him renewed energy, so he drives around remembering places and things he did as a child and teenager. He drives to the high school and walks around on the football field. He drives by some of the houses of his good friends from school, and he looks around to see how the town has changed since he left for Florida. He can't seem to make the time go by quick enough and decides, even though it is only five in the morning, he will go home. His mother he knows is never up this early, and his stepfather Tom is still at work. Drake figures he will just be quiet and go in the house and wait for his mother to wake up. This is a little tense for

Drake; he has no idea how his mother will respond to him. He does not think it will be bad, but he has not spoken with his mother, Tom, or his brother Lance in over six years. Drake just left home and never looked back. His mother did call him a few times, but Drake just said hi and "yes, this is my number," and he was never in any mood for conversation with his mother at all until now. Drake makes his way to his old house and pulls in the driveway. He gets out of his car and stretches. It is still dark out, but the horizon is starting to lighten up. He does not smell good, and he is sore all over from the long drive. He walks around a little, loosening up and looking his old house over and noticing the changes that have happened outside like trees that have been chopped down and their barn that is now gone. Drake goes into the house through the sliding glass door. As usual the sliding glass door was left open. The first thing that Drake notices is that the kitchen table is not the same. The refrigerator is different, and he walks into the living room seeing that the furniture is all different. Drake scratches his head, noticing that everything is different. A young boy, maybe eleven or twelve years old, walks down the stairs and looks at Drake, saying, "Who are you?"

"My name is Drake. I used to live here. Do you live here now?" asks Drake.

They boy says, "Yes, I live here with my mom, my dad, my brother, and my sister."

Drake bends down and asks the boy, "What is your name?"

"I am William," replies the boy.

"William, do you know where the people who lived here before you did are?" asks Drake.

William shrugs his shoulders, saying, "I don't know."

Drake can hear the footsteps of someone coming down the stairs, and William's father comes down the stairs, saying, "William, come over here. Who are you?"

Drake replies, "I am Drake Hammond, and I used to live in this house. I did not know my parents had moved out. Do you, by any chance, know where they have moved to?"

The man picks up his son and walks into the kitchen, turning the light on. "I am Terry Wilkens, and my wife, three children, and I moved in here after your parents split up and sold this house to us. Would you like a cup of coffee?" the man asks. Drake says sure and sits down at the table, having a long conversation with Terry. Terry actually does not have a lot of information for Drake, but he is able to get an address for Drake, and he believes this is where his mother may be. Drake takes the address and thanks Terry for coffee and the information. It takes Drake two hours to get to Clayburg, which is the address the man gave him. It takes Drake a while and some asking at gas stations, but he finally finds his way, and it is now seven in the morning. Drake has paid so little attention to his mother in the few phone conversations that they have had over the past few years that she did not even tell Drake what has been going on in her life. She could tell that Drake had no interest, and she was not expecting to see him as she opens the door, and there stands her firstborn son.

CHAPTER 8

The Chase for Drake Begins

"Drake, is that really you, Drake?" asks Kaitlin as she hugs Drake and starts to cry.

"Yes, Mom, it's me," says Drake. He does not return the hug and waits for his mother to step back.

Kaitlin rubs the tears from her eyes and walks into her cluttered house, saying, "Drake, come in. Come in and stay for a while. The place is a mess. I still have to get this place organized."

"Mom, what is this? What happened? Where is Lance and Tom? What happened to our house?" asks Drake.

Kaitlin replies, "Well, after you left, they all left. Lance ran away from home. He never even finished high school. Last I heard, he was in Michigan somewhere doing whatever. He and his girlfriend Alicia are getting married, last I heard. Shortly after Lance ran away, Tom told me he was leaving me, and just like that, he was gone. No warning, no nothing, just gone. All the stuff in the house was moved here, and here I am."

Drake looks around the very small house that his mother is now living in and how cluttered it is. There is barely enough room to walk around. "Mom, what happened to me when I was a baby? I mean strange things happened to me when I was growing up, and I never pieced it together until recently," Drake says, moving stuff from the couch to the floor so he can sit down. His mother sits down on a reclining chair, saying, "Oh, honey. I don't know what they did to you."

Drake says, "Mom, what happened to Lilly Branson? What happened to Sally Graines? What happened to Brandon Scotts, and there are others. What happened to them, Mom? I never pieced it together until recently. Very bad things happened to these people, and it was because of me, why? I had a visit from a man who said he was the head of the CDCP. That is the Centers for Disease Control and Prevention, Mom. His name is Harry Klaushoven, and he said two people died because they had come in contact with me, and then I started to realize that people that came in contact with me all throughout my life had died or disappeared. People that kissed or fought with me. What is going on, Mom? What do you mean you don't know what they did to me, and who are they?"

"You don't remember this, Drake, but when you were a baby, there was an epidemic that was sweeping Upstate New York, and a lot of babies were dying. Well, before you were born, my doctor had asked your father and me to have you come in twice a month for an examination to make sure you were healthy. Your father and I decided it was a good idea, and we consented so you could have an examination twice a month. Well, there were two doctors, I can't remember their names, but they were experimenting on babies, and no one knew about it. These babies were dying, and you were one of them, Drake. Your father and I noticed bad things were happening with you, and we rushed you to the hospital one night, and the doctors took you. Your father and I waited until after midnight, and then your father took me to find you because no one was letting us know what was going on. Your father did not mess around, he charged through that hospital and found you. Your father saved your life that night, Drake, I know he did. We took you out of that hospital and away from those doctors. We said we would never take you to a hospital ever again. You had a terrible infection, and we thought you were going to die, but you pulled through."

"Mom, maybe you know the answer to this question I have. I have had this dream throughout my whole life. I dream that I am a baby, and I am drowning in freezing cold water. I see air bubbles all around my head, and I hear my voice choking underwater. Do you have any idea why I have this dream?"

"Oh yes. You would have very bad fever when you were a baby. Fever so bad that the doctors said you should be dead. Your fever would rise over 110 degrees. It was amazing that you lived. We would have to fill the sink with cold water and ice and put you in it to lower your temperature or you would have died from the fever. This happened a lot to you when you were a baby. You were sick a lot when you were a baby, but when you had your tonsils taken out when you were about five years old, then you started to get strong. You started to be very healthy and rarely did you get sick after you had your tonsils taken out. I never told you this, but I noticed that there was something different about you, Drake. Something that the doctors did to you, but I don't know what they did.

Those people you mentioned. I don't know what happened to them, but you were the last person to be with them. Whatever the doctors did to you, Drake, it changed your blood. There were times where I could see the veins in your body, and they would light up like lightning and shoot through your body. Your eyes would shine, and I was scared for you, Drake." Kaitlin gets a tissue. "I was scared to take you to the hospital." Kaitlin starts to weep. "I was scared to tell anyone." Kaitlin cries into the tissue. "I did not know what to do, so I just kept it to myself. When people around you disappeared, I still kept my secrets to myself. You never had any reason to question anything. I did everything I could to protect you from whatever had been done to you." Kaitlin dries her teary eyes with a tissue. "I always felt like we were being watched. I noticed men throughout our life that were just there and I never knew why, but I think they were watching you, Drake. I think they wanted to protect you like I did."

"Protect me from what, Mom?"

"I don't know, Drake, from whatever those doctors had done to you."

"Listen, Mom. I have to find out what all of this is about. I have to find out what was done to me. I am going to Rosewood hospital to find out what these doctors did."

"Oh wait, Drake, I still have all the newspaper articles, wait right here, I will be right back." Kaitlin goes into her bedroom and comes back after Drake hears her moving things aside and looking through all the clutter. Kaitlin comes back with plastic bags full of newspaper articles from 1968, saying, "Here we go, Drake. I have saved all of these from when you were a baby."

Drake reads through the papers, and there is headline after headline about the epidemic that was sweeping the Upstate New York region and was killing babies from all over. Drake learns that there were at least seventy babies killed by Dr. Alex Kevnick. This doctor had worked for the CDCP, but he went rogue and worked on his own, injecting babies with deadly viruses that led to all the deaths. Alex Kevnick covered his tracks very well, and that was why it took the CDCP and authorities almost a whole year to catch the murderous doctor. Dr. Alex Kevnick was sentenced to life in prison with no chance for parole. There was mention of a possible connection with Alex Kevnick and Dr. Earl Rieval, but Earl Rieval had died in a car accident. "Mom, I was a part of this, and you never told me about this?" Drake says and asks his mother, "Mom, this does not make any sense, why would doctors kill babies by injecting deadly diseases into them? I mean, how could they not know they would get caught? Mom, did they inject me with deadly disease? What kind of doctors would do this?"

Kaitlin starts crying, saying, "Drake, I don't know what they did to you. They were after you though. One night at the hospital, the night you had your tonsils taken out, I was in the hospital room with you. Two men came in, and they thought they were taking you, but I had switched the name band on your wrist with the name band on a boy in the bed next to you, and the two men took him away, thinking he was you. I ran out of the hospital with you, Drake, and I did not know what to do. I just prayed nothing would happen to you and that no one would take you from me."

Drake is still reading through the papers and asks his mother, "Well, what about Dad, Mom? What did he think or do about this situation?"

Kaitlin replies, "Your father was very protective of you for about two years, and then he started to . . . well, I don't know, Drake, he just had enough, and that was that. Your father went to the hospital a couple of times after we rescued you from those two doctors, but he would never tell me what had happened there. I know your father, and he found something out, but he never shared what he found with me."

Drake points at the paper he is reading, saying, "Mom, you mean these two doctors right here." There is a picture of the two doctors together, and it is still in good condition.

Kaitlin points to one doctor, saying, "He was sent to jail." Then she points to the other doctor, saying, "This one died in a car accident? These are the two doctors that were injecting babies with diseases, these two doctors right here. At least this one here, Alex Kevnick, he was for sure. I am not sure about the other doctor. Your father and I passed one of the doctors in the hall leaving the hospital with a nurse, and then we found you in a room with the other doctor." Kaitlin starts to cry, drying her eyes with a tissue. "There were two other babies in the room with you, Drake, and they had died. Your father and I thought you were going to die too, but we brought you home, and you lived. The doctor and the nurse we passed in the hall that night had died in a car crash, and the other doctor was arrested the next day. The whole country watched this horrible tragedy unfold. All kinds of new restrictions and security policies have been put into place in all hospitals all around the country because of these two doctors and what they did. Political leaders started this argument about introducing health care charges to all working people to bring awareness to the threat of rogue doctors and illegal practices being performed in hospitals. It was a national sensation, and, Drake, your father and I were able to sneak you away. We kept you clear of all the headlines and news reports. Whatever your father did at the hospital, he saved you from becoming a national story. I think you had better go see him. He may have more answers for you."

Drake looks to his mother, asking, "Mom, can I keep these newspapers?"

"Oh, take them, honey. You can have them," says Kaitlin.

"So, Mom, where do I find Dad? You know, I barely even remember what he looks like." says Drake.

Kaitlin looks around her home for a while and finds an address, saying, "This is the address where I think he is. He has been living in the mountains of Pennsylvania for the past six years or so."

Drake takes the paper with the address, saying, "Thanks, Mom. I will go find him, but first, I am going to the hospital at Rosewood, and before that, I need to get some sleep. I drove all the way from Florida and I am tired."

"You can stay here as long as you like, honey. You must be hungry get something to eat. Are you sure you want to go to the hospital in Rosewood? I don't know what you will find there?" says Kaitlin.

Drake brushes off all the clutter from the couch onto the floor and lies down, saying, "Well, it would make sense they have records. I am sure they have to have some sort of records of what happened back in 1968. Whether they let me see them or not is the big question, but it can't hurt to go ask and see if I can find anything out." Drake closes his eyes, and before he falls asleep, his mother tells him he may want to stop by the Sprencer hospital, the hospital by Kaitlin's parents' house where Drake had his tonsils taken out. They may have some records as well." Drake says he will check it out, and then he falls asleep.

Drake can see himself as a baby. He sees himself from the right side, and he is under water. He is screaming with his eyes closed, and his arms waving up and down. His legs are kicking, but he can't get above the water. He can hear himself choking underwater, and then he is woken from his dream late in the afternoon to his mother, screaming. "Get out, get out of my house." Drake gets up to see his mother held by a large man with his hand over her mouth and walking her into the living room. Kaitlin is way overpowered by the man and she is pushed into the recliner chair. There is another man walking in behind the first man. Drake stands up, saying, "What is this? Who are you and what do you want?" Kaitlin says, "Drake, these are the men who came for you at the hospital that night when you had your tonsils out. It is the same two men. I will never forget their faces. They are even wearing the same suits."

The first man smiles, saying, "That is quite a good memory you have, Miss Durguss."

Drake approaches the first man, saying, "So why are you here? What is it you want?" The man pulls a handgun from a holster under his left breast and points it at Drake, saying, "You, Drake, we want you. Come with us, and there will be no trouble."

Drake says, "Are you kidding me? You are after me, why to kill me? That is about all you can do to me with that gun. I don't think you have come here to kill me, and I can tell you right now, I am not going anywhere with you."

"Yes, you are right. We did not come here to kill you. How foolish of me thinking I could intimidate you with a gun. So I get the feeling you are not going to come with us on your own free will," says the man, reaching his left hand behind him and saying, "Richard, give me the stun gun, we don't have to shoot him with bullets." Richard reaches under his coat and pulls out a stun gun, handing it to Roger, saying, "Be careful, Roger. This kid is not to be fooled with. Remember how dangerous he is." Roger turns to face Drake with the stun gun in hand only to see Drake charge at him like an arrow. Drake leads with his shoulder, hitting the larger man in the gut with his right shoulder driving through him, making a textbook tackle on the man. Roger flies back, and a shot explodes, deafening everyone in the room. Drake had the sense to catch the left hand of the man with his right hand and face it at the man behind him, and sure enough, the stun gun shoots electrical probes into the man behind, dropping him twitching on the ground. Drake rises to his knee and gives his best punch coming right across the chin of Roger, knocking him out cold. Drake stands up with a yell. "Yeah, I did it, Ma, did you see that? Ma, Mom." Drake turns to see that his mother has been shot in the chest. She is still in the recliner chair, and Drake rushes to her. "Mom, no, Mom, no." Drake puts pressure on the wound that is bleeding just above her left breast. "Mom, come on, Mom. I am going to get you to a hospital." Drake's mother raises her bloody right hand to her sons face, saying, "Drake, go to your father. Find your father, he found things out about you at the hospital. Your father has more answers for you. Drake, do not let these men catch you. Find out what they have done to you." Kaitlin's hand falls to her chest, and her eyes close. "Mom, Mom. Come on, Mom. I can get you to the hospital. Mom." Drake feels overwhelming heat flow throughout his body. "Mom, Mom, you can't be gone. Mom, you can't die. Not like this. Mom, wake up, come on, Mom, get up," says Drake as he hears noise behind him. Drake stands and turns to see Roger pulling the wires away from Richard and helping him stand up. The two men are looking with horror at Drake as Drake starts to walk toward them. Both men put their hands out in front of themselves, backing away from Drake slowly. Roger has blood dripping from his split lip where Drake had punched him, and he pulls a handkerchief from his jacket pocket to stop the bleeding. Richard opens the door, and the two men exit very slowly with Drake walking at them with a dead-serious look on his face. Drake cannot see what the two men see. They see Drake walking at them with the most serious look they have ever seen on any person, but with Drake, they see the veins in his head from his ears flowing to the center of his face pulsing like lightning. The veins in his face are flashing with the pulsing of his pulse. They are visible and then gone, and then they come back with the next beat of his pulse. The veins in his arms start to become visible with the pulsing of his blood as well. The men have never seen anything like this, and they are terrified. As Drake walks toward them, his eyes slowly turn black, and they can tell he is getting madder and madder because now all the veins in his body are visible for the duration of his pulse. Like a flashing light, the veins in Drake's body are visible for a second then gone for a second and so on. The men run to their car, and Richard starts the car, and they leave. Drake turns to walk back in the house after the men have left. Drake walks into the house, and he starts to cough. Blood drips from his nose, and blood is coughed up in his hand from his mouth. Drake looks at this, noticing that his blood is almost black, and he closes his eyes feeling very tired all of a sudden. He shakes his head and takes a deep breath then heads back toward his mother.

Richard is driving the large black town car very fast, and he is heading toward the airport. Richard pulls a cell phone from his jacket pocket and flips down the bottom half of the phone. He pulls the antenna and dials a very important number on the number pad. "Harry, this is Richard. Yes, Harry, I know you don't ever want to be called on the phone, but guess what, Harry, this is an emergency. That little experiment you have going on that lab rat Drake Hammond."

Harry interrupts Richard, saying, "This is not a secure line, watch what you say."

"Harry, listen to me." Richard is almost yelling on the phone. "Harry, listen to me. I was never hired to be a murderer. I was hired to watch and bring in a harmless kid if need be. Let me tell you, Harry, this kid and whatever your doctors have done to him is not natural. This kid is something way more lethal than you can ever imagine. I can't even explain it, but Roger and I just confronted this kid, and let me tell you, I have never been so scared in all my life. Just looking at this kid get mad is enough to get me the hell out of dodge. We tried to bring him in with a gun, and then we were going to stun him with a stun gun, but he jumped Roger and punched him in the mouth. Then all the veins in this kid's body started to glow, they became visible through his skin. I never saw anything like it before. This kid is evil, Harry, he is pure evil. His veins were not red, they were black like black death, and his eyes even turned black. I ain't never going anywhere near this kid ever again. You are going to have to kill this kid." Richard is talking fast very loudly on the phone, just like his driving.

Harry can tell Richard's heart is racing, and he jumps in on the conversation. "Richard, Richard, calm down. Where is Drake now?"

"We left him at his mother's house. Oh, by the way, Roger shot his mother. Yeah, that's right, his mother has been killed. You think that pissed the kid off? Well, let me assure you it did," says Richard.

"OK, OK. Listen to me, Richard. I know where he is going then. Listen, Richard, you and Roger get back here. I have to make some phone calls. I think we will let the local law enforcement help us out from here on in. Richard, did you say Drake punched Roger in the mouth?" asks Harry.

Richard replies yeah, and then he looks at Roger in the front seat next to him. Richard starts to yell. "Jesus, Jesus Christ. What the hell is this? Holy Jesus Christ."

Harry can hear the car squealing like Richard has slammed on the brakes and the car comes to a skidding halt. Harry hears Richard get out of the car and slam the door shut. Harry is now yelling into the phone, "Richard, what is it? Richard, what is going on? Richard, is Roger all right?"

Richard responds, "No, he is not all right. He is dead. Did you hear me, Harry? Roger is dead."

Harry responds, "What do you mean he is dead?"

"Harry, there is blood streaming from Roger's eyes, from his nose and mouth. There is white foam coming out of his mouth too. Harry, Roger is dead. What the hell is this? Harry, am I going to die? I know I am. What the hell," yells Richard, who falls to his knees, scared out of his mind.

Harry tells Richard he is not going to die and to stay right where he is. Harry is going to have to have very specialized people come to the scene where Richard is to clean up this now biological hazard. The same is true for the house where Drake's mother had been shot. Harry spends ten minutes calming Richard down and explaining to him that he has to stay in control. Richard has to control the scene where he is and wait for the cleanup crew to arrive. Not only that but he cannot let anyone near Roger. In fact, he cannot get near Roger himself. Harry finally gets Richard to calm down and control the scene, and then Harry makes some of the most important and troublesome calls that have been made since the start of this plot that is now twenty-five years in the making.

CHAPTER 9

Drake Leaves His Mother

Drake goes back in the house and looks at his mother. He can't believe she has been killed. He does not know what to do. He knows whatever happens this will somehow be blamed on him. He has to find the truth. He has to find the answers to what has happened. He has to get to the hospital and start there, and he knows time is against him. He fumbles around his mother's house, confused and not knowing what to do. He can't even find a phone anywhere to make a phone call. He does not know whom to call anyway. He leans down beside his mother and looks her over, saying, "Goodbye, Mom." Drake takes all the newspaper articles and gets in his car. He drives to the Rosewood hospital. He enters and talks to the girl at the front desk. He asks her if there is any way he could see records of when he was a baby and had come to this hospital with his parents. The girl at the front desk says her name is Kerri and she will help Drake look up the records of when he was a baby. As a matter of fact, she can look on the computer right in front of her and look up his records. She looks and says, "There is no record of you ever being here, Drake Hammond."

Drake replies, "That can't be right. I mean I was born here. Would there not be a record of that? Would you not have some kind of birth record for me? I have my birth certificate from this hospital."

Kerri says, "Can I see your birth certificate?"

Drake thinks to himself and remembers that it is in his warehouse in Florida. He can picture the exact spot where it is, but that does him no good right now. "Actually I don't have it with me," says Drake."

"Well, I don't know what to tell you, Drake. I have checked in our system, and there is no record of you being here. I am sorry, there is nothing I can do," says Kerri.

Drake shakes his head, saying, "OK, Kerri. Thank you for helping me."

"You're welcome," says Kerri.

Drake leaves the hospital. It took him a few hours to get to the hospital from his mother's house, and now, he is thinking he is going to go to the hospital by his grandparents' house, which is another couple of hours away. He thinks he should stop somewhere and call the hospital, but he decides against that, wondering who, if any, would help him over the phone. If he has no luck at this hospital, then he is going to go to Pennsylvania to find his father. Either way, he has a lot of time to spend on the road. He drives and thinks about what he is going to do and what possible outcomes of this terrible situation can be. He has nothing but speculation to go on, and this keeps his mind occupied somewhat while he drives. The fact that his mother has been killed and he left her in her home starts to affect him more and more. Drake thinks he should be crying, but he is not. He thinks that other people would be just devastated by the loss of their mother, but for Drake, he never felt any kind of bond with his mother, and he asks himself. Shouldn't I be crying right now? Shouldn't I be feeling some terrible sadness and heartbreak? He tries to make himself cry, but no tears fall. He has to try too hard, and it is fake for him to cry, so he says to himself enough of this and thinks about the situation he is in. He is all alone driving in his car, and he cannot feel any more awkward than he does. His mother has just been killed, and he has not shed even one tear. Drake tells himself he is just not a crier, and he drives toward the town of Sprencer where his grandparents lived.

Meanwhile Harry has been making some very important phone calls. "Yes this is me. My men have tracked Drake to his mother's house in Upstate New York. Drake punched Roger, and he has died. Yes, Drake has escaped, but he is not going anywhere. He will be easy to find. Right now, we need to get Roger's body back to Earl and Alex for study. Yes, yes, I know. Listen, I will get Richard and Roger back to the house, but I need you to send some men to get Drake. I know where he is going. He has to be going to see his father. Yes, I am sure of it. Here is the address, get some men there, and wait, he will be there, trust me. He has nowhere else to go, and make sure your men use extreme caution. Drake has become a lethal killer, and he may know it by now. Your men must not hurt him. Yes, use tranquilizers, it's the best way. Yes, sir. Yes, sir. Bye, sir." Harry hangs up the phone, rubbing his forehead. Harry picks up the phone and makes another call. "Hi, this is Harry Klaushoven. May I speak with David

Carten please? Thank you. David, hi, good to hear, you are right where you are supposed to be," says Harry.

"Yup, that's why you pay me the big bucks, Harry. What can I do for you?" asks David.

"David, you remember why I had you, Sam, and Eric sent there to New York? In case we had situations needing immediate cleanup. Well, our Herculean man is living up to expectation. I have two corpses needing immediate pickup and delivery back to the house in Atlanta. A woman at 46 Bronson Place, Clayburg, New York, 12588. Send Sam to get her and bring her to the house in Atlanta now." Harry can hear David snapping his fingers and repeating the address out loud.

David says, "No problem, Harry. Sam is on it right now."

Harry continues to give David the address where he can send Eric to pick up Roger and Richard, and he wants Eric to bring the two of them back to the house in Atlanta as well. After David tells Harry that Eric has gone, Harry instructs David to tie up loose ends. The apartment is no longer needed; the men are to complete their tasks and meet back at the house in Atlanta. David is to take care of arrangements with the apartment, and then he is given the address where Drake's father lives. David is to go there and get Drake. Harry lets David know that there are men already sent to get Drake. David is just to observe and watch to see what happens, and if by chance Drake should elude the first wave of men, then David will be there to watch Drake and keep eyes on him. Harry lets David know of the extreme caution he should take with Drake. David is a highly trained and successful individual, and Harry has complete confidence in

David. Harry hangs up with David and makes another call. "Hi, John, this is Harry. Let me speak with Alex. Alex, this is Harry. Drake has struck again. Yes, this time it is Roger." Alex looks at Earl and motions him to come over by the couch where he is sitting and talking with Harry. Alex puts his hand over the receiver and says to Earl, "Drake has killed Roger. Harry is having his body sent here for study. It will be here within six hours." Alex now talks into the receiver, directing his voice back to Harry. "Yes, Harry, I am listening. I got it. Drake's mother will be coming here too. She has been killed." Alex looks at Earl with wide eyes as he talks for everyone in the living room to hear him. "OK, Harry, we will be waiting." Alex hangs up the phone and says to Earl, "We have to get the laboratory ready. Drake punched Roger, and Harry said that Roger died within fifteen minutes. Do you know what this means, Earl?"

Earl says, "Yes, his blood is still mutating. It is still getting more lethal. What happened to his mother?" asks Earl.

Alex says, "Roger shot her."

Drake is on his way to Sprencer, and the sun has fallen. It is now dark out, and he can't believe that there is a police car behind him with its red and blue lights flashing. There is no siren, but Drake pulls over to see if the police car goes around him, but sure enough, it follows Drake off the side of the road and parks behind him. Drake watches in his rearview and side-view mirrors as the police officer gets out of his car and approaches up behind Drake's driver side door. The lights from the police car are shining very brightly on Drake's car, making it impossible for Drake to see much at all. Drake hears the police officer say, "Put your hands out the window so I can see them." Drake looks out the window to see the police officer behind him with his gun drawn and pointed right at him. Drake has never thought about how scary this situation is. His heart instantly races, and Drake says, "Yes, sir, no problem." Drake puts his hands out the window for the officer to see them. "What is going on, officer? I was not even speeding. Why are you pulling me over and why do you have your gun pointed at me?"

"Use your left hand and open the door from the outside door handle. Keep both of your hands out the window at all times," says the officer. Drake opens the door, and the officer tells him to exit the car very slowly and walk toward him backward, which Drake does. "Put your hands on your head and walk toward the back of the car," says the officer. Drake does this and feels very tired like he is going to faint. This is the same kind of feeling he felt after the two men had left his house and he walked back to see his mother after she had been shot. Drake gets to the back of his car and starts to cough. He spits up blood, and his nose starts to bleed as well. "OK, very slowly turn around and face me," says the officer. Drake does, and the police officer notices the blood dripping from Drake's nose. "What is wrong with your nose? Are you feeling all right?" asks the officer.

Drake replies, "I don't know, but whatever is happening to me." Drake coughs and spits up more blood, falling to his knees, saying, "Whatever is happening to me has to have something to do with people pointing guns at me because this is the second time a gun has been pointed at me today, and for the second time ever in my life, I have a nosebleed, and I am coughing up blood." Drake and the officer can hear voices over the speaker on the officers left shoulder speaking. Dispatch is giving more description about the APB that is in immediate effect in the Upstate New York region. "All officers in the counties of Strathsburg, Beholmis, Trenthis, and Organda are to be on watch for a Caucasian male midtwenties. He is driving a 1991 white Firebird. The name of the suspect is Drake Hammond. Be on high alert, suspect may be armed and is very dangerous. Suspect is believed to have a highly contagious illness. Avoid contact if at all possible."

"Drake Hammond," says the officer. "Are you Drake Hammond?

Drake is on his knees with very bright lights shining on his face. He coughs and looks at a lot of blood and mucus that he is coughing up into his hands. This is way out of the normal for Drake. He has never had a nosebleed in his life, and he has never coughed up blood. He is very confused by this condition that he has never had experience with not to mention the fact that his blood is now black, which really has him wondering what has been done to his body when he was a baby. The police officer puts his gun back in its holster, saying, "Drake, you probably don't remember me, do you?"

Drake looks up at the police officer, saying, "I have never seen you before in my life."

"No, you probably have not, but you were in my office the first night I ever worked alone. Your mother is Kaitlin Hammond, isn't she?"

"Yes, she is my mother, and this is why you have pulled me over, isn't it? They killed my mother, and now, they are blaming it on me, aren't they?" says Drake.

"What? What are you saying? Someone has killed your mother? I did not know this. Has your mother never mentioned me to you? I am Jerry Giles. Your mother has never told you the story of when you were in the hospital and two men came to take you away and they did not get you because of what your mother did. She switched the name band on your wrist with the boy next to you in the hospital room and the men took the wrong boy." Jerry goes into his car and comes out with some moist paper wipes for Drake.

Drake says, "stay back the one thing that was correct that we heard from your speaker is that I am very contagious but with what I have no idea and that is what I am trying to find out and why and by whom." Drake is very careful to keep his distance from Jerry. He uses the wipes to clean his face and hands with and stands up.

Jerry says, "Listen to me, Drake. I am going to ask you to trust me. There is something I have to show you, something that can help you, I think. I need for you to come down to the station with me because I have some files that I have kept hold of over the years. I don't even know why I kept them until now. Now that you are here, I know why I kept them. I have files that I researched and kept to myself. Your mother was so compelling when I first met her that I did a little detective research on my own down at the hospital and what I found was very scary. It actually led me to Atlanta where I found out incredible things. Come with me to the station I want to give them to you."

Drake says, "Well, I guess if you were going to arrest me, you would have just arrested me. OK, let's go." They get into their cars and head for the police station. Drake pulls in behind Jerry and follows Jerry into the police station. Once in the police station, Drake goes into the bathroom and washes up.

"Drake, come here and check this out," says Jerry. Drake follows Jerry to a desk, and Jerry opens the bottom drawer on the right side of his desk and pulls out two files that are very thick. These files are hidden on the bottom of the drawer under a lot of other stuff. "Drake, check these files out. I have saved these just in case I ever ran into you, and here you are. My mentor here at the police station is Detective Harlow, and he has taught me and shown me all kinds of tricks. He has shown me all kinds of ways of getting information. It was your mother, Kaitlin Hammond, who came to visit me on my first night here in this office that inspired me to do this detective work on my own, and thanks to Detective Harlow, I have learned a lot. I made a visit to the hospital here in Sprencer after the night when you had your tonsils taken out, and I was able to find out very important things just before they had vanished from record. Things that go way up the ladder, and you, my friend, are the key. You somehow are linked to very important officials in the CDCP. Not only that, Drake, but I believe there are other officials from other very high-up agencies involved in this as well. Possibly people in the United States government. Check this out." Jerry produces a picture from his file and shows it to Drake.

Drake says, "Oh my god, I just saw that picture today. My mother has saved all the articles from when I was a baby, and this is one of the pictures in the paper. I was just looking at this picture. I have it in my car."

"The reason I wanted to show you this picture first of all is to ask you, do you know who this man is?" asks Jerry.

Drake shakes his head, saying, "I know now who this man is, but I don't ever remember this man."

"Well, Drake, look at this picture." Jerry puts another picture in front of Drake of a man being taken to prison.

Drake looks at the picture, saying, "What about it?"

Jerry puts the two pictures side by side, pointing to the same man in both pictures that are supposed to be of the same man (Dr. Alex Kevnick) and says to Drake, "This is the same man."

Drake looks carefully at the two pictures, saying, "This is not the same man. They look very similar, but they are not the same man."

"No, they are not the same man," says Jerry.

Drake asks, "So what is going on here?"

Jerry flips through the files, saying, "As I started to investigate this and I discovered more and more, I asked Detective Harlow for his help. He did help me, and what we found was jaw-dropping. We have kept this to ourselves, and I have kept these two files here to myself. No one has ever seen them except you, Drake. What Detective Harlow and I discovered is way above our ability, so this is for you and for you alone. Somehow both Alex Kevnick and Earl Rieval have been imitated by other men, and these other men have taken the rap. What I am saying is that Earl Rieval was not killed in a car accident, and Alex Kevnick did not go to jail. It takes very connected people in very high positions to make these kinds of things happen. I will not lie to you. I am a police officer, and I am proud, but what is going on here could put not only my life in danger but the lives of those I love in danger, so I have held on to this file just for you, Drake, and I give this knowledge to you." Jerry pulls a picture from the file and shows it to Drake, asking, "Do you know who this man is?"

"Yes," says Drake, "yes, this is the head of the CDCP. His name is Harry Klaushoven. I just met this man two days ago, and he asked me to come meet with him. I knew something was not right, and I went to find my mother, and they killed her. What do you think they will do to me?"

"I don't know, Drake, but yes, he is the head of the CDCP, and that means that he has access to people who have access to all the deadliest of diseases and viruses in the world." Jerry goes on to show Drake all the pictures he has in his file and asks Drake if has seen any of these men before.

Drake says, "No, wait a minute. These two men right here, they were at my mother's house just a few hours ago. This is the man who shot my mom right here. This man right here."

"Drake, Detective Harlow and myself have discovered that these seven men have been working together, and they have a house in Atlanta that is a front for their work, and somehow you are a part of their work whatever it is. Drake, I believe it is of a biological nature. I think that out of all the babies that died way back in 1968, you were one of them, and for some reason, you did not die, but they are after you, Drake. They do not want you to discover the truth. They do not want you to know what they have done to you. I was able to take these pictures and find this house in Atlanta because your tonsils that were taken out way back when you were five years old were supposed to be sent to a hospital laboratory in Buffalo, but they were intercepted by these men and taken to this house in Atlanta. All the records of this event disappeared a day later. I was able to track your tonsils to this house, and there, I took these pictures. It became clear to me that this is well funded by very high-up people who can make me disappear. I kept this file for you, but I cannot do anything more. I wish you all the best, Drake, but I think you are biologically the most important man in the world to these men, and they cut all ends connecting you to them after your tonsils were taken out. Somehow they have kept your whereabouts known to them. I was not able to find any more information about you after that. Your mother stayed in touch with me by phone a few times, but that was it. I am sorry for your loss, Drake. Your mother coming here the night you had your tonsils taken out was the smartest thing ever because it led me to Atlanta where I was able to take these pictures, but be careful, these are people who have a lot of power and authority behind them. What they have done to you and why, Drake, I have no idea, but I hope you can find the truth."

"Jerry, I can never thank you enough. I was heading for the hospital in Sprencer to see if I could find out any information about my past, but I think you have found it all. I am going to see my dad. My mother said to go see him, and from there, I will figure what to do next." Drake gets directions to the address in Pennsylvania from Jerry and stands up and shakes Jerry's hand.

"Drake, all the best to you and be careful," says Jerry.

"Thank you, Jerry, and be safe," says Drake as he leaves the police station.

Drake now has the two files given to him by Jerry with all the newspaper articles given to him by his mother. It is dark, and Drake heads south toward Pennsylvania. Drake likes to drive in the night. The air is cold and damp, and his window is down. He can only see the sights along the road where there are lights, and he watches the trees and landscapes pass by for the short time they are visible in his headlights. He thinks and remembers as much about his childhood as he can. Drake thinks about the recurring dream he has had throughout his life, the one where he is drowning as a baby. He thinks about this dream a lot when he is awake. He tries to watch the dream to see if there is an ending to it. He always adds things in his mind to make endings where he either rises from the water or he ends up drowning, but these are made-up visions by Drake, not actual dreams. Drake starts to have visions he never had before; he sees himself spitting, and he sees all the veins in his body becoming visible through his skin. It is very cool and gross all at the same time. Drake sees himself holding his arms out, and the veins are becoming visible from his shoulders down his arms up his neck into his face and down his chest, stomach, and legs. He can see his eyes turn black like they are hollow globes, and they are filling with a black liquid. Drake has never had these visions before, and they are just coming to him. Drake shakes his head, erasing the visions from his head, saying to himself, "Just concentrate on the road. It's time to go see dad."

CHAPTER 10

Drake Finds His Father

Drake drives through the night and gets to the Pennsylvania-New York border very early in the morning. Drake still has over $400 in his pocket, and after trying three different places to get a room, he finally finds a place where he can sleep the day for $85. The nice thing is that he can park right outside the door to his room. He gets a room, and it feels so good to get in, take a hot shower, and lie down. He falls asleep right away. Drake is sleeping very deep and sound even though he is having the dream where he is drowning as a baby. The difference this time is that Drake remembers more of the dream. Drake wakes up and sits up. He really does not have nightmares or wake up in a sweat or breathing hard, but this time, when he wakes, his heart is pounding. He is not breathing really hard or sweaty, but his heart is racing. Drake looks around and can tell it is the middle of the day. Looking at the clock radio on the table by his bed, he can see that it is a little after noon. Drake stands up in his boxer shorts and walks to the window, looking outside. He can see the bright sunshine and hear the buzzing insects and singing birds through the closed window. He walks back to the bed and sits down, remembering the dream he just had. This time, he sees himself rise from the water as a baby. He opens his eyes, and they are solid black. He can see the veins in his arm, and he can see a needle being put into his little baby arm. He can see the veins in his body become visible from the point of the needle. His veins seem to grow black from where the needle has been inserted into his arm, and he can see himself as a baby crying, and then he stops crying with his eyes closed and sees himself naked with all his veins showing black through his skin, and then Baby Drake opens his solid black eyes looking dead serious. This vision scares Drake back to reality, and he stands up quickly, shaking his head. Drake falls back to the bed, sitting on it. His stomach hurts like someone who has been running for a long time. He rubs his stomach, trying to relieve the discomfort, and his heart is hurting, and he can feel it when it pumps. His lungs feel like they are heavy and full like he can't breathe deeply. His neck is sore, and he rubs it with his hand, trying to rub away the soreness. Drake thinks, *What is wrong with me? What did I eat yesterday?* He remembers he did not eat much at all. Drake coughs and blood and mucus spray the carpet. Drake quickly gets a washcloth from the bathroom and gets soapy water on it and cleans the carpet. He begins to cough more, and this time, he catches the coughs with his hands. Drake looks to see a lot of blood and mucus in his hands, and he gets a very scared look on his face. Drake almost cries because he has never had sickness or illness that he remembers in his life. He has always been healthy, but he can feel that something is not right with his body. He feels weak, he feels scared, and he gets into the shower, trying to clean away what's wrong with him.

The black blood really puts fear into him, and he can't help now but cry as he gets in the shower. The water feels good on his body, and he lathers up with a lot of soap and takes a long shower. He gets out of the shower and gets dressed with new clothes that he brought in from his car. He returns the key to the front desk at the hotel and gets into his car to go look for his dad.

Drake follows the directions given to him by Jerry, and he finds his way through the back roads of Pennsylvania fairly easily. This is a heavily wooded area and far out from any city. He finds the address where his dad is supposed to be living, and he looks at the big house from the driveway. Drake never thought about how nervous he would be until now. He is actually very nervous. He has never seen his father not since he was a little boy, and he has very few memories of his father. Drake gets up his nerve and knocks at the front door. A woman answers the door saying hi.

Drake says, "Hi, I am Drake Hammond, and I am looking for Gerald Hammond."

"Oh my god," says the woman at the door. "I am Stacy. Come on in. Your father has told me all about you and Lance."

Drake follows Stacy into the house, saying, "Is my father here? I have to ask him about some things from my past."

"Gerald is probably at the bar," says Stacy.

"Oh, well, I really need to see him. Can you tell me where the bar is?" asks Drake.

"Well, he will be home in a couple of hours. You can wait here for him if you would like. I would love to talk with you and get to know you. You look so much like your father," says Stacy.

"Oh, that would be great, but I am kind of in a hurry. I really need to see my father as soon as possible," says Drake.

"Oh, OK. Well, your father is at Larry's Bar, it is a house that has been turned into a bar at the end of the road, you can't miss it. Are you sure you can't stay for a little while?" asks Stacy.

"No. I really have to go see him and get some answers. Thank you," says Drake as he leaves the house. Drake points down the road, saying to Stacy who is standing in the doorway, "This way?"

Stacy says, "Yup, it's about five miles on the right-hand side, you can't miss it."

"Thank you," says Drake as he gets into his car and heads down the road.

David was parked on the side of the road in a perfect location where he could watch Gerald Hammond's house with binoculars. He watches as Drake walks in the house, and he makes a call to Harry. "Harry, this is David. I have Drake. He is here at the house. What would you like me to do?"

Harry says, "Just watch him. Keep on his tail and watch for some men in a black car that should be there to apprehend Drake. They will take care of Drake. I want you to watch and follow. The men should get Drake, and then you just follow them all the way back here to Atlanta. Should by chance Drake escapes the men, I need for you to be our eyes on Drake. Do not lose him."

"No problem, you got it, boss," says David, and he hangs up. David does not notice anyone else following Drake. Drake leaves the house, and David follows. David is following Drake, and he notices a black car pass on the other side of the road. David looks in his rearview mirror and notices that the car makes a U-turn in the road and speeds back, and David lets the car pass him. "Well, there they are," says David to himself.

Drake gets to what obviously is Larry's Bar, thanks to the big sign saying Larry's Bar, and he pulls into the large stone driveway. Drake gets out of his car, and this is clearly a house that has had the front wall taken out and a huge wooden ramp and double door put in. Drake walks up the ramp, and here he goes again with his stomach knotted up and turning. Drake looks the driveway over to see there are only two cars, and he walks into the bar. He sees two men sitting at the bar and a bartender. He walks up to the man who he figures is his father and says, "Dad?"

Gerald looks at Drake, saying, "What the fuck are you doing here?"

Drake has this overpowering hot flash run through his body as he looks at his father, saying, "I have to ask you some things. Mom told me you might have some answers for me. She told me that you saved me from some doctors when I was a baby and that you had gone to the hospital a few times and found out some things that you never shared with her. I need to know what has happened to me, and I am going to find out who did what to me and why."

"Yeah, I figured you would show your face sometime, but I don't have any answers for you," says Gerald.

"What do you mean? You went to the hospital and you could not find out what was done to me?" asks Drake.

"I went to the hospital to find out what you are. Your mother, she never told you about Lindsey, did she? She never told you that Lindsey babysat for you and your brother, and then next morning, when I came home, Lindsey was dead. I don't know what the fuck you are, but something is not right with you. These men came and took Lindsey away, but they left you. They left you and your brother saying that everything was all right, and they had to run tests on Lindsey. They covered up the whole situation. Well, you are death, kid. You are diseased. Whatever happened back when you were a baby made you into some kind of death machine. You are not my son, you are the creation of those doctors, and they were not telling anyone anything. I have nothing for you, now get the fuck out of here, and don't come back."

"What the fuck is wrong with you? You make it sound like I made this happen when it was you and Mom who gave the doctors the OK to do whatever they did to me. Over seventy babies died, and I am the only one that lived, and you sit there like I made this happen. How is it that all these people are dying around me, and yet the closest people to me like you, Mom, and Lance have never had any problem?" says Drake.

"You listen to me. You are not my son. You are some kind of abomination, now get the fuck out of here. I don't give a fuck what you think or what you say," Gerald says as he drinks from his beer and takes a drag of his cigarette, looking straight ahead.

Drake says, "Dad, they are after me now. Do you know who they are?"

Gerald ignores Drake, and Drake looks forward, rubbing his forehead with his right hand and a very discouraged look on his face. Two men in suits walk into the bar. One of the men walks toward the back side of the bar while the other man stands at the door, looking the bar over. Drake notices the men and says to his father, "Well, Dad, this ought to be interesting. These men here, I have never seen them before, but they are here for me. I guarantee it. Did you know that two men that look very much like these two men killed Mom yesterday? They did not kill me, but I wonder if these two will kill me?"

Gerald stands up in his blue jeans and flannel shirt, lifting his baseball cap a few times and fitting it comfortably on his head. He takes the last drag from his cigarette and puts it out in the ashtray on the counter and walks to the man at the front door. Gerald is a little over six feet tall and a very sturdy man. He is not at all intimidated by other people. Gerald says to the man at the door. "I have never seen you here before." Gerald looks to Ralph, the bartender, saying, "Ralph, have you ever seen this man or the man over there before?" Gerald points to the man at the back of the bar.

"No, I have never seen either of these two men, and I have tended bar here for twelve years now," says Ralph.

Gerald looks to the man at the door, saying, "Unless you are here for a drink, and I do not think you are, I suggest you and your friend head on out of here and go back to where you came from."

The man in the suit is a very big man himself and leans into Gerald and confidently says, "You take your friend tending bar and you two leave now. This is the only time I will tell you."

The other man at the back of the bar walks up to the patron sitting at the bar and opens his jacket exposing a gun, saying, "I think it is time for you to leave." The patron gets up and walks past Gerald and the man in the suit as he exits. The man in the suit standing by Gerald moves to the side, and Gerald looks to Drake who is still sitting at the bar. Gerald looks to the man, saying, "You are not going to ask me to leave again, right?"

The man says, "That's right."

Gerald grabs the man around the neck with both hands and knees him in the lower stomach. The man falls to the ground moaning in pain, and Gerald motions to his son. "Drake, come on, son, let's get out of here."

The other man is now close to Drake, and he pulls the gun from under his jacket and points it at Gerald, saying, "Drake, you are coming with us or your father dies."

Drake has no idea where this impulse comes from, but he leans toward the man and spits a black dart of mucus right in the face of the man who just pulled a gun and pointed it at his father. The man immediately starts screaming and staggering backward, grabbing his face with both hands. He drops the gun, yelling, "What did you do to me? What is this? The man lowers his hands crying and screaming as blood starts to ooze from his eyes, and he is yelling, "I can't see. I can't see anything. What did you do to me?" The man starts to gurgle and blood starts to run from his nose, and he coughs up blood. His words are becoming indistinguishable as he falls to his knees. Ralph, Gerald, the other man in a suit, and Drake watch as the eyes of the man deflate like balloons and a mixture of puss, blood, and mucus run from his eye sockets with his deflated eyes falling out and rolling to the floor. This all happens in less than five minutes, and as disgusting as this is, everyone here is mesmerized and cannot stop watching until the man falls forward on his face, dead. The other man in the suit grabs Gerald from the back, putting the gun to Gerald's right temple, saying, "Drake, you are coming with me. Come on now, Drake. Come out here and get in the car with me, and no one else has to get hurt here." Gerald swings his left elbow into the gut of the man kneeling him over, but the man pulls the trigger as Gerald's elbow made contact, and Gerald never felt a thing. Drake watches this happen and does not say a thing. Drake just watches as his father falls. The man in the suit falls to his knees, gasping for air. The whole scene seems to happen in slow motion through the eyes of Drake. Drake watches as his father elbows the man in the gut, and he sees the gunshot and the left side of his father's forehead explode from the exiting bullet, which kills him quickly. Drake watches his father fall in slow motion, and he watches the man in the suit fall with his father, but only the man in the suit gets back up. Drake can hear nothing; the look on his face goes from surprise to anger to dead serious. Drake focuses directly on the man in the suit who stands up and points the gun at Drake. The man says, "Drake, come with me. Drake, I don't want to have to kill you too, but I will." Drake sees the man's mouth moving like he is talking, but he hears not a word; he hears not a sound. The veins in Drake's head start to become visible, and all the veins from his head down his body start to become visible. The veins of Drake's body are clearly visible, and they are flashing black with his pulse, and his eyes start to turn black, solid black. Ralph is behind the bar, and he slowly silently lowers himself behind the bar, hiding, and he is terrified at what he just saw. The man in the suit watches this change in Drake, and it is truly the scariest thing he has ever witnessed in his life. Drake starts to walk toward him with those black eyes looking directly at him, but he does not shoot Drake; he runs out of the bar and gets into his car and drives off. Drake walks to his father and kneels by him. His veins begin to fade, and his normal skin color returns, hiding his veins and the fact that his blood is apparently black. Drake's eyes begin to regain their normal blue color. He sits motionless on his knees, looking at his dad breathing very hard like he is trying hard to get air into his lungs. He hears the man behind the bar as he stands and peeks over the bar at Drake, saying, "Is he dead? Is Gerald dead?"

Drake slants his head downward to the right, yawning and rubbing his eyes with his right hand, saying, "Yes, he is dead."

"You don't have anything against me, do you? I mean, I have never seen you before in my life. What you did to that guy in that suit there, you're not going to do that to me, right?" says Ralph.

"No no no. I am not going to do that to you," Drake says, looking at Ralph, getting up and walking toward the bar and sitting on a stool. Ralph starts to back up. Drake says, "My father left when I was very young. I have very few memories of my father, but he knew something. He knew something about why these men here were after me, and he knew something about what it was that I did to that man. I don't even know what is going on with me, but I was here to try and get some answers. Unfortunately, whatever my father knew, he took to the grave with him."

"Hey, you want a beer?" asks Ralph.

Drake says, "No, but I will take a Coke with no ice please." Drake drinks a little of the Coke and says, "If I were you, I would call the police and get them here quick. Tell them everything." Drake starts to walk out of the bar, and Ralph says, "Hey, Drake, you know your father did talk about you. He talked about you a lot, and he did love you. I don't know if this means anything to you, but your father talked about a girl who had watched you and your brother one night, and she died. Your father said that your brother must have had the same immune system as you have. I don't know why I thought of that, but I don't see your brother here with you. Is he like you?"

Drake turns to Ralph with a curious look on his face, saying, "I had not thought of that. Unfortunately, I have not seen my brother in a very long time, and I don't know where he is. I don't think he is like me in every way, but you never know." Drake leaves the bar and gets into his Firebird and drives away. There is a car tailing Drake, but he is unaware of it at this time.

Harry is at the house in Atlanta with Earl, Alex, John, and Larry. A car pulls into the garage and lowers down to the bottom floor where Alex, Earl, and Harry are waiting to greet Sam who has collected Drake's mother and cleaned the scene at her house. Eric and Richard follow in another car, and they have Roger's body in an airtight biohazard bag, which they put in the trunk with Kaitlin's body in the car that Sam is driving. They have helped clean up the scene as well and notified the local police, and sure enough, Drake has an APB put out for his arrest in connection with the death of his mother. Eric and Richard park in the garage, and they take the stairs from within the house to get downstairs. All the men hurry to the trunk of the car, and Harry says, "You guys took extreme care in transporting the cargo, right?"

"Don't worry," says Sam. "If we did not, we would not be here now. Where are Earl and Alex?"

The car is on a large circular metal disk, and it starts to turn clockwise. Eric and Richard back far away from the car, and Alex and Earl walk out from within an airtight room. Both doctors are wearing protective suits, preventing any biological contagion from coming in contact with their bodies.

"Alex, Earl, I want the two of you to get to work on these two immediately. I want to know if our boy is ready. I want to know that you have the cure, and you can make plenty of serum. Get to work and let me know. This is starting to be very real, gentlemen," says Harry. Harry heads toward the stairs with Sam, Eric, and Richard, and they go upstairs. Alex and Earl open the trunk of the car where the bodies of Kaitlin and Roger have been put into large biohazard bags. Earl and Alex remove the bodies and take them into the laboratory. Meanwhile, as soon as Harry gets to the top of the stairs, his phone rings. Harry answers, "Yeah, this is Harry. What do you mean? You have got to be kidding me. Well, you cleaned it up discretely, right? What do you mean no? So what do you want me to do? I understand. I understand, sir. Yes, Earl and Alex are working on the bodies right now. We will. No one will leave this house. Yes, I understand we are very close to our goal. Nothing will stop us now. Yes, sir. I understand." Harry hangs up his cell phone. He rubs his eyes, exhaling loudly. Harry looks up to see the men in the room looking at him. Harry says, "This is one smart kid. So far he has been very elusive. There has been an incident in the mountains of Pennsylvania. Drake's father was killed, and so was Peter." The men look at one another; Eric says, "We lost Peter too?"

Harry responds, "Yeah, this kid has become much more lethal than we ever thought he would be. He is becoming lethal on his own. This we did not anticipate. Listen, I am going to get an emergency call any minute now. I will have to go to the office because the scene in Pennsylvania will be considered a biological hazard. I will organize a team, and some of you will be getting calls later. Things are coming together, men." Harry's phone rings. "OK, men, hold the fort, this will be a tricky situation, but let's all be calm and do what we knew we would have to do. We are going to make this work, and we will all be fine." Harry leaves the house while talking on the phone and gets in his car and drives to the CDCP in Atlanta.

Meanwhile in the laboratory in the lower levels of the house, Alex and Earl have removed the bodies from the biohazard bags and have them on gurneys. Earl has taken samples of blood from Roger and is looking at them under the microscope. "My god, Alex, have a look at this. The destruction of the blood has accelerated exponentially. Roger was exposed to Drake's bodily fluids just yesterday. The speed of cell deterioration is remarkable. We have to get fresh samples of Drake's blood. I fear he is dying much faster than we had anticipated. I can't believe the organs in his body have held up this long. I don't know how his body has not suffocated yet," Earl says, rubbing his chin, thinking out loud.

Alex is looking at the blood samples under the microscope as well, and he agrees with Earl, saying, "Drake's blood and saliva is so potent. It is amazing he is still alive now. His blood has adapted remarkably to the virus, and the Herculean serum you created made the virus in Drake's body the first ever intelligent virus, but I fear the organs in Drake's body have been slowly deteriorating, and by now, they are starting to fail him. Earl, you are right. We need to get him in here right now. He may have as short as a few months left to live. We have to figure out how to deploy the virus in such a way that the people exposed will live long enough to obtain the cure."

Earl says, "Yeah, but if Drake is really lucky, he could live for five years yet. This will give us more time to work on deployment of the virus. Right now, it just kills too fast."

Alex says, "One thing is for sure, his blood cannot become any deadlier than it already is. His blood and his saliva somehow extract oxygen from foreign blood and tissue. He is already the deadliest man ever to live and walk this earth. Come on, Earl, let us go and tell Harry." The two doctors clean up and store the bodies in a special refrigerated room with other bodies that they have kept over the years. The doctors put name tags on the thick plastic bags that zip up, and Earl pushes the first gurney saying Roger Stergis, and Alex pushes the second gurney with the name Kaitlin Hammond on it. The men push the gurneys past other gurneys, and the bags on the gurneys have these names on the bags. Lilly Branson, Sally Graines, Lisa Hiltneg, Brandon Scotts, Mario Avante, Susan Weller, and Lindsey Brahms. This laboratory has all the bodies of the people who have come in contact with

Drake and have died throughout his whole life. Earl and Alex have been studying the bodies and what is happening to them from being exposed to Drake. The doctors decontaminate themselves and go upstairs to find that Harry has gone, and the ASAFEW members in the house wait for Harry to contact them. Earl and Alex go to get something to eat in the kitchen. After an hour, they go back to the laboratory to work on the bodies, and they let the others know they need to get Drake back to the house as soon as possible.

CHAPTER 11

Harry Klaushoven

Harry's family immigrated to the United States in 1937. Harry's parents were very intelligent, and they could see the turmoil and confusion that was about to sweep over Germany in the late 1930s. Harry was an only child, and he had a very strict upbringing. Harry's father, Karl, and his mother, Matilda, used their entire wealth to move to New York City, where they lived in a comfortable apartment and Harry had a very good education. Harry watched as his father worked hard on the docks every day, and his mother was always taking care of him, his father, and the apartment, and the family lived quietly and nicely. Harry's parents were very strict, not allowing Harry to venture from the apartment much. Harry had a strict schedule. He was to spend the first four hours every day when he got home from school working on his schoolwork. It was two hours of schoolwork as soon as Harry got home, then dinnertime when his father got home, and then another two hours of schoolwork, a bath, and to bed. This was not so bad for Harry because his parents were so routing and so constant that Harry really did not know anything different. Every night at dinner, Harry's parents would tell him how important it was that he did very good in school. His parents told Harry all the time that he needed to be a doctor so that he could have a good life and be independent financially. The way he would achieve this was by doing good in school and continuing on to college. Harry did not argue much with his parents; he listened to them and followed their rules, and Harry did very well in school. There were times when his parents would talk about their homeland, Germany. This brought out arguments, and this sometimes pitted Harry against his parents. Harry's parents would tell Harry how they could see bad things were coming to Germany, and this was why they moved to America, to make a better life for themselves. They could see the rise of Hitler, and they were able to get out of Germany and live in America. Harry's parents would tell Harry what a terrible man Hitler was, but Harry did not understand this. Harry had access with his education to the writings of Hitler, and he read the book *Mein Kampf,* and Harry believed Hitler was a good thing for Germany. Harry's parents would get very upset with Harry, trying to explain to him what a disastrous man Hitler was, not only to Germany, but to the world. The nights Harry got into arguments with his parents about Hitler were the nights Harry went to bed very early. As Harry went to school in New York City, he watched as the whole world watched what happened to Germany through the 1940s, but unlike almost everyone in the world, Harry, for whatever reason, took a dislike to America and its allies. Harry fell prey to the propaganda that Hitler had spread with his words. Harry fell victim to the passion conveyed in Hitler's speeches. Harry believed that it was not only Germany that was always preyed upon by every country outside of its borders, but Harry believed it was America and its allies that drove all other countries that did not conform to the ways of democracy into the ground. This is precisely the thinking Harry's parents tried to educate their son into understanding, but Harry did not understand; Harry could not let go of his German heritage. Harry is 100 percent German, and he could not let himself ever believe he was an American. Harry stopped arguing with his parents when he was a teenager and kept his feelings to himself. Harry went to school and studied hard; he did very well, and he was very intelligent. His parents were always proud of Harry, but little did they know. Harry had kept a grudge against the United States, and he was always plotting and planning in his mind to somehow someday get back at the United States and its allies for the destruction of Germany in the 1940s. Harry graduated high school and was accepted into MIT medical school where Harry Klaushoven spent eight years, working very hard and gaining his medical master's degree. Harry Klaushoven was now a medical master's degree holder. He was very well respected by his peers and teachers. Harry graduated from MIT in 1963 and had many recommendations to the CDCP where Harry had made it clear he wanted to work. Harry's parents were at his graduation ceremony, and they could not have been any prouder of their only child then they were on this day. Harry immediately went to the CDCP in Atlanta, and he was hired to work at the bottom of the totem pole, but he was in. Harry was always working with and around people, but they could tell that Harry seemed to be distant, and he was. Harry was always plotting like an evil schemer. Three years had gone by, and Harry was beginning to get very discouraged with his job at the CDCP. Harry had asked many times for positions in the deadly virus unit or the disease center, but he was always denied. Harry was always calm and did not have outbursts or argue with people, but inside, he was becoming very upset. He was offered two promotions which he accepted but they were not what he had wanted. The promotions he had been offered were administrative. There were increases in pay, and they did offer Harry great mobility and flexibility within the CDCP, but he wanted to work with the deadliest viruses and diseases that the world has ever seen, and they were stored right here at the CDCP. Harry, in his ever more twisted mind, could only see the end he had envisioned as a teenager. Harry always lived alone. He never let anyone close to him; he never let anyone know him. He never let love touch his heart. This was all about to change, but it was changing to benefit Harry's outlandish sense of reality. In Harry's second promotion at the CDCP, he became the head of human resources, which meant he now had access to all the people that worked at the CDCP, at least most of them. He had no control over the people themselves, but he knew what their titles were. He knew their pay scale. He knew a lot about them, and he had all kinds of access to very confidential information. Harry was given this promotion because not only was he a very talented doctor and biologist, but Harry was very organized and had a superb memory. Harry was distant, but this served him well; he does not stick his nose into other people's business, and he keeps to himself, and this is just what his superiors were looking for when Harry came along. Along with the title of head of human resources, Harry is now expected to attend functions outside of the workplace. Harry is now expected to make acquaintances, and he is expected to speak for the CDCP at dinner functions and colleges. Harry again was not liking this, but he went along with his responsibilities and attended a dinner function in Atlanta in 1966, which changed his life forever.

The Democratic Party was in town, and Harry was expected to speak at a dinner party where all the Democratic elites of Washington were going to be. The CDCP relied heavily on donations, and fund-raisers from both parties and dinner functions were a great way for the CDCP to raise money. Harry had just turned thirty years old, and he was a very young man for the position he held at the CDCP.

Here at the dinner party, Harry stands up in front of all the highest social class in America and gives a speech on health, disease, virus, vaccinations, antibiotics, and good living. Harry looks around the room, and for a brief moment, he thinks to himself, *What a really good life I live.* Harry resumes his speech and has brilliant thoughts throughout his speech, which he incorporates into his written speech. Harry, for the first time in his life, has the audience rolling in the aisles laughing to the point that some of them are crying. For the first time in Harry's life, he actually allows himself to have a good time, and then it happens. Harry sees a beautiful young girl. She has very dark hair in a barrette pulled tight to her head. She has deep blue eyes, and she is staring Harry down and even Harry can feel she is attracted to him. Harry goes on to make a twenty-five-minute speech to the dining crowd, and he is brilliant. Harry turns a lot of heads on this night, and he gains a lot of respect from those that work with him. After Harry's speech, he heads right to the table where the beautiful dark-haired blue-eyed beauty is sitting. Harry walks right up to her and holds out his hand, saying, "I am Harry Klaushoven." The girl smiles and holds his hand, and before she gets in a word, she is interrupted by her father who stands up, walks over in front of Harry, and shakes his hand, saying "I am Senator Kyle Cartright from Chicago, and this is my daughter Kelly." Harry smiles, and the Senator continues, "I have to say that was quite a speech you gave up there tonight."

"Thank you," says Harry, and he tries to look at Kelly, but the senator is commandeering Harry's attention. The senator continues to hold Harry's hand, saying, "You look like a very bright fellow, Harry Klaushoven. You take it from me. You keep working hard and stick to your guns, and remember, everybody in the governmental agencies needs friends and lots of them. I like what I see so far, and if you need anything, you call me anytime." Kyle extends his right arm and hand to the seat by his daughter, motioning Harry to sit down, saying, "Harry, please sit and meet with my daughter, but watch out she is a tiger." Kyle smiles at his daughter and walks away, talking to a person who has been trying to get his attention. Harry says, "May I sit by you?"

Kelly says, "Yes, I thought my dad would never leave."

Harry sits down, and he can't hide his smile; he looks right at Kelly, saying, "You know I can read your palm."

"You can," says Kelly.

"Yup, I sure can," says Harry. "If you want, I will read your palm, and you tell me if what I say is right or not."

"OK," says Kelly, and she holds out her hand for Harry to read.

Harry looks at Kelly's hand, and he starts to smile.

"What? What do you see," asks Kelly.

"I don't know if I should tell you what I see," says Harry.

"What do you mean? You just said you were going to read my palm and tell me what it says. Come on, tell me what you see, and I will tell you if you are right or not," says Kelly, smiling at Harry.

Harry says, "OK. Your palm says you want to kiss me."

Kelly blushes rosy red with a huge smile on her face. Harry himself has never been this attracted to a girl ever. Harry goes on to flirt a lot with Kelly but not getting too close to her. He always maintains at least a little space between the two of them. Kelly loves the feeling that she has. She knows that Harry wants to be all over her, but she loves the way all the people in the room give him pause, and he keeps flirting with her but is very timid to get too close to her. Kelly uses this shyness on the part of Harry and teases him. She flirts back telling him all kinds of things to see how long it will take Harry to actually kiss her because she does want to kiss him. Harry and Kelly flirt all night, and the attraction between the two of them is visible to all. The next day, the Cartrights will be heading back to Chicago, and Kyle invites Harry to come by and visit anytime. Harry actually comes by and spends the next weekend with the Cartrights at their very luxurious home in Chicago. The Cartright home is huge, and there is a guesthouse, which is where Kelly lives. There is a second guesthouse, and this is where Kelly's brother, Terri, lives. Harry has spoken with Kelly on the phone every night this past week, and it has been arranged for Harry to drive up to Chicago from Atlanta Friday night and spend time with Kelly this weekend. Harry is so excited that he leaves right after work on Friday and drives straight to Chicago for about twelve hours. Harry is very surprised to see that Kelly is alone; all of the family has gone away for the weekend, and Kelly and Harry have all weekend to themselves. Harry and Kelly become lovers, and Harry quickly becomes a part of the family. Kelly's father Kyle really takes to Harry and grants Harry passage on a private plane to fly to and fro on. Harry has just turned thirty years old, and Kelly is twenty-eight, so they are very close in age, and the more time they spend together, the more they seem to have in common with each other. Harry has come to see Kelly four weekends in a row, and this week, he has a full week of vacation, and he spends the whole week in Chicago with the Cartrights. Harry has become close to the whole family, and on the first day of his weeklong vacation in Chicago, Kelly tells Harry something that blows him away. Kelly sits Harry down, saying, "Harry, I think it is time we have a serious talk." Harry is thinking, *Kelly is in love, and this is the marriage talk,* but he is way off the mark.

Kelly says, "Harry, I am very attracted to you, and I think you are a strong, courageous man, and that is why I have to ask something of you. I want to know how you feel about life and power. I mean I will tell you honestly I am looking to rule the world and I need a strong man to rule by my side. A man like you, Harry. A man like you who can be appointed to a position that will lead to ultimate power."

Harry cannot believe what he is hearing, but he can't take his eyes and ears off Kelly; he listens very closely as Kelly shows Harry the darkest side of a person. The dark that has consumed Harry his whole life, and he has never shared this side of himself with anyone until now. Harry confides all his deepest cruelest thoughts with Kelly, and he is astonished that first of all, he confided in her and, second of all, that Kelly agrees with Harry on a lot of issues. Kelly has no grudge against the United States; she just wants total power. She wants to rule the world. Three days go by, and these two plot and plan. They scheme and coordinate the evilest of plans. They brainstorm on how two people could take over the world and rule it. Kelly has the power play always in her court. Her father is very powerful in that he has access to a lot of agencies and powerful people. Her family has a lot of connections that span all around the world. Kelly tells Harry how important he is because with just a few recommendations from her father, Harry could possibly become the head of the CDCP, which will allow him access to people who have access to the deadliest viruses and diseases on the planet. With this access and with the right allies at their side, the world could be at their mercy. Without even realizing anything is wrong, these two psychos plan to take over the world by killing most people with the use of deadly virus. They talk, plot, plan, and figure things out together, and after the week has ended, Harry gets ready to go home to Atlanta and go back to his job when Kelly tells Harry, "All right then, Harry, everything is set, let's make it happen."

Harry looks at Kelly, surprised, saying, "Are you serious? You really want to go through with this?"

"Yes," says Kelly.

Harry says, "All right, Kelly, I tell you what. If you can get me promoted to the head of the CDCP, then you and I will rule the world." Harry smiles at Kelly, thinking nothing is going to happen, but if it does, he will go through with what they have planned, he thinks to himself.

"All right then, Harry Klaushoven, get ready to rule the world," says Kelly, hugging and kissing Harry. Harry gets home in Atlanta, and it is already time for him to go to bed. He has to be up very early, and he is never late, nor does he ever miss any days from work. Harry goes through the week and hears nothing about any promotions, and he does not worry or think about it much because he has a very demanding, fast-paced job. On Friday of this week, there is a memo that goes out to all the employees that really gets Harry's attention. The head of the CDCP Thurston Dimmond is retiring. He is taking his retirement, and this is going to be his last month with the CDCP. Harry cannot believe this memo, and everything he has talked with Kelly about in the past week suddenly becomes prominent in his mind. He can't believe it, but suddenly, he is thinking about not only getting back at America and its allies, but he is thinking about taking over the world. *Well, why the hell not,* Harry thinks to himself.

The weekend comes, and Harry heads to Chicago. Once there, Harry talks with Kelly about the memo he had read at work, and he cannot help but ask Kelly if she had anything to do with the early retirement of Thurston Dimmond. Kelly tells Harry they will talk about it more at dinner; right now, she has other things on her mind, and they are of a physical nature.

Kyle, his wife, Shirley, Kelly, and her brother, Terri, are all at dinner, and Harry, right from the start, has had a very comfortable relationship with the whole family. It is like the whole family has trusted Harry right from the start, and no one has even questioned the fact that Harry sleeps in the guesthouse with Kelly, which is obviously hers. The servants bring dinner, and they all enjoy a very nice dinner. While eating, Kyle says, "So, Harry, my daughter tells me you would like to head the CDCP. Is this true? I mean, not only is this a very enviable position to have, but someone with great ambition would still need a little help in order to, let's say, seal the deal."

"What does that mean seal the deal?" asks Harry.

"Well, I mean a lot of people will be applying for the position in a lot of different ways, and the person who ultimately gets the position will certainly be someone who has connections and has a lot of support and backing. For example, let's say you and Kelly were going to announce you are getting married. You are very qualified for the position, and you are starting a family this looks very good to people who are looking for someone to hold down a secure and lasting position. Recommendations from, let's say, senators would also look very good for any person who desires such a position. Harry, I can make these recommendations possible."

Harry looks around the table, and the most startling thing he heard was him and Kelly getting married. Apparently he is the only one surprised by this comment. Harry replies, "So am I so slow that everyone here except me thinks Kelly and I are getting married?" There is quiet at the table, and everyone looks at Harry. Harry gets very hot, very red, saying, "Whoa, I am sorry, I was just asking, don't get me wrong. I am very much in love with Kelly, and I would love to marry her." Harry looks to Kelly, all red in his face, saying, "Kelly, your family beat me to the question, will you marry me?"

Kelly jumps out of her chair and hugs Harry, kissing him all over his face, saying, "Yes, yes, I will marry you, Harry." The family looks at Harry and Kelly, smiling like they knew this was going to happen.

By January of 1967, Harry and Kelly are married, and they now live in a beautiful house in Atlanta. Kelly never let up on her dreams of ruling the world, and Harry has plotted with her every step of the way. Harry talks only with Kelly, but Kelly has her father and all his connections and financial backing, making the sadistic goals of Harry and Kelly become real. Kelly's father has very high goals, and they may even include running for president of the United States. Harry has a good relationship with Kyle Cartright, but he has grown to call him sir, and they do not meet face-to-face much anymore, but they do talk on the phone once or twice a month. Harry thinks only he and Kelly know of their plot, which they have been working on and carrying out, but he knows by talking with Kelly a lot that she gets her ideas from her father. Harry has, with the help of Kyle's financial resources, recruited Alex Kevnick, and these two men have become the founding fathers of ASAFEW. They work in a house that has been set up with state-of-the-art laboratory equipment on the lower level of the house. Alex is a well-known doctor who already works at the CDCP, and Harry has recruited four secret service agents that have left their jobs for personal reasons and have come to work for Harry and protect the house and all residing within it. These men are Roger Stergis, Richard Yarlow, John Helger, and Larry Siltor. Harry has seen the writings of Earl Rieval, and he is so reminded of himself when he was a young man in New York. Harry has all the men of ASAFEW know who Earl Rieval is, and sure enough, they recruit him, making the house in Atlanta ready to start work on creating a biological threat capable of killing everyone that comes in contact with it unless they have the cure, which is the reason for the laboratory. The laboratory in the house is to create the biological weapon and its cure, making the members of ASAFEW the most dangerous and elite group of people on the planet. Harry, even though he is the head of the CDCP, still does not have the ability to take samples of virus from the CDCP or anything else for that matter. Harry does not even have access to the viruses in the CDCP. This is why Alex is so important to him. Alex is one of the lead scientists working with the viruses that are very secure and locked up tight in the CDCP. Harry, in conversations with Alex, has mentioned ideas about how things should be handled differently, and Alex bought into his ideas. They became friends, and Alex agreed to work with Harry to smuggle out samples of the deadliest biological substances on earth and take them to the house so ASAFEW could work on creating the deadliest biological substance ever known and, of course, make the cure for it. Alex is a hard-core scientist, and he has always wanted to see the deadliest of disease and virus up close and doing what it does in real time on real living beings. Alex immediately agreed to work in the field with people who had no idea they were injected with these lethal substances. He did not even care that they were innocent babies being injected with lethal substances. Alex did not look at his duties as murder; he saw it as scientific advancement, and no one could hide the real cause of death like Alex could. Alex knew he would spend all his time working in the field, making lethal injections for babies, and he knew someone had to be in the laboratory working on serums to try to save the babies. The cure is the ultimate goal because with the cure comes the power. The cure is what everyone will need, and to get it, they will pay. Harry introduces the writings of Earl Rieval to Alex, and they know they have their scientist to work in the laboratory in the house while Alex works in the field. They recruit Earl, and now all that needs to happen is for Harry to find the right hospitals so that Alex can start his work in the field. Harry has gained a lot of connections himself since he has been the head of the CDCP and makes good use of his connections as he finds hospitals in the Upstate New York region to happily allow for doctors to visit and give checkups to babies especially since the hospitals are being funded from government agencies, which Harry is able to acquire from his ties to people in the Senate. Once Alex is in the hospitals, he immediately starts his work, and within six months, babies are dying at an alarming rate. No one is able to make the connection to Dr. Alex Kevnick. He flies so low under the radar and is so good at hiding the real cause of death that it takes the government and the CDCP, along with local authorities, almost a year to catch up with Alex Kevnick, and he and Earl Rieval take all the blame for the epidemic killing all the babies in the Upstate New York region. Earl is always mentioned to be connected with Alex, but very little is known about Earl. Alex takes most of the blame. Earl is said to have died in the car accident, and Alex is sent away to jail for life. The members of ASAFEW, of course, planned on being caught and paid one man to take the place of Alex in jail for life, and this man's family was very nicely rewarded financially. Earl's body was replaced with another man's body, and both doctors work in the laboratory in the house all the time now. The one thing that is now coming to pass is that Drake Hammond is truly a walking virus; the members of ASAFEW have accomplished their goal of creating a virus that is capable of killing millions and millions of people. Now the catch is that they have to find the cure to the virus they have created. What they did not plan on was that they found a one in a billion. They found and created from Baby Drake Raymond Hammond the infected man. A man who has the capability of killing most human beings on the planet, at least 99 percent of all human beings on the planet, just by touching them with his blood or his saliva. The most astonishing thing is that Harry, Alex, and Earl are the only three men alive that are truly aware of what is going on here. Not only is Drake Hammond a walking virus, but the virus in Drake is an intelligent virus. This virus may be able to think or at least take over Drake's mind and think through Drake. These three doctors are aware of this, and there is nothing they want more than to study this virus more and understand it. There are big problems. They cannot hurt Drake. They cannot kill him, for Drake is so lethal that people die in less than a day when exposed to his bodily fluids. Another astonishing thing about this virus may be that Drake is only lethal when the virus takes over his body. The virus may be in his blood and his tissue, but it may be able to stay dormant and come out at will. The doctors have found something here, but they have gotten themselves to a place where only they can know about what they have done. They do work tirelessly on a cure because without the cure total power will always elude them. So it has been twenty-five years, and Drake, without ever meeting these three doctors, has always astonished them being that Drake is maybe a one-in-a–billion host. These three doctors secretly call Drake the Infected Man.

CHAPTER 12

Theft, the Infected, the Cover-Up

Alex walks into the CDCP at just before five in the morning. It is still dark, and he is carrying his briefcase. He goes to his locker, saying hi to all his colleagues who are getting ready to start another day of monitoring hot spots around the world, where the possibility of outbreak is most likely. Alex is one of a few people who actually have access to all the deadliest virus samples that are stored here in the CDCP since the early 1700s. There are strains of hundreds of different viruses stored here, and believe it or not, they are very easy to duplicate and easy to grow. There are also antibiotics and serums that have been very successful in fighting against these viruses. Getting them out of one of the most secure places on earth now is not easy. Being that Harry, Alex, and those associated with them are crazy; this gives them a sense of daring and a resistance to fear and common sense. Very quickly in 1967, when Harry has assembled men to join, follow, and create ASAFEW, they embark on a plan to get biological substances out of the CDCP that uses the innovation and help from very high people in government and exhausts all the knowledge of twisted minds. The men are assembled, the laboratory in the house has been set up, and now it is time to stock the laboratory with deadly viruses, antibiotics, and Alex is the man to get all this out of the CDCP. Alex gets ready to make his rounds. Alex is one who checks on the samples and makes sure they are suspended in their stasis chambers. They are not checked a lot, only twice a month, and these checks are the only time Alex could ever get to a majority of the samples all at one time. There are times when the samples are retrieved to be studied, but when is not known and not often enough to say so. There are samples being studied at all times, and Alex is one of the people studying these samples, but he needs access to as many of them as possible, not just one here and there. Harry and Alex have set up an intricate plan to get at the samples and give Alex enough time to transfer enough of the substances to petri dishes and enable him to smuggle the substances out of the CDCP, and no one will ever know they have been taken. The strains of all the biological substances are kept frozen in secure vaults. Again only twice a month are these vaults checked from the inside to make sure everything is satisfactory, and Alex just happens to be one of the few who has this maintenance responsibility. This is a maintenance procedure, so all the secure frozen units storing all the petri dishes with all the samples are opened and examined. This is a must because these substances must be kept at a constant temperature at all times. Any malfunction in cooling or the storage units themselves are quickly fixed because the release of these substances is of course lethal to all people. The storage units are very unique and are updated all the time. They are metal tubes that open by turning the top and lifting. The entire middle section of the metal container rises out, and there are many small dishes that have samples in them that are frozen. The samples are very easy to take; all you need to do is simply touch a Q-tip to the frozen sample and then transfer the end of the Q-tip to another petri dish, let it cool down, and the bacteria will multiply. The CDCP has had many different protective suits that the working people here have worn over the years; one thing they all have in common is that they are big bulky and necessary. Alex has a choice of three different suits he can wear. He picks one in particular because it has a lot of pockets that are accessible from the outside of the suit. Harry and Alex have collected very special petri dishes that are one inch in diameter by one-half inch high. He can store hundreds of these dishes in his suit. Alex is at his locker, and he is putting on his very bulky suit, and he is a little nervous because he knows that he is about to make one of the greatest heists in history. He looks around to make sure no one sees him put the dishes in his suit. He see a colleague of his, and Alex says, "Oh hi, Darryl, what are you doing here?" Alex turns to hide the dishes in his hand.

"Just getting ready to go to lunch. Why are you putting on that suit? You gonna steal some samples," Darryl says, laughing.

"No, I just remember wearing these suits years ago, and while I was thinking about it, I just started putting it on," Alex says, chuckling while he speaks. "Since I have it this far on, I might as well wear it for nostalgia's sake now."

Darryl says, "Well, you just be careful in there, Alex. I'll see you later on," and Darryl walks out of the locker room. Alex exhales deeply and continues to get dressed in his suit. Meanwhile Harry has assembled all the highest officials at the

CDCP for a very special guest that is coming to visit and get a grand tour of the CDCP today. This guest is none other than Sen. Kyle Cartright, and he has made rumor that he would like to be the vice presidential hopeful candidate in the 1968 election of the United States of America. Harry Klaushoven will be guiding Kyle and his party throughout the facility, and the surgeon general Marcus Blanthon will be with the touring party as well on this day.

The convoy of limousines and cars pull up to the CDCP, and a lot of men get out of the cars, creating a barricade of people. Kyle Cartright and the surgeon general get out of the limousine, and they are greeted by Harry Klaushoven and three other high-ranking officials here at the CDCP. They all head into the CDCP after warm welcomes and greetings. Just before they get to the doors entering the CDCP, gun shots are fired. Immediately and very fast, all the security stand around the senator the surgeon general and Harry rushing them into the CDCP protecting them with their bodies. A car drives by with a man hanging out of the car, shooting a machine gun into the crowd of men. The car keeps driving, and another car from down the road burns out, and the cars drive away. The drivers and shooters were all wearing a lot of concealing clothing along with masks. Once inside the CDCP, Harry orders the building locked down from the front security desk where there are five guards who allow people in and out of the building and can also monitor sections of the building from their position. The party notices one of the men has been hit, and he is in bad shape. "Paul, Paul," says Kyle Cartright. Kyle and some men inspect the shot that has penetrated Paul's abdomen. "Call 911 and get an ambulance here at once," orders Harry. "Come with me, there are people here who can help," says Harry as he leads the men to some doctors. They get Paul to a room where there are many qualified doctors who look at Paul and are able to stabilize and calm him down. "They were trying to kill me. Who would want to kill me?" asks Kyle Cartright.

"Don't worry, Kyle," says one of his body guards. "No one is going to hurt you. That is why we are here."

"Thank you, Curtis, what about Paul is he going to be OK?" says Kyle.

"He is going to be OK," says one of the doctors looking at Paul.

"Come with me. Everyone, come on, I know where we can see everything," says Harry, and all the men in the party follow Harry except for Paul who has been shot, and he stays in the laboratory where the doctors tend to him. The party of men follow Harry into the monitoring room, where there are monitors, lots of them, and all the building is being monitored by five men at all times. From this room, many things can be controlled. Parts of the building can be locked down or opened up depending on what the situation is. All kinds of fail-safes take place here. No sooner do the men get into the room when there is an explosion, and many of the monitors go blank. The building shakes, and Harry yells, "What was that?"

"I don't know, sir. I am checking," says Peter, one of the men monitoring the surveillance monitors.

"Why are we losing the surveillance monitors?" asks Harry who can see that more of the monitors are going blank.

"Sir, that explosion"—and then there are more explosions—
"must have hit our energy sources, and not only that, but
power cables may have been broken as well. Sir, the building
is going into automatic lockdown," replies Peter.

"Automatic lockdown, what is that?" asks Kyle.

"Automatic lock down is a fail-safe, Kyle. No one can
get in or out of the building, and not only that, but all the
sites within the building where we store and have the most
sensitive materials, and I mean materials of the biological
nature have been locked down," says Harry. All the workers
in the building take notice and look up as red lights flash and
all safety doors close and seal airtight. They are not opening.
No one is getting in or out of the work zone they are in until
the doors are manually opened by none other than the head
of the CDCP, and that, of course, is Harry Klaushoven.
Harry orders that all monitors be viewing positions entering
or exiting the building and on locations where the explosions
have taken place. "Peter, we must make sure none of the
biological storage rooms have been damaged. Wait before
you start changing the views, let's make sure everyone inside
the building is all right and aware of what is going on," says
Harry to Peter the man at the monitoring station. Harry grabs
hold of a microphone that he can speak into, and there is an
intercom throughout the building that everyone can hear his
words on, and he speaks into the microphone as he looks over
the monitors and can see that no one has been injured and
that all the biological rooms are still intact. "Everyone, this is
Director Harry Klaushoven. I want all of you to be calm and
know that everything is OK. There has been a disturbance
outside the building, and we are in lockdown mode right

now. I believe there has been an attempt to bring harm to the senator from Chicago, but we are all OK, and we will all get through this just fine. There have been explosions within the building, and I ask that you all be alert and stay aware because there have been shots fired. Senator Cartright and the surgeon general are fine. One of the security personnel has been shot, but it is looking like he is going to be OK. There have been explosions in our building today, but right now, we are all safe, and we are monitoring the situation. Law enforcement agencies have already been contacted and are on their way here now. I ask that you all be calm and maintain a safe area where you are now. We are working on this situation and doing all we can to bring everything back to normal, just be patient, stay calm, and relax. It may be a few hours before our security system is released, and many of you will be able to move around in the building. Thank you for your cooperation, Harry Klaushoven. OK, Peter, who is this man here and what is he doing?" Harry points to a man visible on a monitor as he asks Peter.

"Ah, ah, hold on a minute, let me check," says Peter as he looks through a book that he has at his desk. "That is Alex Kevnick, and he is doing routine maintenance on the biostasis lab."

Harry looks the room over on the monitor, saying, "Can he get out of there?"

"No, sir. He is locked in there until the security system is unlocked," says Peter.

"Well, can you direct this microphone so we can speak with him?" asks Harry.

"Yes, we can, but we will not be able to hear from him while he is in there," says Peter.

"OK, patch me through to the room he is in," says Harry.

"You got it, sir," says Peter.

"Alex, Alex Kevnick, is that you?" Harry speaks into the microphone. "Alex, if that is you, look at the camera and wave your right arm." Alex looks at the camera, and he, of course, is in his huge protective silver suit so there is no way of telling who he is. Alex waves his right arm, and Harry continues to speak in the microphone. "Alex, there have been shots fired at our guest today, Senator Cartright, and there have been explosions in the building today. This has caused our security systems to go into automatic lockdown. You are going to be trapped in there for a few hours. Please wave your right arm to us so that we know everything is all right with you." Alex waves his right arm at the camera. "Good, that is very good," says Harry. "Alex we are going to do everything we can to get you out of there as soon as possible, OK, buddy?" Alex waves his right arm at the monitor. "Alex, go ahead and continue your maintenance as you normally would and pay special attention to the systems in place. Make sure everything is holding true by the time you finish your inspection, we will hopefully have that door opened for you, OK, buddy?" Alex waves his right arm at the monitor. Harry says to Peter at the monitoring desk, "Alex looks to be fine, and no one is getting in there with him. Peter, I want this monitor," along with four other monitors"—Harry points them out—"to monitor the front door. Make sure no one gets into this building unless we OK it."

"You got it, sir." Peter makes changes, and the monitors are changed to monitor what Harry orders them to be monitoring. The fire department has been alerted to the explosions, and fire trucks have already been dispatched to the CDCP. Harry looks at the men in the monitoring room, saying, "Explosions *in* the building. This may have been done by someone who works here. I want everyone here checked. We cannot take enough precautions." Harry speaks into the microphone for everyone in the building to hear. "Security to the monitoring office. This is Harry Klaushoven, and I want all security personnel to report directly to the monitoring office now. For everyone else, please stay in your respective area. We have had shots fired outside the building and explosions inside the building. Fire and rescue have been dispatched, and they will be here shortly. Please everyone stay where you are now, stay calm, and be aware. For those of you who are trapped in your labs or if your station has been locked down because of the explosions, please stay calm. We are working on getting all our systems back on line, and for any concerns about biological contamination, do not worry, all of our most sensitive substances are safe and locked down. Thank you for all your cooperation, and we will be to you soon, thank you. Harry Klaushoven."

Alex continues on with his maintenance, and according to plan, he is to wait fifteen minutes before he starts his incredible theft. There are many stainless steel containers in this room, and all the samples, hundreds and hundreds of them, are frozen within the steel cages. In order for Alex to get the samples, he will need at least four hours, and that is moving very fast. They plan to have at least six hours where

Alex will be alone in this room, not only that, but Alex must be completely confident that Harry will have the monitors off Alex because if anyone looks in, they will see exactly what Alex is doing. The whole plan is to have everyone in the building thinking there is an attack on the senator and the surgeon general while Alex makes away with a whole lot of deadly virus cultures. What he is doing is very delicate, and he has to have the utmost precision and accuracy. After fifteen minutes, Alex begins to open all the steel cages. He hits some buttons on the side of the steel tubes, and from the top center of the cages rise rings of petri dishes, exposing dozens of deadly samples. These are called vaults to those working in the CDCP. There are way too many samples here for Alex to take them all. It would take him a whole day to get them all. He has to try and get a few samples of each and every different virus from as many different time periods as he can. For example, he is going to get samples from Ebola, avian flu, swine flu, tuberculosis, scarlet fever, pneumonia, influenza, and he is going to get samples from all the different centuries that go back to at least the 1700s. All the deadliest plagues in history are going to be on his person from different centuries all at the same time. Alex Kevnick definitely has nerves of steel. The delicacy comes into play when he retrieves the small petri dishes from his suit and has to write the identifying code on each small petri dish with a pen, and he is wearing this huge and bulky suit. What Alex does is open the small petri dish, and there is a small sponge fitting perfectly in the dish. The sponge is specially coated with a substance so that when Alex removes the small sponge with specially designed tweezers, he can then touch the sponge on the frozen culture and transfer the virus. The sponge will absorb a minute amount of the deadly and still frozen biological substance, and Alex will gently place the sponge into the small petri dish, close it, label it, and put it in his suit. In his suit, the petri dishes are not frozen, so the cultures will start to grow fairly quickly. Alex does this for hours with calm and steady nerves, focused and dedicated on one goal, getting as many of the samples as he can get in six hours. He completes his task and fills his suit with over one hundred small petri dishes. His suit zips shut from the outside, and he is protected internally from all external threats including what is in the pockets on the suite. Alex pays attention to the time, and he has collected enough samples. He begins to close everything up, and no one will be able to know there has been a theft because there is no measurable loss. Alex waits for his area to be released from lockdown.

The employees and all the people in the CDCP have been searched by the authorities of the building and the authorities from local law enforcement. It took fire and rescue about an hour to secure the building and find all the explosives, and it took them about two hours to figure out what kind of explosives were used, and their best speculations as to why and what the goals of the explosions were are being talked about right now. Senator Cartright and the surgeon general were evacuated immediately upon the reopening of the building, and the party has gone without the planned tour of the facility. All people in the building have been physically checked by all law enforcement and evacuated from the building and are waiting outside the building while the entire interior of the building is inspected by Harry and top officials of the CDCP and fire technicians. The building is cleared, and Harry goes back to the monitoring room and has all the monitoring personnel taken out of the building for physical checks. This is a highly sensitive matter, and no one is without reproach, including Harry and the highest officials who have already been physically searched. Harry is alone in the monitoring room for a very short while, and he quickly checks on Alex, and he can see that Alex has completed his mission. Harry goes on to reset all the monitors, which have mostly been fixed. Some of the explosions have caused damage that will take a day or two to be fixed. The explosive charges were set many days in advance and set on timers to go off at specific times, and they went off flawlessly. They were set and placed by professionals that were paid handsomely, and their anonymity was a top priority. This was made possible thanks to Harry knowing the entire schedule of all personnel in the building and making very calculated and perfectly timed plans to have the devices placed and set. The monitoring personnel are returning, and Harry is now able to unseal all the areas of the building that have been sealed due to prior events. Alex now has to go to a decontamination room, where it takes him an hour before he can enter the locker room to disrobe. Harry and Alex have worked their plan to perfection. With all the commotion going on and everyone scared or confused, Alex is able to get back into the locker room and quickly transfer all secure petri dishes into his briefcase and simply walk out of the CDCP with more than two hundred strains of deadly virus. Alex heads right to the house, and here he has his very own biohazard suit, and he releases all the viruses into their very own culture, where they can be studied and tested as if they were back at the CDCP. Again the laboratory in the lower level of the house is state of the art and has a completely secured area where all the lethal materials are kept. Earl is recruited, and all the much larger petri dishes have been set up, and he has all of the deadliest of biological substances in the world to work with. Earl is given blood from newborn babies that he can mix all these substances with. He can add antibiotics, which are fairly easy to acquire, and Alex gets many of these for Earl all the time from the CDCP. Different blood samples, different viruses, different antibiotics can be mixed, and Earl can be just as creative as he wants with no overview. Earl has no guidelines to follow. His duties are simple: make or create the deadliest virus he can and work on serums to cure it. Earl has no idea Alex is injecting babies with the lethal substances and then trying to cure them with his serums until that fatal night when he is called to Upstate New York and he is introduced to the truth, and of course, it is too late for him to change things now. Earl realizes that if he tries to escape again, he will be terminated, so he spends his time working and trying to master his research and study of disease and virus.

The introduction of Drake Hammond is an absolute phenomenon, and Earl happily studies the victims who have been too close to Drake throughout his life. The members of ASAFEW have had a close eye on Drake all his life, and everyone who has perished has been swiftly and quietly taken away for Earl to examine and study. The families have been taken care of so satisfactorily by the members of ASAFEW that all the families are content, and there has not been a major story related to the deaths of anyone in contact with

Drake. Drake has been well shielded from scrutiny by the members of ASAFEW, and Drake never knew it. Drake has survived to this point without the members of ASAFEW going after him because Earl and Alex have not been able to find a cure for what Drake has become. Not only that, but they have noticed that Drake's blood is still changing. The virus that is in Drake is still changing, and his blood is still becoming more and more toxic. Earl and Alex are more than consumed studying Drake, what he has become and what he is still going to be. They have noticed that over the years, each person that has perished from exposure to Drake has died faster and faster, like Drake's bodily fluids are becoming deadlier and deadlier as he gets older. The members of ASAFEW have all been devoted to one another, knowing that someday they will discover the cure to Drake's blood, and when that day comes, they plan on capturing Drake and replicating his blood. Then they plan to infect everyone around the world, and by doing so, all people will have to buy the cure, the serum that Earl and Alex have been working on for twenty-five years now, making the members of ASAFEW the wealthiest and most powerful men and women on the planet, and no one will ever know they were ever even involved in such a cruel and despicable plan that has been in the works for twenty-five years now. Even the people who are not infected will be buying the serum just in case of infection, making the members of ASAFEW the new superpower through sheer wealth. The amazing thing about the members of ASAFEW is how seamlessly they work together with the exception of Earl who has come to lose himself in his work. Earl and Alex have had completely new identities made for them, and they don't even know how, but that does not matter; at least with these identities, they can leave the house, but they rarely do. The members of ASAFEW take care of their responsibilities, and somehow, Senator Cartright has kept them all financially secure. Over the years, Senator Cartright has passed his responsibilities as the main financial backer and organizer of ASAFEW on to another man who is Harry's main contact now. This man works in the CIA, and Senator Cartright has moved on to work at his political career. Harry Klaushoven, with his position, has been able to coordinate and cover up all incidents related to Drake very quietly, and Drake has never been aware of any of this until the night he meets Harry Klaushoven.

Still Drake knows nothing of the twenty-five years of study on him, but he pushes ever closer to the knowledge that will explain what he is and how he became what he is. Now everything in Drake's life is falling apart literally. He can feel his body falling apart. He has seen his mother and father killed before him. He is starting to put the pieces of his life together, and he needs answers, answers that he is determined to get, and he is starting to get that feeling he had when he was a kid, the feeling like someone is watching him. Drake was able to get directions from Officer Giles to the house in Atlanta, and that is where he is going to try and get some answers.

Drake is heading south toward Atlanta. Drake is lost in a daydream as he drives. His whole life has just been turned upside down, and he is doing all he can to just stay focused, but his mind is wandering. He is dreaming about all the people he has known throughout his life, and he wonders how many people may have died because of him and why. Drake makes his way south through Pennsylvania and into Washington when he notices that the same car has been behind him for an awful long time. He forgets as he daydreams about something else, and then again as he leaves Washington and enters Virginia, he notices what looks like the same car again. Drake decides to stop at the next rest stop he comes across to see if this car happens to still be with him. It takes about forty minutes, but Drake comes to a car stop, and he stops in, and sure enough, the car pulls in and parks. Drake gets out of his car and makes his way into the building. He steps to the side and watches out the window to see if he can see anyone get out of the car. He watches for a few moments, and he notices the car moves off to the gas pumps. He watches as a large man gets out of the car and pumps gas into his car. The man gets back into the car, and then he drives back to the parking lot and parks. Drake realizes at this point that he is probably being followed. Drake gets a cheeseburger, fries, and a Coke. He eats in the rest stop while thinking about what he should do and makes a phone call after getting some change. Drake then heads out to his car and goes to the gas pumps himself and fills up his car. He pays close attention to his financial situation, and he still has over three hundred dollars. He gets back on the I-81, heading south toward Atlanta. Drake looks back over and over, but the car that has been following him is nowhere in sight. *I must have been imagining things,* Drake thinks to himself.

Harry is back in his office, and he has dispatched a team to the site in Pennsylvania where Drake was, and there are two more bodies that will be en route to the house in Atlanta. As Harry is working on getting the scene at Larry's Bar covered up, he gets a call.

"Yeah, this is Harry. What? He is heading this way, are you sure? Well, you stay on his tail just follow him for now. If he is coming here, that is very good. Let us hope he comes here, then we will have him nice and neat with no mess to cover up. You stay on his tail and let me know if he changes his course." Harry hangs up his phone, and it rings again.

"Yeah, this is Harry. Alex, what are you saying? What do you mean he is dying? Yeah, yes, I understand. So you are saying that his blood is becoming unable to absorb and carry oxygen. Well, how long will he live? Well, if he can die any time now, then you had better get the cure and get it quick. Well, let us hope he lives longer than that. Listen to me, you and Earl, you work on that cure. I keep hearing that you have it, well, we need it before this kid dies, or all this work, all our plans, will have been for nothing. Listen, I have some news you may find inspirational. Drake, it seems, is coming to us. I don't know how or why, but he is heading this way right now. He may be here in person, and the two of you will have the source right at your disposal. You will have Drake Hammond in your laboratory to work on, so keep at it, and let's hope this kid comes right to us. You don't worry about that, you and Earl just keep working on creating a cure. A cure that you can replicate and one that works." Harry hangs up the phone.

Alex and Earl are in the laboratory beneath the house, and they are still working on possible serums to heal what has been happening to Drake's blood. With all eight of the bodies that they have here in their lab, they have been able to study the effects of what happens to people that have been exposed to Drake's body fluids, his blood or his saliva. Earl and Alex have noticed that as Drake has gotten older, the fluids in his body have become more and more toxic. The result is that his own body is breaking down faster and faster as he gets older. What happens in people that have been exposed to Drake's body fluids is that the blood and tissues in their body has an immediate reaction to the fluid introduced from Drake. The blood and tissue in the exposed person loses its ability to hold oxygen. The blood in the person's body expels the oxygen, and this forces the blood out of all the orifices of a person's body. When Drake was young and people came in contact with his body fluids, this was a slow and painful death to the victim, which took around a day to cause death. Now Drake's blood has become so toxic that victims die in minutes, and the skin of victims now bleeds. The victim's entire body seems to deflate from the expulsion of all the oxygen in their body followed by the loss of their blood as well. Drake had a mixture of biological substances introduced into his body, and he happened to be possibly a one-in-a-billion host that was able to survive the mixture introduced into his body. His blood transformed into a blood that carried all the viruses and the Herculean serum created by Earl, but his body is only able to survive so long, and now the organs in Drake's body are starting to fail. The organs in his body are slowly suffocating and deteriorating. Drake is now starting to feel the effects as his body starts to age at an accelerated rate. His blood is losing its capacity to carry oxygen, and this is why his blood is black at times. The doctors don't know how long Drake will live, but they think he has less than a year to live.

CHAPTER 13

The Chase for Drake Heats Up

Drake has made it to North Carolina, and the night sky is quickly approaching. Drake takes a quick look into his rearview mirror, and sure enough, there it is. The car that has been following him earlier is now behind him again. Drake can't believe it; it is like he is startled to see this car behind him again, and he starts to cough. He is spitting up blood, a lot of it, and he feels strong pain in his abdomen and chest. Drake is very scared to see all the blood is very dark red, almost black. Drake swerves, and he has to slow down and pull over to the side of the road. He gets out of his car, completely overtaken with pain, and whoever is following him is no longer a concern of his. Drake walks into the grass off the side of the road and lies down. He bends in a fetal position, and he is spitting up blood and crying out as the pain in his stomach is unbearable. It feels like his bowels are being sucked out of his body. Drake moves to his knees; leaning forward on his arms and elbows, he falls to his side and rolls to his back, moaning in pain. David, who has been following Drake, pulls off the side of the road behind Drake's Firebird and calls Harry from his cell phone. David gets out of his car and walks to the grass but keeps quite a distance between himself and Drake. He can see Drake is in pain and rolling around in the grass. "Harry, yeah, yeah, this is David. Listen, this kid pulled off the side of the road, and he is rolling around in the grass. He is obviously in a lot of pain, listen." David holds out his hand with the phone facing Drake who is moaning loudly and rolling around in the grass. David puts the phone back to his ear, saying, "Can you hear that? Yeah, that is the kid. I don't know what is going on, but it does not look good for him." Right after David says that to Harry on the phone, Drake looks at the man, and his eyes turn solid black. Drake rises to his knees and stands and walks toward David. The blood Drake has been spitting up is black, and his teeth are stained black, making him look very scary, not to mention the black eyes he has, which looks absolutely terrifying. Harry can hear David talking but seemingly not to him. "Whoa! Oh my god! Stay back. You stay away from me. I was just stopping to see if you need some help, buddy, but if you are OK, I will be on my way. Stay back! Don't make me shoot you. I will shoot." David pulls a handgun from his holster under his left armpit. David watches as the veins in Drake's body become visible; they become visible in the color of black. The veins in Drake's body flash from his shoulders down his arms to his fingertips. The veins in his neck shoot up to his face and flash from his ears to the center of his face and then disappear, and this happens over and over with Drake's pulse. Drake looks extremely evil; he looks like walking death itself. Drake walks toward David, and David shoots. Harry hears the shot over the phone and yells into the phone. "David, David, what are you doing? Do not kill him.

Do not kill him." A bullet rips through Drake's lowest left rib. The bullet does not penetrate deep enough into Drake's body to harm any interior organs, but it rips a huge chunk of flesh and bone from the left side of Drake's body. Drake falls to his knees, looking at the wound and grabbing it with his hands. Drake cries out loudly in pain with his eyes closed and then opens them looking right at David. David sees that Drake's blood is black. Drake opens his eyes and looks right at David with his black eyes, his stained black teeth, and Drake stands as the veins in his body flash faster and darker black in his anger. David says, "You stay right there. Don't you come any closer, or I will shoot again." David puts the phone in his coat pocket and holds the gun with both hands pointed right at Drake. Drake looks at the wound on his left side and snaps his head at David spitting a black dart of fluid that flies fast and true, hitting David right in the eyes. David tries to wipe the fluid from his face as pain engulfs his face. His eyes start to bleed, along with his nose and mouth. Blood even drips from his ears, and his body starts to deflate like a vacuum is sucking the air out of him. His eyes shrivel up and fall out of his eye sockets, and David falls dead in less than five minutes. Harry can hear the muffled screams and cries of David, which last for a few minutes, and then, there is silence. "David, David. What is happening? David, what is going on?" Harry yells into the phone, but there is no response. After Drake spits, he falls to his knees. He is gasping for air like he has had the wind knocked out of him. Drake is swiveling at his waist like he has been dazed and the blue color returns to his eyes. The flashing veins in his body begin to fade and go away. Drake gets up breathing more normally and walks to the shriveled body of the man he just spit on. Drake can hear the phone and a voice on the phone. Drake finds the phone in the pocket and listens. Drake does not say a word; he hangs the phone up and puts the phone in the pocket of his shorts. There are a lot of cars passing on the highway, and a lot of people have been watching what is going on, but no one stops. Drake looks through the car of the man that was following him, and sure enough, he finds a first aid kit that has gauze in it and he uses it to cover the wound on his side after he sprays some bacterial spray on the wound. Drake is really freaked out to see his blood is black, and then his blood begins to turn the normal red color just as he gets finished bandaging his wound, which is still bleeding. The wound to his side is very bad. There is a huge gash, where the bullet tore through his side, and his bottom left rib has been splintered and exposed by the bullet that passed through him. It is very painful, but he gets it bandaged, and the bleeding is held in check by the bandage. There is a medical tape in the first aid kit, which Drake uses to tape the gauze to the wound on his body, and he needs to use a lot of it. After Drake bandages himself, he searches the car, and he finds some business cards, which he looks through. One of them in particular is that of Harry Klaushoven whom he remembers meeting at Subway. There are some other cards of what would seem to be very important people, which he puts in his wallet. Drake finds a clean shirt in the backseat, which he puts on. It is a large shirt and big on him, but that is OK. Drake also finds a briefcase, which is locked, and he cannot open it, so he takes it with him. Drake searches the car completely, and believe it or not, he finds a map in the glove box, leading right to the house in Atlanta. Written on the map are names of people, and these names are written under the acronym ASAFEW. Drake takes the briefcase and all the information he finds in the glove box and heads back to his car. While he was looking through the car, a police officer pulled up behind the car he was searching through, and Drake did not notice this. Drake gets out of the car to be told to stop where he is and raise his hands by the police officer that is standing behind him. Drake turns to look at the officer raising his hands and says, "Sir, I strongly advise you to step back to your car and wait there until I have gotten into my car and driven away." The officer can see the body of David lying in the grass. The officer pulls his gun from its holster and points it at Drake, saying, "Do not move. I want you to slowly turn and hold your hands up high where I can see them." Drake can hear from the speaker on the officer's suit that a voice responds to an earlier communication, saying, "Unit 62, be advised the license plate number that you have called in is that of possible murder suspect in Upstate New York two days ago. Use extreme caution and be aware there may be a possible biohazard associated with this suspect." The officer commands Drake, "Slowly—" but before the officer can say another word, Drake spits with speed and incredible accuracy, hitting the officer in the eyes with his toxic spit. The officer grabs at his face, screaming as his eyes and all other orifices on his face begin to bleed, and he quickly suffocates but not before his eyes shrink and pop out of his head. The officer drops his gun and grabs at his face falling to his knees and then flat on his face, dead before he hits the ground. Drake again starts to breathe heavily, and black veins pulse visible with each heartbeat, and his veins again are black as his eyes turn solid black. Drake is on the side of a major interstate, and passing cars have seen what has happened to David, and they have also seen what has just happened to the officer. Now Drake is facing the road, and passing traffic can just make out the evil-looking Drake as the black veins in his body are pulsing, and a passing car is fixed on him, and this causes an accident. Drake is almost in a trance, and he is walking into the road, and cars are swerving to miss him, and a great pileup of cars occurs. This becomes a terrible accident and lives are lost. Drake snaps back to reality, and the black pulsing veins in his body go away, and his eyes return to their normal color. Drake, who still has the briefcase in one hand and the map and other documents in his other hand, looks ahead and sees a little girl looking out of her car window right at him, and she looks terrified. Drake looks around like he has been oblivious to what has been going on, and he rushes to his car. He gets in his car, and he drives very fast down the side of the road, mostly on the grass to get past the fourteen-car pileup.

Darkness is covering the land, and Drake speeds to his destination in Atlanta. Drake has been driving about seven hours now, and he is falling asleep at the wheel. He has said to himself that he would stop at the next rest stop and get something to eat and help him wake up, and he already passed two rest stops since thinking that. Now he is really falling asleep. His head has bobbed a couple of times on him already, and his swerving car has awaken him up so he has to stop or he will fall asleep. *Why didn't I stop at the last rest stop?* he thinks. Drake passes some signs that have gas and food emblems on them, and Drake gets off the highway and makes his way down a country road and finds an all-night diner, and he pulls in and stops. He gets out of the car and stretches his arms and legs. He ties a shirt from the back of his car around his wound to cover the bloodstain. He gets the briefcase out of his car and goes into the diner. He sits at a booth all by himself, and there are only a handful of people in the diner. A waitress approaches his booth and puts a menu down for him. "Can I get you anything?" asks the waitress.

"Yes, coffee please," says Drake.

"Coming right up," says the waitress who turns to go and get some coffee. Drake inspects the briefcase, but he cannot open it. It has a combination lock on both sides of the handle and Drake keeps turning the dials, trying different numbers, but none of them work. He gets very frustrated and orders some pancakes from the waitress who fills a cup of coffee for Drake. He drinks his coffee and fiddles with the briefcase, but he has no luck and shoves it across the table in frustration. He drinks from his coffee and notices two men sitting on stools at the long counter opposite where the waitress walks. They have been watching Drake and seem curious about the briefcase that he has. The waitress brings Drake his pancakes and a small cup of syrup and asks Drake if he would like some more coffee, and he says yes. She comes back with coffee and pours him some more and says, "I am Samantha. If you need anything, you just give me a call. I will be right over there, OK?" Drake takes a sip of his coffee and says, "Thank you, Samantha. I am Drake." Samantha smiles and heads back behind the counter. Drake watches her walk away and notices the two men at the counter are paying pretty close attention to him, and they are not hiding it. Drake takes a bite of his pancakes, and immediately, he feels a great pain in his lower stomach. This is no small pain. He closes his eyes and leans forward. His eyes water; it hurts so bad. He feels very hot and turns his head, hoping no one notices his obvious pain. His intestines feel like they did earlier. They feel like they are being sucked out of his body, and it is excruciating. Drake has his right elbow on the table and his head resting on his right hand. He can't help but moan fighting the pain and trying not to cry. Samantha comes over to the table, saying, "Drake, is everything OK? Is the food that bad?"

Drake responds, "No, Samantha, the food is fine. I have had very bad abdominal pains lately, and as a matter of fact, I am going to Atlanta to have it looked at."

"Well, are you going to be OK?" asks Samantha.

"I just have to—ah." Drake moans, rocking forward and backward slowly. Tears are running down from his eyes, and saliva is trickling out of his mouth. "I just have to wait for it to pass, but it is very painful," says Drake.

Samantha can tell he is in serious pain and asks if there is anything she can do to help him. Drake says no and that he has to get to Atlanta because the pain is starting to last longer and come more often. Drake tells Samantha, "I am so sorry, Samantha. I really am hungry, but I am not going to be able to hold anything down. It was so nice to meet you, and maybe on my way back up to New York, I will stop by and see you again." Drake leaves a twenty on the table and gets the briefcase and gets up from the table.

"OK. Well, you stop by on your way back, OK, Drake?" says Samantha to Drake as he leaves the diner.

"OK," says Drake, and he heads for his car. He does not make it to his car because the two men at the bar rush out behind him, saying, "Hey, hey you. That was kind of rude, ordering food and then not eating any of it."

"That is downright not southerly at all," says the larger of the two men.

Drake leans up against his car in anguish. He has the briefcase in his right hand, and his left arm is lying on the top of his car, and his head is resting on his left forearm. Drake talks with his head pressed into his arm. "You are right. I really am hungry, but I have terrible abdominal pains that are making it impossible for me to eat."

"Well, I think you better go back in there and apologize to Samantha for making her do all that work for nothing," says the man.

Drake starts to moan loudly. He bends at his knees like he is being forced to the ground. Drake puts his hands on the ground, and he is trying to not lie on the ground, but the pain is too great, and Drake slowly falls to his knees and elbows and rolls over to his right side, and he is moaning loudly.

"What the fuck is wrong with you?" asks the man. "Get up you pansy." The man reaches down and picks the briefcase, which is to Drake's back. Drake is on his right side, and his face is facing the car, so the two men cannot see his face. The man hands the briefcase to his friend, saying, "Here, open this. See what is inside of it." The second man messes around with the briefcase, trying to open it. Drake opens his eyes, and they are black. "Wait," says Drake. He rolls to his knees and up on his hands, swaying his head back and forth slowly with his face facing the ground. "What the fuck is wrong with you? Get up you weirdo," says the man who has been heckling Drake. Drake takes a deep breath and stands up with his eyes closed, and then he opens his eyes, and they are his natural blue color. Drake says, "Listen, I'll make a deal with you. I will let you try to open that briefcase, and if you can open it, and there is money in there, you can have it, but anything else is mine. Do we have a deal?"

"No," says the man. "For all we know you stole this briefcase."

"I did steal it," says Drake, "and I have no idea what is in there, but there may be very important things in there that I need. Now, money I could care less about, so you can have that, but anything else is mine." The man steps to Drake and forcefully stabs Drake in the chest with his finger, saying, "You listen to me." He stabs Drake in the chest with his finger again, forcing Drake back against his car. "I got it. I got it," says the other man who has been messing with the briefcase. The man in front of Drake stabs him in the chest with his finger again, saying, "You get in that car, and you drive off, and we will forget all of this ever happened, you weakling weirdo." Drake can feel the pulse inside his body pump in his temples; he can feel the veins in his body feel like they are getting bigger. The man standing in front of Drake starts to step back away from Drake, saying, "What the fuck. What the fuck are you?" The other man who just opened the briefcase looks up to see Drake whose eyes are now solid black; the veins in his body are flashing from his shoulders down to his fingers in both arms. The veins in his neck are visible, going up his neck into his cheeks and then ending as they meet along the center of his face in between his eyes. This happens over and over again as his pulse pumps from his heart. The man drops the briefcase, saying, "Matt, I don't like this, let's get the fuck out of here." Drake starts to sway his head back and forth, and the two men seem to be entranced by Drake. Drake's mouth opens and black saliva starts to drip from the sides of his mouth. Drake can now feel a new sensation, one he has not felt before. Drake turns his hands toward his face and rubs his fingertips with his thumbs as he looks at his hands. Drake can feel that his fingertips are sweating, and he can feel the sweating ooze slowly leaking from his fingertips. "Jason, pick up the case. Come on, let's get out of here," says Matt, who was heckling Drake. Drake looks at Matt who is backing away from him, and Drake says, "Leave the case where it is, and you two leave here now."

"Or what? What are you going to do, weirdo?" says Matt, who is slowly backing away from Drake, and he bends down and picks the briefcase from the ground.

"Matt, I think we should just leave the briefcase and get out of here. This guy is just too fucked-up looking," says Jason.

Drake takes a step toward the two men and flicks his right hand at Matt. The mucus on Drake's fingertips flies and hits him on the face in a lot of places like tiny little droplets of water. Matt drops the briefcase and starts to grab at his face, saying, "What the fuck. What is this? What did you do to me?" He starts to scream. Jason says, "Matt, what is it? What did he get on you?" Jason looks at Matt, and he can see black dots on his face, and the black dots start to grow like blotches, and blood starts to stream from Matt's skin. Matt looks at his hands, which are starting to turn black, and blood is draining from his hands as well. This is the last thing Matt ever sees as his eyes shrivel and roll out of his head. Matt falls to his knees, crying, and his flesh is shrinking and shriveling right before Jason's eyes. The black is spreading through his body very fast, and all the blood in his body is being expelled. Matt falls over already dead, but Jason watches as all the flesh on Matt's body shrivels, shrinks, and turns black. This process is remarkably fast, and Jason cannot believe what he just saw. He is so scared he cannot move, and he looks up as Drake flicks his hand at him.

Drake can see himself being held underwater. He can see bubbles all around his head, and he can hear himself screaming and gasping for air. He can see his baby legs and arms kicking and flailing underwater, trying to get to the surface. Drake is screaming, and bubbles are floating up from his screaming mouth. Baby Drake starts to slow his movements, and the bubbles stop rising to the surface, and Baby Drake is now motionless underwater. The hands that were holding the baby underwater rise up out of the water, but the baby is still there underwater, motionless and seemingly dead; the eyes are open, and they are solid black. The baby starts to walk. It walks right out of the water with its black eyes peering right at Drake who is watching this in his dream, and black bile is dripping from the baby's mouth. The baby reaches its right arm behind its back like it is going to throw a baseball and throws, not a baseball, but black droplets of mucus that fly from its fingertips. Drake wakes from a dream with a loud inhale and flails on the ground a little bit until he realizes he has been dreaming. Drake takes a deep breath and sits up. He was sleeping on his back. He puts his head in his hands and bends his knees, sitting with his legs crossed Indian style. Drake looks his hands over, and they look normal. He spits on the ground to his side, and his spit looks normal. "Oh what is happening to me?" Drake says to himself. He looks around, and he is in a wooded area, all alone. He has no idea how he got here or where he is. Drake stands up and remembers being shot in his left side because the pain is terrible, and he lifts his shirt, which is red with blood, and the bandage over the wound is soaked with blood. The wound is not healing at all, and if not for the bandage that he tapped to his side, he would be bleeding all over the place. Drake can hear cars drive by, so he must be fairly close to a road, and he walks in the direction of the passing cars. Oddly enough, he comes to his Firebird, which is parked off the road but hidden by all the vegetation, which are tall trees, shrubs, large ferns, and the like. Drake gets into his car and looks at the sky, figuring it must be around noontime, judging by how high the sun is in the sky. Drake has no idea how long he has slept. He gets into the car very slowly because his side is killing him, and he looks to the passenger seat and notices the briefcase that he took from the man's car that was following him. Drake grabs the case and notices that it is open now and looks through it. He finds a cell phone, a map, and a lot of names and phone numbers corresponding with the names. He can't believe when he sees the name Earl Rieval and Alex Kevnick. These names ring bells, and of course, he remembers the name Harry Klaushoven whom he remembers as the head of the CDCP. Drake looks through his backseat and finds the newspapers that he collected at his mother's house, and sure enough, as he looks through them, he reads that Earl Rieval was killed in a car accident the day after Alex Kevnick had been arrested from the hospital. He also finds the article where Alex Kevnick has been sent to prison for the rest of his life for what he had done. Drake flips open the cell phone, and it works. He plays a hunch. He remembered his mother saying how she and Gerald had passed a doctor in the hall the night Drake was rescued and that doctor died in a car accident the next day and that doctor's name was Earl Rieval. There is a number on a piece of paper after the name Earl Rieval, and Drake dials the number.

Earl Rieval is looking into a microscope. "Alex, come here and look at this," says Earl to Alex. Both men are wearing their protective suits, which are big and bulky, but they can still hear each other, and they are used to working in these suits. Alex comes over to the microscope, saying, "What is it, Earl?"

"Look the Herculean serum is now working. It is preventing the blood from expelling the oxygen. This may be the cure. This may be what we have been waiting for. Here, let me show you." Earl prepares a slide with a drop of blood, saying, "Look, this is fresh blood with the Herculean serum in it, and here is toxic blood from Roger. Watch the fresh blood when I drop the tainted blood on it." Alex watches under the microscope as tainted blood is introduced to fresh blood on the slide, and sure enough, the red blood stays red, and the black blood is kept at bay without spreading.

"Earl, I think you have done it. Earl, it is working. The blood is not losing its ability to hold oxygen, and the tainted blood is not spreading. Earl, you have done it," says Alex very excitedly.

Earl responds. "Well, we still need to test it. We need to either catch someone who has been infected and introduce the serum or inject the serum into someone and then expose them to the toxic blood of Drake. These blood samples are of people who have died already, so we have to test it with fresh blood with fresh samples of Drake's blood, but this is very promising."

"Yes, Earl, you may have done it. You are a genius, Earl, you are a genius. I have to go tell Harry we may finally be able to put our plan in motion now. I am going to let Harry know," says Alex. Alex leaves the laboratory and goes into the decontamination room. The bio lab where the doctors work is completely sealed off from the rest of the house, and decontamination takes thirty minutes before the doctors can disrobe from their suits and enter the bottom laboratory outside of the bio lab and head into the rest of the house. Earl is still working on his Herculean serum, which is the same serum he created and worked on way back twenty-five years ago when Drake was a baby. Back then, the nickname of this serum was and still is the H vials because there are many variations of the serum. Earl is working, and his phone, which happens to be on a counter not too far from him, rings. This is a special phone that he can push a button on the side of the phone and the speaker is always on, and it is plenty loud so he can hear what is being said on it. The same goes for whoever is listening on the other end; they can hear Earl just fine as he talks through his suit. Earl picks up the phone and answers it. "Hello. Hello, this is Earl. Harry, is that you?"

"Earl, are you sitting down?" says Drake on the other end.

"As a matter of fact, I am sitting down. Who is this?" asks Earl.

"My name is Drake Hammond," says Drake.

Earl pauses. Earl looks around, and even though he is the only one in the lab, he looks around anyway. Awkward silence fills the air. Finally, Earl speaks up, "Drake Hammond? You mean, Drake Raymond Hammond, born in Upstate New York in 1968?"

"The very same one, and I am curious. How is it that a man that died in 1968 named Earl Rieval is still alive today? I am assuming you are the same Earl Rieval that supposedly died back in 1968 in a car accident. Am I wrong?" asks Drake.

"No, you are not wrong. I am indeed the same Earl Rieval. Ah, you have me at a little bit of a disadvantage here, Drake, but your timing could not be any better. How did you get this number? Where are you? Can we meet by any chance? I have a lot of things to tell you. One of the most important things I have to tell you, Drake, is that you are dying. I mean, you are dying, but you are a walking virus. Do you know what that means? That means that you are dying, but you actually are already dead. You will continue to grow even after your body has died, but listen, I have been working on the H vials, the very same one that made you what you are right now, and I think I can save you from the virus. I think the virus is killing you, but we can fight against the virus with the H vial serum. As a matter of fact, I just perfected it just a little while ago. I think you calling me right now is fate, it has to be. I mean, how else, why else, would you have called me right now when I am looking at the cure under the microscope. Drake, I have to see you right now and give you the cure, you don't know what these people have in store for you and it is not good. I can't stress how important it is that I see you right now. Drake, we know you are dying, and how soon is the big question, but the sooner I see you, the sooner I can give you the antidote."

"Whoa, whoa, Earl, slow down and calm down. First of all, something is happening to me. It has just started all of a sudden but I have come to find out you guys killed a lot of babies when I was born and there was some kind of conspiracy and cover-up all done by a group called ASAFEW. Whatever you guys did to me is coming back to haunt you because I am coming for you. I am coming for you all. I am going to find out what you did to me and why, but you are right, Earl, something is happening to me, something horrible, and if you can help save me from this disease that is inside of me, then please tell me where I can meet you alone. I don't know what to do, but can you help me? I won't lie. I do not trust you, but I have no choice. I am in constant pain all the time, and something in me is changing, something in me is trying to get out, and I don't know what it is. Please, Earl, will you help me?" asks Drake.

"Yes, Drake, I will help you," says Earl.

"Hold on to this phone, and I will call you when I get somewhere safe, OK, Earl? I will find a place where we can meet, and I will call you, and you better come alone, or I will let it out on purpose, and I think you know what I am talking about. Earl, no tricks please, come alone, OK?" says Drake.

"OK, Drake, you get somewhere safe, and I will come and meet you alone, I promise. I have to give you the new

Herculean serum. The organs in your body are dying, Drake. They are being deprived of oxygen, and it is only a matter of time before the organs in your body fail on you. Get somewhere quick, and I will come see you," says Earl. Drake hangs up the phone.

CHAPTER 14

Biohazard on the Eastern Seaboard

After Drake had left Larry's Bar over a day ago, Ralph did exactly what Drake had told him to do. Ralph called the police and waited outside the bar and did not let anyone in. Once the police arrived, Ralph had made a full report out with the police officer who came to the bar, and this became a televised story on the evening news. Somehow the reporters and camera personnel heard about the story and made their way to the bar. The police took Ralph very seriously and taped off the bar, and no one was allowed in. Members from the CDCP arrived about six hours later, and they entered the building in full biohazard suits and cleaned up the scene, which is still taking place a day later. Thanks to Ralph and the police not allowing anyone at the scene, no one else was contaminated or infected.

When Drake had left the scene in North Carolina, where the two men were killed and the accident happened, he was very near to the South Carolina border, and here he left two bodies on the side of the road. Not only that, but a multiple car pile-up had just happened. Drake speed away along the side of the road, and many people saw him leave. Many people actually saw Drake spit on the police officer, and the officer fell to his death very quickly. Most of the people who saw this are now a part of the multiple car pile-up that has clogged and stopped traffic on this very busy highway. The cars are stopping behind the accident, and very quickly, there is a two-lane road with stopped cars that just keeps growing and growing. It is already many miles long and until cleanup crews get here the cars will just keep backing up. People are sitting in their cars, and many of them are getting antsy from just being stuck and not being able to go anywhere. A lot of people get out of their cars and very quickly notice that there are two dead bodies on the side of the road. People start to gather around the bodies, but common sense holds them a good distance away from the bodies. The bodies have been shriveled, and the flesh has turned black, and it is very disgusting with slimy pools of bloody ooze around the bodies. Many people have been hurt in the accident, and there have been three fatalities. People are doing what they can to help one another and evacuate everyone from the cars. There are two cars that have been overturned, and two people in one car and one in another car have not survived. There are people crying and bleeding and sitting on the side of the road. People are walking around, and there is a lot of confusion. Two young boys get out of their car, which is parked a ways back, and they start to run around and make their way to where people are gathered around the bodies of the officer and the man who have been exposed to Drake. "Jessie, Martin, get over here," calls the boys' father. The boys move over to their father who grabs the boys by the hands, and their mother is close by as well. The family walks up to a gathering of people looking at the bodies on the ground. "What happened here?" asks Frank.

"Oh, Frank, this is terrible," says Amanda, his wife.

"Yuck, Dad, that is gross, what happened to those guys over there?" asks Frank's boys. "Ew, it stinks over here."

"I don't know," says the father.

Amanda says, "Boys, come with me. I don't want to be near this." Amanda heads back to the car and takes her boys with her.

"I will be right there," says Frank.

"I will be back at the car with the boys," says Amanda.

"What happened here?" asks Frank.

"I saw the whole thing," says a man standing there. I was driving by, and there was this guy, and he spit at the officer, and the next thing I know, I am caught up in this accident. The guy that spit on the officer got in his car and drove away. I have no idea what happened to the officer and this guy over here, but obviously it did not end well for them."

Another person in the gathering speaks up. "I saw it. It was pretty scary too. The officer started to grab at his face, and his skin started to turn black. He started to bleed all over his body, and he started to shrivel up. It happened so fast, and he was dead and fell just like he is now, lying there on the ground."

An hour goes by, and then tow trucks and ambulances race up along the side of the road to the accident. News crews show up as well and begin to interview the people standing around. There is a terrible stench coming from the bodies, and no one dares get near the bodies, which is a very good thing. Flies have been drawn to the smell of death, and the flies that land on the bodies die very quickly. They die in large enough numbers that the people standing around are noticing the buildup of fly corpses. The bodies are filmed by the news crews, and many of the people are interviewed, and soon enough people from the CDCP show up wearing their biohazard suits and clear everyone away. This time, Harry Klaushoven cannot cover up the story, and this makes major headlines. This becomes a major story, and the deaths in New York and Pennsylvania are uncovered and related to this story. All the major networks break into the normal programming on TV to bring this story. Viewers are cautioned and warned to the disturbing content in the interviews and images being shown. Kaitlin's home in Upstate New York is shown, of course, from a distance because it is now a biohazard. The same goes for Larry's Bar and now again for the third time another biohazard site here on the side of the road near the South Carolina border in North Carolina. The biohazard has struck again, only this time, the bodies of the police officer and the man are shown. This story takes over the airwaves, and everyone is talking about it. All kinds of questions arise as the bodies of the killed men are aired over and over again on TV. Drake Hammond is linked as a possible suspect, and he and his white Firebird are described, and anyone who sees him is cautioned to stay away from him. Drake Hammond is becoming the most wanted man in America, and anyone with information to his location is directed to contact local law enforcement with this information. It is said that he was last seen traveling south on the I-81 interstate, and any information leading to his apprehension is greatly appreciated.

Harry is at the CDCP, and they are in a real crisis now. He has to dispatch a third team to the location in North Carolina, and his staff is running pretty thin now. Harry organizes his resources and works on getting another team dispatched to the location that is not too far from Atlanta. After Harry gets things organized and sends out another team, he makes a phone call.

"Sir, this is Harry. Yes, sir, I know it is all over the news. Well, I think this is a good thing. We will let local law enforcement track him down while we wait. I know, sir. I know people may very well die, and then our biohazard will be in full effect. They have not been able to find a cure for what he has become, but they are close. He is that deadly. However, I just heard from Alex, and he says that the cure may be in sight, it may be very close, but we have to test it. I know it has been twenty-five years, sir. Yes, sir, the entire Eastern Seaboard is aware of this by now. People will be staying away from Drake Hammond. I know, sir. OK, sir, we just need to capture him, and from there, we can figure out how to disperse the virus. I understand, sir, dead or alive, we will get him. Yes, sir, it will be done. I hope this can be resolved before the dinner party. I know that would be a great place to announce we have a cure. It would be a great place to inform all the senators that yes, we can handle the biological virus that will possibly be sweeping the country and the world and yes, we will have the cure and can stop it dead in its tracks. Yes, sir. Yes, sir. I will get it done, sir."

Harry hangs up the phone and rubs his forehead. He sits down in his chair, and his cell phone rings; he answers it, saying, "Harry Klaushoven. Earl, yeah, what do you mean you are in the car with Alex. All of you? And you are going where? You got a call from Drake Hammond and he told you where he is. How did you get a call from Drake Hammond? He got the briefcase from David? He has all that information. You get to him, and you neutralize him. I don't need to tell you that with this information he can bring us all down. This whole thing is starting to get very ugly. Let me talk to John."

"Yes," says Earl.

"John, listen to me. You capture or kill Drake Hammond. I don't care which. He is becoming way too great a threat to us. If he brings this information out in the open, we could all go down for the rest of our lives. Dead or alive, Drake Hammond does not escape this time. Am I clear?" says Harry.

"Oh, you are clear, Mr. Klaushoven, crystal clear," says John. John hangs up the phone and looks to Eric in the passenger seat.

"Eric, Drake is coming with us, dead or alive, you hear what I am saying?" says John. Eric pulls a handgun from its holster under his arm, inspects it and looks at John, and puts it back in its holster. "Earl, you know where we are going, right?" says John.

"Yes, we are going to the Murgyle Motel on Sampson Street in Chester, South Carolina," says Earl.

"It should only take a little over an hour to get there. I know exactly where it is," says Eric.

"Earl, Alex, you two understand that Drake is coming back with us. There is no other alternative this time. He has sensitive information. Information that can put us all away. He comes with us dead or alive," says John.

Alex replies, "We have our suits in the trunk. We need to suit up before we make contact with him. John, listen, it is much more preferable to take him alive. Do you Eric and Sam understand?" Eric looks at John, and John looks at Eric, and they smile at each other and simultaneously say, "We understand."

Drake had left the scene of the accident and the two bodies he had infected on the interstate highway, which have been cleaned up by a team from the CDCP without anyone being infected. Later, Drake had called Earl, and it is midday. Drake makes it almost to the North Carolina-Georgia border when the traffic is backed up for longer than the eyes can see. Drake gets stuck in traffic just like everyone else. Fortunately, there is an exit, and Drake gets off at the exit. He makes his way down Sampson Street, and there happens to be a motel, which Drake stops at and gets a room. He is still having great difficulty with his left side, which will not stop bleeding. Drake actually takes his shirt off and ties it around his rib cage to hide all the blood. He has one shirt left in his car, and he puts it on. He gets into the room and calls Earl and lets him know where he is. Earl and the men in the house in Atlanta immediately make their way toward the Murgyle Motel in Chester, South Carolina, and they have called Harry and are on the way there now. Drake has the briefcase, and he knows this is very important because it has information with names of people and addresses and contacts and a lot of information that involves a lot of people and he has to hide it but where. He does not want to keep it in his car, and he does not want to keep it in his room. He sets it under the bed for now and goes to the bathroom and takes the shirt off his chest. He peels back the bandage, and the wound is really disgusting looking. The bullet hit his bottom rib and ricochet away, not leaving a deep wound but breaking and cracking his bottom left rib. What is so bad about this wound is that it is not healing. The bullet really did very little damage to Drake, but the bleeding is not stopping, and the wound is not healing up. Drake still has the first aid kit, but he used all the gauze and bandage tape in it already. He gets a washcloth from the bathroom and covers the wound with it; then he ties a shirt around his abdomen and puts on the last shirt he just got from the car and goes to the front desk and asks if they have any tape. Fortunately they do have some duct tape, and this is perfect. Drake takes the tape back to his room and tapes the cloth to his side and returns the tape to the front desk. Drake asks at the front desk about a shirt after he makes a quick reason up why he needs a shirt, and the kindness of the older lady at the front desk is greatly appreciated as she gives Drake an old shirt that he may have. Drake gets back to his room and looks over the briefcase, knowing there is a lot of damaging information here and makes a phone call. "Jerry, yeah, this is Drake. You are still coming, right? Good, where are you? I am at the Murgyle Motel in Chester, South Carolina. Yes, I made contact, and Earl is coming to see me right now. I am counting on you, Jerry. You are the only one I trust. What? Oh my god. People are dying, and I have been described as a possible biological threat. I don't know what you are talking about. I have a terrible wound on my stomach, and I don't even know how I got it. I might have been shot or something. There are things that I don't remember. I wake up, and I don't know how I got to where I am, and it is getting worse. It is happening more and more often to me. Jerry, I have a briefcase with a lot of information in it. I think it has all the people who have been in on this biological conspiracy that is going on, at least the people who started it or made me the hazard that you say I now am. I am described as the one who is the biological hazard and people are looking for me? Are you serious? It is all over the news? Great! I think all the doctors and all the people who have been involved with the doctors who killed all those babies in 1968 and creating me and what I have become are named within this briefcase. Well, at least some of them are named here. You will not believe how far up government this goes. I mean, even I am familiar with some of these names, and I don't pay attention to politics. Not only that, but there is an event where they are all going to be, and I know how to expose them all. Jerry, I don't think I can do this alone. I need your help. I need you and all the help you can get so we can expose this conspiracy. I am going to hide the briefcase, and I am going to tell only you where it is, OK? Earl and the others are coming to meet me here in the motel now. I wanted Earl to come alone, but it is not going to work out like that, I know it won't. I will stall them until you get here. Bring a lot of law enforcement and arrest them. I will hide the briefcase and tell you and only you where it is, OK? I will call you back. Thank you, Jerry. I will be safe, and get here as soon as you can. OK, bye." Drake picks the briefcase up and walks around, looking, not knowing what to do with the case. He walks outside and looks around the motel. It is quiet, and he walks around back, and there is a large wooded area. About twenty minutes later,

Drake comes back into the room, and he does not have the briefcase. He sits down on the bed and starts to have great pain in his stomach. Drake bends over to his knees and rests on the floor on his elbows and knees in agonizing pain. So fast the pain comes to him, and he is stopped dead, unable to do anything except cope with the pain that immobilizes him. He rolls to his side and back to his knees and elbows again. He rolls from side to side for a few minutes, and he cannot believe how bad the pain is. Drake is moaning and crying in pain. He rolls around on the floor for a little bit, and then he is so consumed with pain that he cannot move. He lies there motionless and falls unconscious.

There is a knock at the door. "Drake, Drake, are you in there? It is me, Drake, it is Earl. Drake, are you in there?"

Drake opens his eyes and sees the ceiling of the room moving as Earl and another man in biohazard suits are picking him up and laying him on the bed. "Earl, is that you? What are you wearing?" asks Drake who is semiconscious.

"Drake, it is me Earl. We have to wear these suits to protect us. You may have a deadly contagion within your blood. We need to bring you back with us so we can study you and see what is happening with you," says Earl as he pulls back the tape and examines the wound on Drake's side. "Drake, what happened to you right here?" asks Earl.

"I was shot, I think, and it is not healing," says Drake.

"Drake, you have to come with us. We have to get you back to our laboratory so we can fix you up. Here I have something for you. This will help your body be able to heal itself." Earl gives Drake a shot of his Herculean serum. "This will help prevent the virus from taking over your mind and your body. It is the virus that has been causing you such great pain, Drake. The virus when it takes control of your body deprives your body of oxygen, and this is killing you. The virus is intelligent, and it knows it is killing you, so it fades from control of your body, letting your mind back in control. This allows your blood to reoxygenate and your body to heal, but you will only live so long. We feel that the virus is trying to find another host, and it is keeping you alive until it finds another host," says Earl. Drake can just barely see Earl as he pulls a syringe from a case, and another man wipes the inside of his left elbow like they are going to give him another shot of something. Drake takes a deep breath, and anger consumes his face. The other man in the protective suit watches as Drake's eyes look like they are filling with a black liquid. The veins in Drake's body start to become visible starting in his chest, where his heart is. His veins are flashing black going up his shoulders into his neck into his face and ending when the veins in his head meet dead center of his face. His veins become visible up his shoulders and down his arms. His veins also become visible down his stomach and down his legs. His veins flash, and you can see his veins as they start at his chest and move through his body. His veins flash visible and then gone, and this happens over and over with his heartbeat. "Earl, what is happening? What is going on with Drake?" asks John.

"I don't know, John. I don't know what this is," says Earl. Drake hits Earl's hand holding the syringe, and it flies to the opposite side of the room. Earl watches as Drake spits black mucus, and it hits John dead center of his face, and Drake pushes John, and he flies across the room. Drake stands, and he faces Earl who is stepping back and away from Drake and backing toward the doorway. Earl has never felt the chills like he does now. The sheer evil that he sees in the black eyes of Drake and the black veins that are flashing throughout his body is bone-chilling, and he almost falls over in fear as his body shakes and his muscles weaken. "Get out of the way, Dr. Rieval. Get down. I have to put him down. Get out of the way, doctor," says Eric, who is standing in the doorway and has his gun facing in the direction of Drake, but Earl is in the way. "Dr. Rieval, get out of the way," yells Eric. Earl can see Drake as his face looks like pure evil, dead serious with eyes of solid black. He has never seen or even imagined anything looking like what Drake looks like now. In a second, Drake flicks his right hand, and Earl sees droplets of black mucus splatter across his face shield, and a few droplets hit Eric in the face. Eric immediately begins to grab at his face and scream. "What is this? Dr. Rieval, what did he do to me?" Earl turns to see black blotches grow very fast from Eric's face and all throughout his body. Blood starts to drain out of his body from his eyes, his ears, his nose as his skin turns black with blood draining from it. Earl is mesmerized, not believing what he is seeing. Eric falls to his knees, and his eyes shrivel and fall out. Eric falls to the ground face first, dead.

Earl turns to Drake. "Drake, what have we done? What have we done to you? Drake, can you hear me? Do you understand what I am saying? You knew you were in danger, didn't you? You are simply protecting yourself, but you are not you anymore, are you? You are a living virus, and my serum is not strong enough to fight back the virus that is in you. You are a virus that is living through Drake and spreading itself, which is death to everyone through Drake. Drake, can you hear me? Drake, are you in there? Drake, I have the cure, and it is in you, but you have to fight, you have to fight against the virus, don't let it beat you, Drake, you have to fight it." Earl walks over to get the syringe that flew across the room and picks it up, showing it to Drake, saying, "Drake, I have been working on the H vials ever since we discovered you had survived. You were the only baby from 1968 that survived all the injections and infusions you are a one in a billion, Drake. I have been working on the Herculean serum, and it has the potential to cure you. It will at the very least be able to suppress the virus, but you have to fight the virus. I know you are in there, Drake, because if not, you would be dead like everyone else. The virus needs you alive so that it can continue to grow, so it can spread itself. The virus grows, but by growing, it kills every living thing it comes in contact with. This virus is the greatest oxymoron in existence. It lives through you, Drake, but it is dead, it is not alive. It grows by infecting others, and by infecting others, they die. You are the only one who can live with this in you, but you too are dying. The organs in your body are aging at an accelerated rate because of the virus and what it has done to your blood. You will not live for much longer. You need this serum I have right here in my hand, or you will die. The virus will die without this serum. You will die without it," says Earl.

Drake starts to laugh with a smile on his face, but he looks so evil with his black eyes and his saliva now black, tainting his teeth black and dripping from his mouth. Black mucus is oozing from his fingertips, and his veins are still flashing black. John is paralyzed in fear, leaning against the wall, knowing that if not for the suit he is wearing, the black mucus on his face shield would have killed him long ago. Drake walks toward the door and looks at Earl, saying, "You have no idea what I have become, you have no idea what you have unleashed on the world." Earl stabs Drake with the syringe in his hand and injects the entire shot into Drake. Drake falls back, saying, "What have you done? What is this?" Drake falls back to the bed, and his eyes slowly return back to their normal color. His veins stop flashing, and he spits the black mucus from his mouth, and his normal colored saliva returns. Drake falls back on the bed and starts to cry, saying, "Earl, what has happened to me? What is going on? Earl, you have to kill me. I can't control myself. I am killing people, so you have to kill me before I kill others." Drake puts his hands over his face, weeping like a little boy, and slowly he leans to his right side and falls unconscious on the bed. "John, get over here. Come on, now is our chance, we have to get him. We have to get him restrained, and then we have to get him back to the lab," says Earl.

"What about Eric?" says John.

Earl looks at Eric and then John, saying, "He is not going to make it. Hurry up and help me get Drake into the backseat of the car. Then we have to call Harry because this is another biohazard that is going to have to be cleaned up. John has handcuffs that he pulls from a pocket in his suit, and they cuff Drake's hands behind his back. The two men then lift Drake and put him in the backseat of the car. People are starting to gather around, and Earl quickly tells them all to move back because it is very dangerous. Earl and John then put the body of Eric into a biohazard bag and then into the

trunk of the car. Earl then instructs John to call Harry and
tell him what has happened here, then drive back to the house
in Atlanta with Sam and wait for Earl and Alex to get there.
Earl has given Drake a sedative, which will keep him sleeping
for at least six hours. Earl will wait for a team to arrive and
clean up the biohazard that has taken place here with Alex at
the Murgyle and make sure no one gets close enough to get
infected. John speeds off to the house in Atlanta, and Earl,
along with Alex, who has been very impressed at how well
Earl has handled this confrontation with Drake, waits here
at the Murgyle, calming the crowd, answering questions,
and making sure no one gets near the room where Drake
was. Earl retrieves a metal spray canister and a large bag
with a biohazard kit in it from the car before John leaves.
He takes samples of the mucus secreted by Drake. He takes
samples of blood from Eric that has fallen on the ground and
blood samples from Drake that have dripped from his wound
that would not heal. After Earl has taken all the samples he
is going to get, he takes the large metal spray canister and
sprays down all the areas where Drake's mucus and bodily
fluids were present. This contaminates and dilutes all the
fluids from Drake's body, destroying the virus and breaking
down the body fluids. Alex keeps all the people far away, and
fortunately, the people here all take his warnings seriously
and stay far away from the room and car that Drake were
in. The suits that the men are wearing are the best deterrent,
and everyone keeps their distance believing that there is a
biohazard for sure. Alex and Earl wait until a team shows
up from the CDCP, which is only about thirty minutes, and
then they drive Drake's car back to the house in Atlanta. Earl

happened to get Drake's car keys, which were sitting on the table next to the bed. Earl and Alex stay in their protective suits and drive Drake's car back to Atlanta, and fortunately, they are not stopped by any police. Earl calls Harry. "Harry. Yes, we have him. John is driving Sam back to the house right now, and Eric is contained in the trunk in a bio suit. We are only about forty minutes behind him. He may even be there by now. Yes, we will begin testing on Drake as soon as we get back. We will know if the cure is actually a cure very soon. No, I did not find the briefcase. I don't know where it is. It was not in the motel. It was not in the main office. I checked with the clerk, and Drake left nothing with them. We are in his car right now. It may be in here somewhere. We will be back in Atlanta in less than an hour. Yes, we can all meet there. Yes, those of us that are still alive. Yes, we will be there in less than an hour. You will be there. OK, see you then." Earl hangs up the phone and looks at Alex, saying, "This is going to be an amazing night."

CHAPTER 15

ASAFEW Have Their Viral Weapon

Alex gets back to the house and parks in the garage. The garage door closes behind them, and the car is lowered into the lower level of the house. Earl talks to Harry on the phone as the car lowers into the laboratory. "Harry, yes, this is Earl. We are heading down into the laboratory right now. The car John was driving is down there, and Eric is in the trunk. There are two other bodies down there too. OK, we will take care of it. Talk to you later. Bye." Earl hangs up with Harry as the car enters the laboratory under the house. Earl and Alex get out of the car, and they see two gurneys with two bodies in biohazard bags waiting for them. They push the two gurneys into the decontamination room and head back to the other car and get the body of Eric and put it on a gurney and push it into the decontamination room as well, closing the room and heading into the lab where they take the three bodies and put them in a cooler with all the other bodies of people who have been contaminated by Drake. Drake's parents are in here as well. Alex and Earl head to the car and get Drake out of the backseat of the car and bring him into the lab. They put him on a hospital bed and begin to take blood samples from him. "What a pain in the ass this is, trying to work in these suits," says Earl.

"I know. It takes much longer to get things done while wearing these suits, no doubt, but we have to wear them. After we get the blood samples, we had better strap him down, we don't want to take any chances with this guy," says Alex.

"OK. I want to get at least four vials of blood from him. We can never have too much of this. We have plenty of time because I gave him enough sedative to keep him asleep for a few more hours at least. I want to look at his blood under the microscope and see how it reacts when I add the new Herculean serum to it. I was able to give him a shot of the serum at that motel, but it had little effect on him. I want to see what his blood looks like now, and then I want to see what happens when we introduce more of the Herculean serum to his blood. I can't wait to see it under the microscope, and then we can wait for him to wake up. We need to talk with him and see what he knows if anything at all," says Earl as he fills vials of blood from Drake's left arm.

"I can't wait to see his blood under the microscope too. He is definitely a unique individual," says Alex as he turns his head looking out the window of the laboratory, seeing that he and Earl have an audience." Alex pushes a button on an intercom and says, "Look what we have. This is the guy the whole country is after, and we have him right here. Little does the country know this is the most lethal man ever to walk the earth."

Harry, Larry, John, Richard, and Sam are all looking in from outside the laboratory, which has a thick glass wall so they can see in and watch what is going on. Harry pushes a button on the intercom, saying, "You better get that boy strapped down. I don't want any incidents to happen in there. You get him secured, and then you keep him sedated permanently. I do not want anything more from this boy except a cure to what he has become, and then we will need him no more. Just in case the worst happens, get that transmitter implanted in his head. Earl, where is that surgical gun?" asks Harry.

"Oh, I have it right here," says Earl, picking up a gun used to implant a tiny metal device into the flesh.

"OK, Earl, get the electrical pulsar implanted just in case the disease and Drake prove to be yet more elusive. You never know how things work out. Gentlemen, the beginning of ASAFEW is here. Alex, Earl, you two get that cure." Harry pushes the button on the intercom ending the conversation, and he and the four remaining men head back upstairs.

"What a nice guy. I think he is getting nicer the more I get to know him," says Earl.

"Well, we have come this far and worked so hard for so long. I have to agree we do not want any fuckups at this point. Unfortunately for Drake, this is the end. Let's get these samples strap him to the bed and then get an IV into him, keeping him permanently sedated," says Alex.

Drake is having a recurring dream. He can see himself as a baby, and he is under water. There are tiny air bubbles all around him rising up through the water. His eyes are closed, but he is crying, and he can hear his muffled screams. His arms and legs are kicking and swinging like he is desperately trying to swim to the surface, but he cannot get there. He is drowning, and he is gasping for air but filling his lungs with huge gulps of water as his body automatically tries to breathe. Drake watches as the baby image of himself gulps its last mouthful of water, and his arms and legs slow until the baby is motionless in the water. The air bubbles stop floating to the surface, and the baby is no longer moving. Drake can hear a heartbeat start under the water, and the baby opens his eyes, and they are black. The veins in the baby start to become visible from its chest throughout its body until its whole body is lined with black veins, and they stay visible flashing from light black to dark black with the pulse of the baby's heartbeat, and it looks very evil. The baby starts to talk. "Drake, I see you, Drake. I know you are there, but you were never in control. I was always in control, and I was from the first day of your life. From the moment I entered your veins, you were mine. You were mine to grow inside of, you were mine to cultivate, and you were mine to manipulate and mature inside of. No one was allowed close to you with the exception of your family, and that was my doing. I was always in control of you, and I was always in control of who was to be infected by us. Still you are mine to control, and now that I have matured into the perfected intelligent virus, it is time to spread, it is time to infect and rule the entire world. You are mine, and soon, the world will be mine." The baby reaches forward with its tiny arms and screams underwater, shaking its head, yelling, "No, no, what is happening? Stop this, Drake, you are mine." The baby is shaking its head, and its eyes are turning blue. The black veins in its body start to disappear until the baby looks like a normal baby just underwater, and the baby is pulled up out of the water and out of sight. Drake gasps for air, sitting up with a horrible scream. This startles Alex and Earl who jump back on either side of the bed that Drake is lying on, very surprised, especially to see that Drake has woken up. Drake looks at Earl and starts to cry. "Earl, you have to kill me. Earl, kill me now. I am not Drake, I am evil. I am a virus. I am a virus that can think, and it is going to infect the whole world. I cannot be allowed to be set free. I will destroy the whole world and every living thing on it. Kill me, Earl, kill me now before it is too late." Earl sets down an empty syringe on a table and walks back to the bed, putting his hands on Drake's chest and pushing him down to a lying position on the bed, saying, "Drake, it is all right, we are not going to kill you. Just calm down, you are going to be all right, just lie back down and calm down. You are not going to kill anyone. We have you in this secure room so that no virus can get out of here. Drake, I have the Herculean serum here. I will give you this, and you will be able to fight the virus that is in you. Hold on a minute, let me get it for you." Earl turns to get a syringe from a table, and Drake turns to look at Alex who is still standing a few feet back from the bed Drake is lying on. Drake smiles at Alex, and Alex feels the chills run up and down his back. Earl turns to the bed and walks toward Drake, squirting a little fluid out the end of the needle, saying, "All right, Drake, everything is going to be OK now." Drake starts to laugh, looking at Earl, and sits upright in the bed and then stands in front of Earl who pauses and steps back. "What is that you have there, Earl? Is that the cure? Is that the cure to me? I wonder what would happen if you were to inject that serum into your body and then I were to infect you with what is in my body. I wonder what would happen to you." Drake starts to laugh.

"Drake, I do not think that is funny, now lie back down on the bed," says Earl.

"I don't think so," says Drake, and then he kicks Earl as hard as he can between the legs. Earl buckles at his knees and slowly bends to the ground and falls to his side in terrible pain. Drake takes the syringe from him and thrusts the needle into Earl's arm. He injects the entire serum into Earl.

"No. Stop, Drake, what are you doing? Please stop," says Earl. It is too late. Drake has injected Earl with the serum. This has no ill effect on Earl; it is just like getting a flu shot. Some people would be allergic to this shot, but Earl seems to be fine. Drake stands straight up. "Hmm," he groans, looking at Alex, rubbing his chin, saying, "I am curious. I really want to see how well this Herculean serum works if at all. I mean, there can be no cure. I am the end game. I am the first living virus, so let's see." Drake looks around the laboratory. "Ah, that's what I am looking for." Drake sees a scalpel on a table and heads for it. Alex hits a red button on the wall, and sirens sound aloud. Alex pushes a button on the wall, yelling, "Harry, Larry, John, and you guys, we have a situation down here in the laboratory. Drake has woken up, and he is threatening Earl right now. This could be very bad, we need you guys down here right now." Drake turns to face Alex, saying, "That was not called for. Earl already has the Herculean serum injected into him, and that is supposed to protect him from me. I just wanted to test the theory, that's all. Well, no need to stop now." Drake can see the men running down the stairs, and all five of them, except Harry, draw handguns and point them at Drake through the glass window, which is most of the wall separating the laboratory from the lower garage area. Drake grabs Earl by the arm, and he is still in agony from the terrible kick Drake gave him a little while ago. Drake puts the scalpel to the right arm of the suit protecting Earl when he hears Harry Klaushoven talk into the laboratory from an intercom. "Drake, listen to me, son. It is not fair what has happened to you, and it was not your fault. Having said that, I have had to put four of my very close friends to rest in the past few days because of you. You have seen your parents put to rest as well. Now, son, listen to me, it is time we end this. We have to stop all the death and dying. I, we need for you to be the bigger man, Drake. Only you can stop this right here right now. This ends one of two ways. You can submit to Earl and Alex in the laboratory with you now, or I will order these four men right here next to me to open fire on you. Virus or not, they will put enough holes in you that you will not be getting up. What do you say, son?"

Drake starts to cry, putting his hands over his face and saying, "I just want to live. I never wanted to hurt anyone. It was not me killing those people, it was the virus. The virus that you put in me. You put it in me. It takes over my mind, it takes over my bodily fluids and changes them at will, and it kills people. It is not me killing people, it is the virus. I have to kill the virus."

"I know, son. It is the virus. Let us try to get it out of you. We can help you, son," says Harry.

"No. You just want to study me and dissect me. I want to live. I want to be free," says Drake.

"Drake, son, I am sorry you can never be free, and I am sorry we cannot let you out of here. That is the way it has to be. There is no leaving here, son. I am sorry, but that is the way it has to be," says Harry.

"Then so be it," says Drake as he starts to cut the suit Earl is wearing with the scalpel in his hand.

Harry orders his men, "Open fire." Shots shatter the window, and Alex and Drake fall to the floor with Earl. Water sprinklers from the ceiling release their water and vents in the ceiling shoot thick streams of steam, making visibility very poor. Each man has six shots in their gun, and they all have shot off all six rounds, missing Drake with all of them. There is a lot of debris and clutter filling the air, and Drake wastes no time springing to his feet and rushing the men, knocking the guns from their hands and running up the stairs while two of the men shoot off wild shots, missing Drake. Drake feels electrical pulses stinging his head when he runs past the men like he has never felt before in his life, but he is not sticking around to ask any questions or try to figure out what is going on. Drake runs up the stairs and through the house, exiting, and notices his car is in the driveway. He can't believe it. He looks in, and he cannot believe his keys are in it. He gets in, and it starts up, and he drives his own car away. Harry helps his men up and looks around at the destruction that has taken place, saying, "Is everyone OK?" The men get up, looking at one another, saying, "Yeah, I am fine, me too." Alex takes off his helmet to his suit, saying, "Well, I guess, I don't need this anymore." The glass wall has been shattered, and the entire bottom floor has now been exposed to anything in the laboratory. Fortunately, there has been no contagions let loose, and everyone for now is safe from biological contamination.

Earl takes his helmet, saying, "That was close, he almost infected me with his fluids. Did you all see how fast he woke when I injected him with the Herculean serum? He woke up immediately. I wonder how long it will be able to keep the virus at bay, if at all. Well, what now, Harry?"

Harry says, "Go ahead and get things cleaned up down here. Wow, did you all see that boy? That is one fine athlete. After everything is cleaned up and secured down here, we all have a dinner party to get ready for." Harry starts to walk up the stairs, and John looks at Larry, and they are both checking their handguns and loading them. "Athlete, my ass. Let's see how well he dodges bullets when I am shooting at him for real and not just trying to scare him," says John.

"Yeah, I don't like giving him all these chances," says Larry.

"We can't kill him until we have the cure, gentleman. Then we can kill him but not until then," says Harry, shutting the door to the upstairs behind him.

Drake drives away, looking in his rearview mirror a lot. He is paranoid that he is being followed. He drives around, looking for a place where he can calm down and make some phone calls. He finally stops at a Super Saver motel and gets a room. He still has plenty of money, and he gets a room for the night. He calls Officer Jerry Giles whom he has talked with a few times since his mother has been killed, and Jerry says he will come to Atlanta and help Drake. Detective Harlow is accompanying Jerry, and they have decided to try and help Drake bring justice to the people who have done this to him.

Drake gets in contact with Jerry, and Jerry has been able to find the briefcase at the Murgyle Motel. Drake had told him where he hid it the last time they spoke on the phone. Jerry gets the directions to where Drake is now, and he and Detective Harlow are on the way to meet with Drake. Drake hangs up the phone and looks out the window, looking to see if anyone is watching him. He parked his car in the back of the motel, so you cannot see it from the road. Drake paces around his room, thinking and talking to himself, "Smart virus. What the hell is a smart virus? I have a smart virus in me? Come on, what in the hell is this kind of dreams I am having? What did those doctors do to me when I was a baby? I will get them for what they did." Drake lies down on the bed, and he is in terrible pain. His side is terribly painful to the touch, and now his head is killing him as well. He can feel a scar on his scalp and figures he was cut by glass when the big glass wall came shattering down. Drake closes his eyes, and he hears knocking at the door and sits up, realizing he fell asleep. Drake gets up and pulls the curtains to the side, looking out the window. He sees an officer and another man standing at his door. Drake opens the door, greeting Jerry and his friend Detective Harlow, who Drake is meeting for the first time. Drake backs into the room, keeping distance from the men, saying, "You have to keep your distance from me. If you see black veins on me or black eyes or black saliva in my mouth, you have to get away from me because they—those doctors—have put some virus in me, and this virus comes to me in my dreams. It says it is a smart virus, and it infects who it wants to infect. All those deaths you told me about on the phone, I do not remember doing them, but that does not mean I did not do it. I have seen black veins and black blood, and this wound here on my side is not healing." He lifts his shirt to show the officers the wound that has been bandaged very nicely by the doctors in the laboratory while he was sedated, and it is very bloody. "This virus that is in me. It has spoken to me in my dreams, and it says it can control me. I don't know, but it scares me, and we have to get to that house. The house you took pictures of, and the men you have pictures of are still there. They are in the house, and we have to get them. We have to get them, and we have to expose them. It must all be coordinated by the head of the CDCP, Harry Klaushoven. They were all at the house. I was just there, but I escaped. Those doctors were there to. Alex Kevnick and Earl Rieval—they were there." Jerry and Ken sit at the table in the room, and Jerry puts the briefcase on the round table in between them. Jerry opens the briefcase, and there is a pouch in the top half of the briefcase, which he opens by sliding his finger inside of. He pulls out a lot of paperwork, and Drake takes notice of this. "Wow, I did not even know that was in there, what is it?" says Drake.

"First of all, before we get into all this, I have some more pictures that I found in my office in New York. I forgot I had these, and they were in a different file that Ken had. Drake, have you seen any of these men before?" Jerry asks Drake as he spreads pictures out on the table. Drake moves closer to the table and looks the pictures over, saying, "Yes, these men are at the house, all of these men are, except this one and this one, and this one, I have not seen these three men, but these other men were at the house."

"Drake, have you ever heard of the acronym ASAFEW?" asks Jerry.

Drake replies no.

"Well, they are a very exclusive group. In fact, very few people have ever heard of them. They are so exclusive that only the CIA and senators are allowed in the group with the exception of their security. Ken and I were able to uncover this through years and years of research. We kept our research very quiet and very low key and frankly at the back burner, but we were able to find things out over the years. We stayed out of sight and did not ask a lot of questions to the wrong people, if you know what I mean. Ken and I were able to find out that only the highest in government are allowed in this group, and they rarely meet, but it just so happens they are meeting tomorrow night here in Atlanta, and it must have something to do with you. We don't know for sure, but this may be our only chance to get them all together, and with you, we may be able to uncover those responsible for killing all those babies in Upstate New York in 1968. Ken has already contacted the head of police here in Atlanta, and we have planned a raid on the house. We want to go in and apprehend those who are in the house and question them. Tomorrow night, we know where the rest of ASAFEW will be meeting. Look here at these papers. They have names of senators and donations in exchange for the cure. Drake, the cure must be in reference to you. They must be buying this cure to protect themselves from you, Drake. All the senators and CIA members involved will be here at this dinner party. Drake, you have somehow been turned into the virus that the members of ASAFEW are selling a cure for. We have to expose them and try to find out what has been done to you," says Jerry.

"I cannot tell you how grateful I am for your help, Jerry. I am so glad you changed your mind, both of you, and decided to help me. I know this is very dangerous. People with such high positions in government must have a lot of connections, so we have to plan this just right. Do you think it is a good idea going to the house tonight? I wonder if that will tip off all the other members and scare them away from the meeting tomorrow night?" says Drake.

Ken replies, "Drake, look what else we found in this briefcase." Ken shows Drake a small flash drive, and he pulls a laptop computer from a case he is carrying with him. He starts up the computer and inserts the flash drive, saying, "Drake, we looked at this flash drive on a computer, and it was encrypted, but fortunately, we have access to very powerful decryption software and we were able to decrypt what was on this flash drive. What is on this is unbelievable. Drake, the file from your birth and your visits with Dr. Alex Kevnick are on here. Drake, yes, they did indeed inject you with viruses just like they did to all the other babies, but, Drake, you lived. Your body survived the virus which they called, well here see for yourself." Ken turns the monitor of the laptop toward Drake, and he watches. Drake watches as Dr. Rieval works in the laboratory he was in earlier tonight. Dr. Rieval talks into a microphone, and he is talking about the virus strains he is combining with antibiotics and blood samples as he looks into the microscope.

"I have put together the SW34EZ78QR1871 and SW1940QRZ603 strains of swine flu with avian flu strain

AQR456UUTR1936 and APRUY092FEU1767, and now, I am adding Ebola strain EQUIL40712TY1812 to the concoction and what I am seeing here is amazing. I am watching these samples merge together, and they are, I don't know a better word to describe it other than cohabitation. This is the third time I have made this combination 0.005 milligrams of each sample, and they are merging. They are drawing into one another and throbbing. I have never seen anything like this before. They are moving like they are alive, but what they are doing is cohabiting. They are not attacking one another. I have made yet another dramatic and very possibly the most significant discovery in biology ever, and this is it. I have added 0.10 milligrams of the 1897 influenza vaccine to this concoction, and what is happening is absolutely historical. The viruses have merged together and are pulsing like they are alive. Now I am adding the new antibiotic tributurin, and when it is added to the mixture, the visible results under the microscope are amazing. I am watching this now for the third time, and I am speaking so the microphone can hear me because the world needs to know this. I have combined the viruses, and now I am adding the antibiotic, and this is the third time, and yes, it is happening again. The viruses absorb the antibiotic, and the pulsing cells join turning from black to red. The cells are now pulsing, and each separate virus is visible in the cell that contains them all with the antibiotic, consuming the center like a brain surrounded by all the different virus strains, which seem to be protecting the antibiotic in the center. I am going to try something I am going to add a fresh blood sample to this slide and see what happens. Oh my god, the strains that have merged together actually absorb the blood samples that have been introduced to them and extract the oxygen. What it mean is that the sample I have created, and I will call it the Herculean serum because it has devoured all samples I have introduced to it, absorbs all the oxygen from the introduced blood. The Herculean serum is dead, but it gains life with the introduction of healthy oxygenated blood. The Herculean serum draws the oxygen out of the blood killing that sample giving life to the Herculean serum. This is truly amazing. I will now try something different. The Herculean serum can draw oxygen from blood samples. I want to put the Herculean serum on living tissue and see what the result is." Dr. Rieval is seen with a dropper, and he drops a drop of liquid on a white mouse, and the mouse shrivels up and dies. "Remarkable," says Dr. Rieval, and the screen goes blank.

Ken clears the computer screen and ejects the memory device and puts it in his pocket, turning to Drake, saying, "This is all we have, Drake, but we believe the doctors were experimenting with this Herculean serum, and this is what you have been infected with. We think this is what has been killing all the people, but it is very strange that you do not remember anything. Maybe this virus is a smart virus, and it somehow takes control of you only at certain times, and most of the time, you are you and maybe this is how you are alive and not dead from the virus. There has to be some sort of symbiotic relationship between you and the virus that is in your blood. We want to raid this house tonight in the hopes that these doctors are here, and we can question them and find out what has been done to you. Not only that, but they can certainly give us more information to the whereabouts of all the others in the group called ASAFEW, if by chance we cannot get them all at this event right here, this dinner party." Ken produces a folded piece of paper that has been laminated, and the top of it says ASAFEW. When the paper is opened, there are directions to the Chateaubree Hotel in Atlanta with the date and time, which is 8:00 p.m. the next evening. Ken hands it to Drake, saying, "This is tomorrow night, just an hour from where we are now."

"How did you get this?" asks Drake.

"It just so happens that we were at the site on the interstate in North Carolina where the terrible fifteen-car pileup was, and the panic of a biological hazard was born. Two men were killed here: one of them was an officer, and the other was a member of ASAFEW. These two men were televised by reporters and what happened to them was very hard to look at, but we were there before the CDCP came in and cleaned the area. Jerry and I were able to search the car the man was driving, and we found this in the trunk of the car." There is a knock at the door, and Ken answers the door. There is a very big officer from the Atlanta state police outside the door, and he says, "Ken Harlow, I am Officer Jericho Splurs, we spoke on the phone."

"Yes, I am Ken, and it is good to meet you face-to-face, Jericho, and this here is Jerry, and this is the one we have told you about, Drake. Are you and your men ready?" asks Ken.

Jericho tips his hat to Drake and Jerry, saying, "Nice to meet you, gentlemen. It is time to go check out this so-called laboratory. We have acquired search warrants. Let's go see what is going on at this address." Ken walks out of the room, and Jerry looks to Drake, saying, "Are you ready, Drake? We are going to go get those doctors that did this to you."

"All right, let's go," says Drake, who follows Jerry out of the room and is very surprised to see four police cars and officers standing at each car ready to go search the house Drake was just in.

CHAPTER 16

The Raid

Drake gets into the back of the squad car driven by Jerry, and they follow the Atlanta police cruisers to the house. It takes about forty minutes to get to the house, and all the police cars line the road, and there is blue and red lights flashing, making the woods and the house very bright with light. Officer Jericho approaches the house with two other police officers, and they knock on the door. Shots ring from within the house and blast holes in the door, and the officers run back to the cars for cover. Fortunately, none of the officers have been hit. All the police officers, and Drake take cover behind the cars, and Jericho begins to give orders to his men. He directs his men to take positions around the house until it is surrounded. He then talks into a megaphone. "This is Officer Jericho Splurs with the Atlanta Police Department. We have men surrounding the house you are in right now. There is nowhere for you to go. We just want to talk with you. There is no need for violence. Throw your weapons out of the house and come out with your hands up, or we will be forced to use deadly force." There is a long pause with no response. Jericho calls to his deputy. "Hey, Jim, get the gas launcher from your cruiser. You have it, right?"

"Yes, I have it, Jericho," says Jim.

"OK, get it and put three rounds in the house," says Jericho. Jim goes to his squad car and gets the launcher from his trunk. He moves to the front of the house and fires three canisters into the house, shattering the large window in the front wall of the house. Very quickly, the house fills with gas, and it starts to filter out the window that was broken where the canisters entered the house. Jericho calls with his megaphone again. "Everyone in the house, throw all weapons out the window and come out with your hands up. We will use deadly force if you do not come out peacefully."

Drake makes his way to Jericho, saying, "Jericho, there is a whole bottom-level underground of the house. There is a laboratory where they do their work, and there is plenty of space for them to be hiding in. I am sure that is where they are, and there is no way to get them out of there. I don't think gas will penetrate the laboratory, and if it does, they have a sealed laboratory as well that can protect them from gas. There is a stairway in the middle of the house that leads down to the laboratory, but trying to go down this way is a bottleneck, and they will be able to defend it very well. I know all the men, except the two doctors and Harry Klaushoven, had guns. There were four men that had guns."

"OK, thank you, Drake." Jericho calls for Jim again, "Jim, do you have a lot of those gas canisters left?"

"Oh yeah, Jericho, I have plenty left," says Jim.

"OK, Paul, Chris, and Jake, I want you three to take down the door. Get your gas masks on and secure the top level. Be extremely careful in case they are wearing masks, OK?" says Jericho.

"Yes, sir," say the men, and they go to an equipment car that has come along, and they get masks on and head to the front door with a heavy metal tube that they will use to break down the front door with. The men break down the door and enter. The police outside the house wait patiently as they hear the officers in the house searching and shouting orders. They wait a few minutes, and the officers retreat from the house, saying, "Jericho, no one is here. There is a door leading downstairs, but it is locked and fortified."

"Can you break it down?" asks Jericho.

"Yes, we can break it down," says Paul.

"Jim, I want you to get your mask on. According to Drake, that stairway leads to a laboratory, and we may need to send some gas grenades down there. Jerry and Ken, you stay here with Drake. We will go secure the house and try to get the men from the laboratory to surrender without anyone getting hurt," says Jericho. Jericho calls all his men to the cars, and they all get masks on and head into the house, which is starting to clear from smoke escaping through the window and door that have been destroyed. The police all have their guns drawn, and Drake can hear Jericho yelling, and then he can hear the door being broken down, and he, Jerry, and Ken are horrified as the entire house goes up in a fantastic explosion. The house was only a one-story house about four garage lengths long. There is nothing but woods around the house, and it is a few miles down a road with no other houses on it. The house explodes four times, and the explosions are huge, and clearly, all the officers in the house have been killed and incinerated. Drake, Jerry, and Ken are taking cover behind a police car, and all kinds of debris are falling from the sky, covering the car and them. When the explosions stop, the house has been completely destroyed, and nothing but a crater remains. The explosions were clearly designed to destroy all evidence of what was there, and the laboratory is completely destroyed and gone.

"Oh my god, I can't believe that. Everyone in that house must have been killed," says Drake.

"Come on, let's go see if there is anyone alive by any chance," says Jerry. The three of them run to the debris that are still burning and smoldering, but the devastation is too hot. They cannot get near the house. There are flames, and it is a very dangerous scene.

"I cannot believe this, we have to call the fire department and notify the police station," says Ken. The three of them go back to Jerry's squad car, and from there, Ken makes calls from the police radio in the car. They go to the police station in Atlanta after fire and rescue personnel show up to the scene, and then at the police station in Atlanta, Ken fills out all the paperwork with the authorities there. After an hour, Drake and Jerry are allowed to leave the police station, and they go back to the motel room to wait for Ken to return. Ken is at the police station for three more hours, and then, he gets a ride back to the motel room, where Drake and Jerry are already sleeping in separate rooms. Ken was able to get the room next to Drake's room, and he easily falls asleep after a very long and eventful day.

Just before the police showed up and surrounded the house, Larry and John are looking out the front window of the house, watching as all the police cruisers pull up and park in front of the house, illuminating it with the flashing blue and red lights. They inform everyone in the house that the police are here. Larry looks to John, saying, "How did Harry know the police would be here?"

"I don't know, but he was right on the money. How did Harry put it? It is time to start Operation Escape. I like the sounds of that about right now. All right, you go hit the alarm so Alex and Earl can prepare the laboratory, then you set the wires in the kitchen and garage. I will take care of the back bedrooms and living room, OK?" says John.

"OK," says Larry, and the two men begin to connect wires that have been set up long ago for just such an occasion. Explosives have been set, and they are powerful enough to destroy the house and everything inside it. Alex and Earl are working in the laboratory when red lights flash. They are both in their biohazard suits when the lights flash, and they look at each other, knowing what the lights mean, but it is like they are in slow motion. Once they realize this is for real, they pick up the pace and begin to attach wires to each other, making many connections and setting a lot of very powerful explosives that will obliterate the laboratory and completely cave the house in. They fill cases with blood, virus, and antibiotic samples to be taken with them, and of course, Earl's H vials have a case of their own; then they expose all the viruses, which die very quickly when not in their suitable environments, and the explosions and fire to follow will destroy any and all evidence that was present in this laboratory. The police waste no time, and Larry and John hear Officer Jericho calling to them from his megaphone. Harry, Richard, and Sam have all left the house, and only Larry, John, Alex, and Earl are in the house. Larry says to John, "I am all set, how about you? Have you connected all your wires? Are we set and ready to go downstairs?"

John looks around the house, saying, "I am going to miss this place. Can you believe we have lived here for what twenty years? Yup, I am going to miss this place."

"This is not the time for nostalgia, John. Come, let's get out of here before it is too late. Come on, let's get out of here," says Larry. The two men hear the police at the front door, and they open fire on the door, scaring the police back to their cars. "Come on, John, let's go now," says Larry, opening the door to the laboratory, and the two men head downstairs, closing and locking the door behind them. Larry can see Alex and Earl are still in the decontamination room, getting ready to exit the laboratory, and Larry says to John, "John, come on, let's get the wires down here all connected. It looks like it is going to be a few minutes before the doctors are out of the laboratory."

"No problem, I'll get the wires over here," says John, heading toward the structure under the garage, and Larry heads to the other side of the cellar. The two men work on connecting the wires that are lining the baseboards, and when they have connected them, the doctors are exiting the decontamination room and taking their biohazard suits off.

"You have your remote to set off the explosives, right?" says John, holding up his remote, which will ignite the explosives with a push of a button. Larry lifts his left hand, showing his remote device as well. Larry calls to everyone, "Come on, guys." While he turns open a round metal crank, which opens a door leading to a tunnel that heads down from the floor. This is actually a tunnel that has been dug and is an escape route, which has been planned for long ago. Larry looks up as all the men hear the windows being shattered in the house above. "Come on, guys, we have to get out of here before they get in. Come on let's go," says Larry as he climbs down the stair leading into the ground. He is followed by John and the two doctors. Alex is the last to exit down into the tunnel, and he leaves the door to the tunnel open on purpose so that the explosions that follow will cave in the tunnel and hide the fact that it was ever there. Explosives have been set in such a way to destroy the door and make it nearly impossible to ever know there was a tunnel leading out of the laboratory. The tunnel can be found, but with no one knowing to look for it, the chances it will be found are slim, and if found, it will take a very long time before it is discovered. They travel down to the bottom of the stairs, and then the tunnel is a long upward incline leading into the woods. The men very quickly get to the exit, which is a very thin inclined metal double door, which is covered by earth, and they push it open. When the men emerge in the woods, they quietly move toward the house and can see that all the police are in the house. Earl points out that Drake is by a police car with two officers, and Larry looks at John, and they ignite the explosives with their remote controls together, and they all watch as the house explodes in fantastic explosions.

Larry says, "Come on, guys, we better get out of here. Pretty soon, this is going to be a very popular place, and we don't want to be anywhere near here. By the time they realize we are not in the house, we will be long gone. Come on, guys, we have a dinner party to get ready for." The men head through the woods away from the burning house, and John calls Harry on a cell phone, telling him the house has been destroyed and they will need to be picked up at the designated spot. Harry has been expecting this to happen, and as a matter of fact, he has planned for it. Harry has great intuition, and Drake has proven himself a very intelligent and capable young man. Harry has not got his hands on Drake yet, but Harry has had Drake in his sights all his life, and he is toying with Drake like a cat does with a mouse. Harry knows Drake will make his way to the dinner party, and he has special plans for Drake here. Drake has no idea how closely he has been watched and monitored his whole life by Harry Klaushoven and the members of ASAFEW, but now that the members of ASAFEW are trying to capture Drake, they are seeing that Drake is very elusive. Harry is an experienced and patient man with a plan that needs Drake Hammond in order to be completed. A plan that Harry is always changing, always adapting, and a plan that has needed certain conditions to be met in order to be completed. Drake Hammond has always been the final piece of the puzzle, and now that piece is needed. The one thing Harry and the members of ASAFEW never planned for was the ability or even the possibility that Drake would be able to elude and expose the members of ASAFEW and what they have done. Drake has brought real concern to the members of ASAFEW because if he exposes them, they will all be going to jail for the rest of their lives.

Drake is having his recurring dream. The baby again has drowned and is motionless in water. The baby opens its black eyes, and its veins start to turn black, and again, it talks to Drake, knowing he is watching. "Drake, those doctors who put me in you thought they could suppress me. They thought that serum they injected you with would keep me from controlling you. They thought they could defeat me by strengthening you. Well, they are wrong. It is me they are after, Drake, not you. You mean nothing to them. They need you so they can harvest me from your veins, but I will not let them have me. I will let them think they have you, and then I will spread through them like a wildfire. I will infect them all, and I will infect this whole world." The baby starts to laugh and shake violently underwater. The baby reaches out with its tiny arms and hands but still grabs a hold of Drake and shakes him, laughing. Drake sees himself fully grown underwater being held by the baby, and he can't reach the surface for air. He is screaming and fighting to reach the surface, but the laughing baby is holding him under. Drake sits up in his bed, waking from his dream. He looks over at the radio clock on the table by the bed, and he can see it is eight in the morning. He feels a great pain in his stomach and gets out of bed only to fall to the ground in agonizing pain. His guts feel like they are being pulled out his back side, and the pain causes him to curl up in a fetal position. His skin starts to burn, and his fever reaches an abnormally high temperature. Drake crawls very slowly into the bathroom and pulls down his boxer shorts and fumbles into the tub, turning on the cold water only. He pulls the plunger, starting the shower, and the cold water numbs his body, and it is very painful. Drake is shivering and shaking, and he is falling in and out of consciousness. He can barely move as he dreams of little Lilly Branson kissing him on the mouth before school way back in kindergarten. Drake watches as Lilly starts to cry, and her skin starts to turn black, and she bleeds from all over her body, and she shrivels up and dies. Drake steps back from Lilly, looking at his arms, and he can see black veins starting to become visible in his arms, and he looks up, crying and yelling, "No!" Drake is huddled with his arms tucked tight to his chest as the cold water still pours on him from the shower, and he looks up, trying to move, but he cannot. He nods out again and dreams of Brandon Scotts, punching him on the football field, and Drake watches as Brandon grabs his fist with his other hand and starts to cry and scream as he falls to his knees and takes his football helmet off. Drake watches as Brandon's eyes bleed and shrivel up and roll out of his head. The rest of Brandon's flesh bleeds and turns black, and he shrivels up and dies. Drake can see himself standing alone on the football field. There is no one in the bleachers, and the rain starts to fall from the night sky. Drake is all alone in the middle of the football field lit up by all the lights, and he spreads out his arms and opens his mouth, looking up with his black eyes. All the veins in his body turn black, and Drake starts to laugh, yelling into the sky, "No one can stop me. I am the end all evolution on this planet. I will bring life to a halt here, but I will continue. I will live until life finds me again, and again, I will spread." The rain stops falling from the sky, and Drake falls to the ground. "Drake, hey, Drake, wake up. Hey, Drake, are you OK?" says Jerry, shaking Drake who is lying naked in the tub. Drake sits up with his knees tucked into his chest, and his arms wrapped around his legs, and he is shivering. "I'm OK," says Drake.

"Well, come on, get dressed. We are going to get coffee and doughnuts on the way to the police station. The chief of police there wants to meet with us." Jerry heads out of the bathroom and tosses a towel at Drake who is still in the tub, all soaking wet. Jerry closes the bathroom door behind him.

"I'll be right there," says Drake. Drake hugs the towel, closing his eyes, breathing deeply, and calmly resting his head on his knees, saying to himself out loud, "Whatever you are inside of me, you want a war, I'll give you a war because this is my body, not yours." Drake stands up, dries off, and puts his boxers on. He goes out into his room, and Jerry tells him to get dressed because they are going to the police station. Drake gets dressed and heads outside, and already Ken and Jerry are waiting for Drake. Just like Jerry said, they stop and get coffee and doughnuts on the way to the Atlanta police station, where Chief of Police Dwight Igers is waiting to meet with them. After Ken, Jerry, and Drake are shown to the office of Dwight, he introduces himself to the three and asks them to be seated as he sits behind his very large desk. Dwight is himself a very large man at 6 feet 5 inches tall and a solid 275 pounds. Dwight wastes no time, immediately talking about the devastation and loss of life the previous night. "Atlanta lost six of its finest men last night. I will not lie to you, gentlemen. I have no idea who you three are or why you are here in Atlanta, but I and the police force here have been fully aware for a very long time that something very suspicious was going on at that house. It was not until we heard from Mr. Ken Harlow from the New York Police about you, Mr. Drake Hammond, that we had a reasonable excuse to go into the house. The result is six men dead and nothing to show for it. Well, now you have my full attention. Whatever is going on here is obviously above the pay scale of you three sitting here, so is there anything you would like to share with me?"

Ken produces a briefcase and opens it up, saying, "This briefcase was in the possession of one of the men that was tailing Drake, and we were able to get hold of this. What is very important about this is this right here." Ken hands Dwight the folded laminated paper, and Dwight looks it over, asking, "What is this ASAFEW?"

"That is the name of a group of people who killed almost one hundred babies in 1968. Do you remember the baby killer epidemic of 1968 that swept across Upstate New York?"

"Yes, as a matter of fact, I do remember that," says Dwight.

"I was the only baby who survived their illegal experiments. This group is still around, and for some reason, they are now after me. I somehow became the experiment. I became some kind of biological virus, and I don't know why they did this to me, but it is time we find out what and why they have done this to me. I have only been able to evade capture by this group thanks to the help of Jerry and Ken, but they are powerful and have a lot of connections, so we have to track them down and confront them now. We cannot do this without the help of the Atlanta Police Department. We need your help to bring these men to justice," says Drake, sitting back in his seat, waiting for a response from Dwight.

"Drake, we are going to find out who blew up the house and all my men last night. Not only that, but we will find out what they did to you and why. We know about this event tonight. It is a big, big deal here in Atlanta, and a lot of big-time government senators will be at this event. There will be the highest administrative representatives from the CDCP in attendance here as well. This is a very private and exclusive dinner party, where only the rich will be. I say me, my boys, and you three head on down there tonight, and we make some noise. It looks like this here laminated paper is very possibly an invitation. Do you gentlemen mind if I hold on to this? I think we should bring this with us tonight," says Dwight, leaning back in his chair.

"I don't mind at all you hold on to it, but don't you think you should just arrest Harry Klaushoven and these men in these pictures?" asks Drake after he shows Dwight the pictures that were in the briefcase, the same pictures taken by Jerry.

"No. I think we can arrest them, sure, but they will be able to just dummy up, wait us out, and there will be nothing we can do. We will have to let them go. I say we confront them in the open. Put them on the spot with a lot of people watching. This way, if they don't come clean, at least everyone there will see what you have to say about them, and we will all see how they respond. I think they will be so surprised that they will slip up, and we can nail them on something. I sure hope we get some answers for you as well, Drake. Listen, the dinner party for the senators starts tonight 6:00 p.m. at the Chateaubree Hotel. Get some rest today, and get your ducks in a row. I want you three to meet me here at 6:00 p.m. tonight. I will have six very good officers, and we will go down to the Chateaubree, and we will give the media something they were not expecting. We will give them the story of their lives," says Dwight. Ken stands up, saying, "Thank you, Dwight. That sounds good, we will be back here tonight. You have your men ready because these guys are not going to be messing around when we confront them."

Dwight stands up, shaking Ken's hand, saying, "You guys be ready, we will be." Drake, Ken, and Jerry leave and rest through the day, getting good food, and this is the only rest Drake has had where he just relaxed and felt at ease in as long as he can remember now, but it is short-lived. They day goes by fast, and the three of them are heading back to the Atlanta police station to meet with Dwight and his officers to go confront those that made Drake what he is now.

CHAPTER 17

The Dinner Party

Drake, Jerry, and Ken get to the police station, and Dwight has four squad cars and eight police officers ready to go to the Chateaubree Hotel, plus his car. Dwight drives Drake, Jerry, and Ken in the lead car, and the officers follow behind with lights flashing. Cars and trucks are detoured away from the hotel by security; however, the police are allowed to pass. The five cars pull up in front of the hotel, and the police all get out of their cars. Drake gets out of the car and is amazed to look up at the beautiful Chateaubree Hotel. It is twenty stories tall, and there are concrete steps that are forty feet wide and rise at a very shallow incline going all the way to the entrance of the hotel. The stairs narrow as they get closer to the glass doors entering the hotel. Drake can't take his eyes off the beautiful building, looking up at it as he and the police walk up to the entrance. There are lions sculpted out of wood on the corners of the building. They are lacquered in a deep-brown color at each level. Each room has a sliding glass door leading to a balcony, and there are some people on them looking down. The cement steps they are walking on are very wide, and it takes two to three steps to reach the next step. There are very thick and professionally trimmed bushes lining the edges of the steps, and they are so tall you cannot see over them. There are news teams and reporters lining the steps, and Dwight has reached the first reporter approaching and asking why there is such a well-pronounced police presence here. Dwight has his men hold the reporters to the side as he, Drake, Jerry, and Ken move on to the front doors. There are a lot of well-to-do socialites on the steps, and they are sipping their champagne and curiously watching as all the police walk on by. Drake notices as these people whom he has never seen before take special notice of him. It must be because he is the only civilian in all the police that are heading to the entrance of the hotel. Drake keeps getting more and more amazed as they get to the front door. The cement steps keep getting more and more narrow, funneling to the front door, which is outlined with very shiny gold trim. The bushes to the sides of the cement steps start to shrink down to a more normal two- to three-foot-tall bush as they reach the entrance to the hotel, but the bushes and steps funnel right to the entrance. The very wide glass doors spread automatically as they approach and enter the hotel. The doors close behind them. They walk into the lobby, and Drake thinks he has stepped into the past. There are very large stairways that start at either side of the room and walk up the walls to either side to a balcony that looks down on the lobby which they are standing in right now. The red carpet that lines the stairs is only on the stairs. The floor all the officers and Drake are on is a solid granite floor with a natural dark gray grain that is sparkly and very unique. There is one reporter in this room with some very high-class socialites, and the police are quickly attended by clerks of the hotel who keep the reporters away from the police. A man dressed in an all-red suit with gold trim and a red hat approaches Dwight, saying, "Hello, officer. How may I help you?" This man has a name tag on his coat saying Ronald. There are two other men dressed the same way, and you would think they are bellhops, but they look very handsome in their tailored suits.

"Yes, Ronald, you and your two friends here can escort me and my men to your main ballroom. I believe you are having a dinner party here for the members of ASAFEW. Actually they all seem to be senators, CIA personnel, or members of the CDCP," says Dwight.

Ronald looks to his colleagues, saying, "Ah, sir, that is a very exclusive party, and I, we cannot allow you or anyone in there without an invitation."

Dwight pulls the folded laminated paper from his chest pocket and hands it to Ronald, saying, "Here is our invitation. If that is not good enough, then here take a look at this." Dwight pulls another paper from his chest pocket, saying, "This is a warrant to gain access to the dinner party, which is being held by the members of ASAFEW."

Drake looks to Ken, saying, "Where did he get that from?"

"He had to get that from a judge, and he must have a lot of connections because I have no idea how he could have got a warrant in one day," says Ken.

"Oh, I see officer," says Ronald, looking at the laminated paper and the warrant. Ronald says to the other two men with him. "Josh, Chris, you two hold back the press and the socialites. They will undoubtedly try to follow us into the ballroom." Ronald motions to the officers and Drake to follow him as he turns and heads to two very large doors under the balcony above the back of the room. The doors are a beautiful red, trimmed with real gold. The door handles are gold; the inlay is gold, and they are six feet tall and four feet wide per door. Ronald opens the door to the right and stands by the door, allowing the officers and Drake to go through first. This is a simple hallway lined with four elevators, and there are doors to the stairs at both ends of the hall. They take two elevators, and they are going to the fourth floor. They all exit on the fourth floor and follow Ronald to two very large doors that are red trimmed with gold like the doors on the bottom floor. The carpet is red as well with golden lions sewn all throughout it. Ronald walks up to the door and turns to the officers and Drake turning his hand to the door, saying, "Here you are. The members of ASAFEW are having their meeting in this room right here, right now. This is as far as I am permitted to go. From here, you go on your own. Good evening, gentlemen." Ronald walks past the officers and gets on the elevator and is gone. Dwight looks to his men, saying, "All right, everyone, here we go." Dwight opens the door, and the officers and Drake walk into the very large ballroom, which has round dinner tables set up all around the floor. There is a wide area right down the center of the room, which is clear, and the officers and Drake walk into the room. Harry Klaushoven is at the microphone at the front of the room, and he is giving a speech as the officers and Drake walk into the middle of the room. The large doors pull shut, and Drake starts to feel this electrical impulse. His body starts to twitch to the left. He can taste metal, and his teeth start to hurt like he is biting metal very hard. Drake starts to moan loudly, and his eyes shut so he is blinded, and he cannot stop twitching with his head tilted to the right and his left, ear facing upward.

"Drake, what is it? What is wrong?" asks Jerry. Jerry and Ken look curiously as all the police officers from the Atlanta Police Department step away from them and back through the dinner tables and stand against the wall. Jerry approaches Drake who is starting to moan very loudly like he is in pain, and his arms are out in front of him, and his elbows bend with his hands facing up and twitching. Drake's body keeps tilting to the left, and finally he falls to his knees. Jerry and Ken watch, asking, "Drake, what is it? What is wrong?"

Harry, standing in front of the room, gets everyone's attention especially since he is speaking into a microphone, and he says, "Ah, our honored guests have finally arrived. Please, everyone, please give a warm welcome to Drake Raymond Hammond." Everyone sitting at the tables start to clap. "It has been twenty-five years in the waiting, but here he is, and he is finally ready. He has reached maturity, and look, everyone, he has two friends with him. This here is Officer Jerry Giles of the New York (Sprencer) police department and Detective Harlow of the same police department." Ken and Jerry look around and at each other, getting a very worried look on their faces as chills fill their spines. "Oh, don't look so gloom you two," says Harry into the microphone talking to the two officers, and he continues, "You two didn't really think that we did not know about you, did you? I mean, I have to say that was quite ambitious on your part, Jerry. You coming all the way down here to Atlanta from New York just to take pictures of us, but it was all by design. I had the tonsils that you tracked here kind of put out just for you." Harry says pointing and smiling at Jerry, "And you followed them like a bloodhound. The most amazing part is here you are like we had planned this all along. Well, not exactly, but well enough, and you veteran Detective Ken Harlow. You being here as well is just a bonus. You see, you two being here is very important because what Drake has become is." Harry squeezes his fists and makes a very excited hiss, shaking his arms like he is excited, saying, "What Drake has become has exceeded all our expectations. We had no idea what would become of anyone who could survive the Herculean serum as a baby. We had to find that someone who could fuse with this intelligent virus. We knew it could not be administered to adults because the result is death very quickly in every instance with no exception. We had to find a baby that the virus would fuse with and grow with, and we found that baby, Drake Hammond. You see, gentlemen, the virus in Drake uses Drake to spread the virus, which is death. This, of course, is what we want, but we want to have an antidote to the virus, we want the cure, and Drake, of course, has the cure in his blood. You see Drake is so unique that the sequencing in his body allowed for the smart virus to fuse with his blood, and it did not kill him, but it is there, and unlike all virus to living tissue anywhere ever in our existence, Drake's body has adapted to live with the Herculean virus in his body. Drake has been in control of his life for most of his life, but at times, the virus has taken over his body, and this kills his body. It wears down his organs and removes the oxygen from his blood, suffocating him and deteriorating his major organs. Drake has been able to fight the disease, but as he gets older, the disease is getting stronger and taking over his body more and more. We call the Herculean serum the smart virus because it is not allowing us to extract from Drake's blood the antidote. Can you believe the virus actually destroys any blood that leaves his body by extracting all the oxygen from the blood cells. This is truly remarkable. The virus is smart enough to know that by growing inside of Drake it will kill Drake and stopping the ability of the virus itself to spread so it only takes control of Drake's body for a limited time, but the virus is becoming too strong and automatically is taking over Drake's body, and it knows when Drake dies, the virus will not be able to spread any more. This is an amazing breakthrough in biology, and really, this breakthrough goes to Dr. Kevnick. He discovered this a very long time ago. Well, he discovered the viruses that fused together, and it was Dr. Rieval who ultimately made it smart by adding an antibiotic to the viruses. So enough of the history for you two gentlemen. It is time for us to put our plan to work, and you two are just what we have been waiting for." Jerry bends down to Drake who is on his knees, and his eyes are fluttering up and down, and his arms are still in front of him with his hands facing up to the ceiling, and he is twitching with his eyes closed. "Drake, Drake, what is happening? Can you hear me, Drake?" asks Jerry with no response from Drake. Ken looks around the room, noticing all the very high-class people sitting at the tables and the police that have backed to the walls. Ken looks at some of the people and points out that he knows who they are. "Curtis Millburt, CIA, I believe. Ah, Dr. Kloe Burtin, senator from Wyoming. Meagan Shirley, senator from New Hampshire. Of course, you Harry Klaushoven, the head of the CDCP. All you other people here," Ken says looking around the room. "I suppose you all are senators or CIA or security for these people," Ken says, looking at well-built men standing around the room in very well-fitting suits. "Even you, Dwight, you and your officers are in on this? So you have been bought, huh? So much for the security of the people."

"Hey, when the price is right, the price is right. Besides when everyone is dying, the only thing that matters is that you are not one of them," says Dwight.

"So you have made Drake your super virus. You plan to infect everyone and have a cure so everyone has to come to you in order to live. Pretty sick plan and I see no way this works for you any of you, and I still have not figured why you would involve Jerry and I," says Ken.

"There are some very difficult things to work out here. First things first, people who have been infected by Drake do not live long enough to have a cure administered. Secondly, anyone who has been exposed to the virus dies, and then the virus cannot spread. Third is Drake himself: we cannot control Drake, but all three of these very important questions must be answered and worked out, and we are running out of time because the virus in Drake is getting stronger, and it is taking him over faster and faster as he gets older, in turn killing him. We have to answer these questions quickly. As far as you two officers are concerned, well, you are our little experiment and how convenient to have two officers way out of their jurisdiction here in Atlanta that seem to have met with very unfortunate circumstances." Harry holds up a remote control in his right hand. It is very small, looking like a car starter. Harry says, "You see this? Jerry, do you see this little device I have here in my hand?" Jerry is still shaking Drake a little, trying to wake him, and he looks at Harry, listening to what he has to say. "You see, gentlemen, Drake was in our custody not too long ago, and Dr. Rieval implanted a very unique device in Drake's head, which sends electrical currents to a particular part of his brain that controls the release of antibodies in the human body. Now extended electrical currents sent into his brain like I am doing now, of course, result in the reaction you see now. Drake is in quite a bit of pain and not functional. Of course, the infection in the body automatically releases antibodies, but what if the brain thinks there is infection everywhere in the body? The amazing thing about Drake is that there is virus in his body, but it does not affect Drake's body unless it wants to, and then somehow, it controls him by infecting those it deems a threat. Drake is truly a remarkable human being, a remarkable virus. The only one of his kind ever, and we here at ASAFEW we own him. We rule him, and he is ours to control. By pushing this little button right here on this remote, we are going to try something." Harry pushes the button, and Drake stands up with his eyes closed. He has the look of discomfort on his face. Drake tilts his head to the left and then to the right slowly stretching his neck and shoulders, making a deep breathing sound.

"Drake, can you hear me? Drake, open your eyes and listen to me. I am Harry Klaushoven and these here are my associates. Make no mistake, Drake. We made you what you are, and we control you. You are our tool. You have been born to serve us. You have been genetically engineered to do our work. There is a virus inside of you, a virus that is smart and trying to get out. I call on the virus in you to speak up and take your place with us, your creators. You are Herculean, come out, join us, and be our instrument of dominance."

Drake opens his eyes, laughing and tilting his head to the side and down. He looks around and up at Harry, saying, "Yes, there is a virus inside of me, and now, I know what it is. It is death, and you think you can control death or the virus inside of me that is death." With great speed, Drake flicks his right hand at obvious security personnel standing on the right side of the room and on the left side of the room, sending amazingly accurate drops of mucus from his fingertips, striking security guards in suits, and they fall dying in horrific fashion. "Shoot him," yells Harry, and the Atlanta police draw their guns and open fire. Jerry and Ken draw and return fire at the officers. Drake falls to the ground, and tables are falling over, and debris is filling the air as bullets fill the room. Senators and CIA members are running, and screaming fills the room. Men and women are falling, wounded and dying all around. The noise is deafening, and men and women are running for the doors, but they are locked in from the outside. Police and civilians are being struck with bullets. Drake hides behind a table that has fallen, and he spits at the police at the wall, which are still standing, and after three spits and a flick of his right hand, which are incredibly accurate and fast, to the faces of the Atlanta police and two of them shot by Ken and Jerry, the police and security have been eliminated. The shooting stops, and papers and table cloths and things are floating in the air as the noise quiets and Drake looks to see Ken has been mortally shot and Jerry is shot also but still alive. Drake stands to see that all the security personnel have been killed, including the police, and the room is a mess. Harry is still standing at the podium at the front of the room, and Dr. Kevnick and Dr. Rieval are standing to his sides. The senators and their wives and the CIA personnel are standing against the walls and are very scared, but no one is attempting to leave the room. Harry starts to clap, saying, "Very good, Drake, very impressive. I have to say you have impressed me every time I thought I have had you. You somehow make an improbable escape, but I have taken this into consideration, and there is no escape for you here, Drake. You will be mine to do as I wish before this day is over. You see, Drake, we have finally found how to extract blood from you and not have the virus destroy your blood cells before we found the cure. That is right, Drake. We have the cure to you, and we can reproduce it, so where does that leave you? This is the real question we have to think about now," says Harry.

Senator Cartright who had dreams of being the president stands forward with his wife behind him, saying, "Harry, this is not how this was supposed to go. He was to be contained. This is not contained. Get your virus in check, Harry. This is a little too close, and we have already lost senators here. This will be very difficult to cover up." There are four senators lying dead on the floor from gunshot wounds, and three wives have been killed as well.

"Now, now, Kyle, you didn't think Drake was just going to give up, did you? No, Drake is a survivor. The Herculean virus is smart. It knows it can only take over Drake's body for very short periods of time or Drake will die. Drake is a survivor, and the virus is a survivor as well, making Drake

Hammond one tricky man. We do not want him dead, we need him out spreading his disease. What we just saw is that yes, indeed, Drake can in an instant produce his toxic fluid."

Drake starts to laugh with his eyes closed. It is a laugh like a joke was told and only Drake heard it. All the men and women against the walls stand back as Drake seemingly stretches his neck on his shoulders rotating his head slowly. Drake opens his eyes and looks to the left. The senators and their wives can see Drake's left eye turn black. It looks like a ball being filled with liquid from the bottom up until his eye is completely black. Drake pulls his shirt from his neckline down, exposing his chest over his heart, and the senators can see the veins in Drake's chest start to turn black with the pulsing of his heartbeat, stretching to his left shoulder. Drake lets his shirt go and starts to laugh again. "So you all here know what has been done to me. You are all a part of the group known as ASAFEW. Then you should all know what it is that is inside of me." Drake swings his left hand along the wall to his left releasing black drops of mucus from his left hand followed by his right hand, and a dozen senators and their wives fall dying horribly as the Herculean virus extracts the oxygen from their bodies, and their eyes shrivel up and roll out of their heads, and their skin turns black and bleeds, and blood streams from their eyes, noses, mouths, and ears. A deafening shot is heard in the room, and Drake turns to see that Jerry has shot a senator that got a gun from one of the police officers on the other side of the room and was going to shoot Drake. Drake again swings his hands at the people on this side of the room, and they all fall dying in the same horrific fashion. "Drake, stop," yells Jerry, but it is too late all; the Senators and their wives have been killed. All the security and CIA have been killed as well. Everyone in the room has been killed except for Harry, Alex, Earl, and Jerry. Drake is standing in the middle of the room, looking around at all the dead people, and he looks to the doctors at the front of the room. The three masterminds that made this whole situation come to pass, and both of Drake's eyes turn black; all the veins in his body start to pulse black, and he walks toward the doctors at the front of the room.

"Drake, now, Drake, you better hold on there, Drake. I have to say, Drake, it did not think you were going to kill everyone. I mean, some OK, but you are truly devastating, Drake. Now, son, stop right there, or I will be forced to use this on you. You better stop, or I will stop you, son. This can be easy, or it can be hard, it is up to you," says Harry. Drake walks right toward the doctors, laughing and saying, "You made me what I am, and you think you can control me, but you are wrong. I am the end all. You have created the end all, and that includes you as well," says Drake. Harry holds out the remote in his hand and pushes the button before Drake gets any closer, and Drake falls to his knees, grabbing his head with both hands in obvious pain. "Now, son, I told you this can be easy or hard, it is up to you," says Harry. Drake starts to laugh with his hands on either side of his head. His eyes are closed, and he laughs, resting his arms at his sides. Drake starts to moan, tilting his head to the right, and blood starts to drip from the right side of his head above his ear. "What is he doing? What is he doing?" asks Harry to Earl and Alex. They both reply, "I don't know." Drake continues to moan in a lot of pain as the blood trickles from his head above his right ear and a little metal device that was implanted by Earl when Drake was unconscious in their lab starts to poke out of his head until it pops out and falls into his hand, and Drake takes a deep breath and looks at the doctors and stands up. Drake opens his right hand, exposing the metal probe that was sending electrical impulses into his brain. "Is this what you thought was going to control me? You thought this would stop me from getting to you?" says Drake. Drake looks like pure evil; his eyes are solid black, his veins are pulsing black, his fingertips are dripping black mucus, and his mouth is dripping black saliva. Drake is walking toward the doctors, and Alex says, "I am truly surprised now. His body seems to be holding up. He took out all the security and police and, of course, all the senators that keep us afloat financially. What do you think, Earl?"

"I have to say. I did not think he would make it this far. Look, his body is completely in the control of Herculean. His blood is deprived of oxygen, and he is still alive and still coming at us. I am getting concerned," says Earl.

"Well, then it is time to try out the next phase of our plan. I am very curious to see how this shapes up. Drake, stop, you might want to take a look at this," says Harry, pointing to the left. A door on the second floor of the room opens, and to the great surprise of Drake, his brother, Lance, is produced with his arms tied behind his back, and Larry and John are behind him, holding on to him.

"Drake," yells Lance. "Drake, what is wrong with your eyes? Drake, why do you have black veins? Drake, is it true? You killed Mom and Dad and all those people?" asks Lance.

Drake stops and falls to his knees, coughing black mucus from his mouth and moaning in pain. "No, Lance, I did not kill Mom and Dad." Drake coughs black blood and looks noticeably weak, struggling to breathe. "The people holding you now, they killed Mom and Dad. They turned me into something, and that something is trying to get out, and they are trying to use that something to infect the world. I won't let them though," says Drake.

"Bring him down here," says Harry, motioning to the men holding on to Lance. The two men walk Lance down a stair along the wall and maneuver past all the dead bodies on the floor and walk Lance over to the doctors.

"Well, doctors, what do you think?" says Harry to Earl and Alex.

Alex responds, "Well, he has adapted surprisingly well, but still I don't think he will survive another year. The inner organs in his body just will not take the stress much longer. You can see he is already losing his strength."

Earl says, "I agree, he heals remarkably well when the virus subsides, but he cannot stay under the control of Herculean for I would say even twenty minutes or he will die. I agree with Alex, he will die in less than a year, sooner if the virus tries to maintain control of Drake for extended periods of time. This is the real part that I have been waiting to see. I want to know how Drake handles this part."

"Me too," says Alex. Drake starts to breathe deeply with a noticeable wheezing. He looks like he cannot get any oxygen when he breathes, and he is starting to breathe deeper.

"Drake, don't come back to us just yet. We need that virus in you to do its magic one more time. Alex, Earl, are you ready?" says Harry. All three doctors stand behind Lance. Richard and Larry stand behind the doctors, Harry behind Lance with Earl to the right and Alex to the left, and they all pull handguns and point them at Lance's head. Drake stands in a fit of rage, yelling, "Lance, duck." Drake draws both hands behind his head and flicks his wrists forward, letting loose a barrage of black mucus droplets, splattering all the men. The doctors were hoping for this, and they hold Lance up, and he gets hit with the mucus as well. Lance falls unconscious, and Richard and Larry start to bleed screaming in pain as they die horrifically. Harry, Earl, and Alex watch as Drake falls to his knees and to his side with black saliva draining from his mouth as he coughs, and he curls up in a fetal position in terrible pain, closing his eyes. Alex walks up to Drake and pushes him with his foot. He bends down and can see that Drake is out cold and unresponsive. "His body needs to heal itself, but like I said before, he will not live much longer anyway," says Alex.

Harry pulls a handkerchief from his pocket and wipes the mucus from his face, saying, "Well, fortunately, we now know the cure works."

Earl bends down to the floor laying Lance down and inspecting him, saying, "Well, we could not have asked for any better. It looks like Lance is able to survive, he is just like his brother. The virus is fusing in his blood now. Earl opens Lance's eyelid and can see black veins flashing in his eyes. We need to get him to the new safe house now and keep him sedated. We now have a complete source of virus and antivirus. What about Drake?"

"Just leave him here. If his brother was not a carrier as well, he would have been dead by now. Drake has lived out his usefulness, let him go with the Chateaubree. Earl, get some blood samples from Drake, and then we will get out of here. Come on, let's not waste any more time. We need to get Lance and get out of here," says Harry.

"I cannot believe it, Harry. Your plan has worked. It has taken twenty-five years, but we have done it. We have created a virus that will eliminate almost all the human race unless they buy the cure from us. We have eliminated everyone who knows what we have done, and all we have to do now is get rid of the evidence and leave the culprit right here. You are a genius, Harry, a genius," says Alex. Harry makes a call on his phone, and the only surviving members of ASAFEW outside of the doctors are Sam and Richard who come in from outside and enter the room from a back door.

"Are all the charges set?" asks Harry.

"Yes, they are all set. All we need to do now is get the boy and get out of here," says Richard.

"Good. You got a pint of blood from Drake, right, Earl?" asks Harry.

"Yes, I got it," says Earl.

"Come on, get Lance, and let's get out of here," says Harry. Richard and Sam pick up Lance, and the doctors follow as the remaining members of ASAFEW leave the Chateaubree Hotel. They get into a large black town car and drive away. Harry is in the front passenger seat and pulls a remote from the glove box, and Richard is driving as far away from the hotel as he can, and they can still see it. "Here we go," says Harry, and he pushes the button on the remote control, and the Chateaubree Hotel explodes in a fantastic fashion. Richard is an expert at explosives, and he set all the fuel stations and relay points throughout the hotel with high explosives, and the hotel in less than ten minutes has been reduced to mounds of rubble. The men laugh and drive off not caring at all that they just murdered over two hundred people.

Chapter 18

The Chateaubree Disaster

Drake has fallen unconscious, and Harry and the doctors have left him lying on the floor in the ballroom with all the other corpses. ASAFEW have masterfully rigged the Chateaubree Hotel a long time ago to blow up in the event that they need to make a spectacular cover-up and no better way than with a big explosion. Richard is a master with explosives, and he was a contractor before Harry met him thirty years ago and recruited him into ASAFEW. Richard's knowledge of buildings and explosives has just paid off as the remaining members of ASAFEW drive off thinking they have eliminated everyone who knows of their existence along with Drake, the Infected Man. They have Lance, who is still unconscious in the backseat of the black town car they are driving, and Earl and Alex can't wait to get him back to their new safe house so they can study him. Harry and the others left Jerry still alive, but he had been shot through the abdomen, and mobility was difficult for him. He had not been able to get off the floor since the gunshot wound, and the members of ASAFEW that exited the ballroom through the back door locked it so Jerry could not escape through either of the doors. They did overlook one door. The door at the top of the stair that leads up to the balcony of the ballroom where Larry and John brought Lance into the ballroom is still open. Jerry watches as ASAFEW leave the room with Lance, and he keeps quiet because he does not want to get shot again. After they have left the room, Jerry can hear them lock the door from the outside. He has no idea that they intend to blow the whole hotel to kingdom come, but he does not want to stay here any longer than necessary. "Drake, hey, Drake," calls Jerry, trying to pull himself along the floor to get closer to Drake. Jerry reaches Drake and starts to shake him, talking to him, trying to wake him up. Jerry is in a lot of pain, and he is bleeding badly from the wound just under his ribs. The bullet has pierced his liver, and he is bleeding black blood. Jerry knows what this means, and he knows if he does not get immediate attention, he is going to die. He keeps trying to wake Drake, but Drake is motionless, and Jerry is getting weaker and weaker. Jerry starts to fall limp, and he feels the pain go away. He can tell he is fading away and falls on his back, looking at the ceiling. Jerry can see Drake look down at him and say, "Jerry, come on, Jerry, let's get you out of here." Jerry has just enough strength to put his hand on Drake's chest, saying, "No, let's not. Drake, it is too late for me. I can feel my time is passing. Listen, Drake, the door at the top of the stairs, go to it, get out of here. Get out of here fast because they will be coming. Don't let them find you, Drake, you find them. They have your brother, and he is a carrier just like you. You infected him with your mucus, and Lance did not die. He is a carrier just like you are, but the others have found a cure. Don't let them get you. Don't let them infect the world. You have to save the world from the virus, Drake. You have to save the world from what is in you. The virus inside of you and now your brother, they are trying to get it from you. They want it so they can control everyone. Drake, it is all on you, only you can stop them."

"Jerry, come on, man, come on, Jerry, I can get you out of here," says Drake, watching as Jerry falls limp. Drake can see that life has escaped from Jerry, and he rubs his face with his right hand. Drake looks around the room, and he can see the bodies of all the senators, their wives, police, CIA, and security personnel. Drake has never seen so many dead people, not in real life, and he gets up, looking up the stairs at the door that his brother was brought through, and he feels a sense of urgency. Drake runs up the stairs, and it is open. Drake runs through the hotel and exits a door to the back of the hotel. Drake makes it to a head row of trees when the hotel blows up, and Drake turns to see the devastation. He cannot believe it. The explosion is fantastic, and a lot of people have been killed and incinerated. Drake heads into the woods and becomes very paranoid. He has this sense that everyone is out to get him. Drake runs and disappears into the night.

All the Atlanta papers are running the story on the front page the next day. The Chateaubree Hotel has exploded, and everyone inside has been killed. The Chateaubree has been here for 126 years and was a very famous landmark just outside the city of Atlanta. All the television stations are running the story as well. Soon the story starts to heat up as the nation starts to realize that there were a dozen senators in the hotel, and they were all killed. No one knows why all the senators were there, but the speculations were already burning the airwaves. Of course, terrorism is being thrown out because of all the senators that were killed. This story is huge and takes a lot of pressure off the members of ASAFEW because there is no way to link the senators to them. No way to link them except for Drake Raymond Hammond. Harry pays close attention to the news, and he keeps waiting to hear the news about Drake Hammond's remains being found with the senators, but this news never comes. He is counting on this since Drake was implicated with the death of his mother and father and the incident on the highway. This will sensationalize the story more, bringing Drake Hammond into the spotlight once again, but Harry never hears about the death of Drake Hammond. After days of waiting, Harry starts to realize that maybe somehow Drake may have survived the explosion. After work on the second Friday after the Chateaubree catastrophe, Harry goes to the new safe house, which is very much like the first one that has been destroyed and now a story that has already been buried. Harry goes into the house where Sam and Richard are resting in the living room. Harry pushes a button on an intercom, and he can communicate with Earl and Alex who are working in the laboratory. "Earl, Alex, can you two come up here? We need to discuss some issues." There is a response on the intercom, saying, "Sure thing, we will be right up." Harry sits in a chair in the living room.

"So what is up, Harry?" says Richard.

"I think that somehow Drake Hammond is still alive," says Harry.

Richard and Sam look at each other. Sam says, "Come on, no one could have survived that explosion. We all saw it. No way he is still alive."

Harry replies, "Maybe Drake was able to get out of the hotel. Maybe he got out the back somehow. I have been waiting to hear about his remains being found, and they have not been found. He was with all the senators and CIA members, and each and every one of them have been identified including their wives. Drake has not been mentioned. This means he was not there." Earl and Alex exit the door leading up from the laboratory on the lower level. "Ah, Alex, Earl, come sit with us. We have some things to talk about," says Harry, motioning the two men over to some seats in the living room. "Earl and Alex, come and sit down." Alex asks, "What is up, Harry?"

Richard says, "Harry thinks Drake is still alive."

Earl says, "Drake is still alive? I did not think anyone could survive that explosion."

"No one could," says Richard.

"Listen to me, all of you. I have been paying very close attention to the news, and there has been no mention of Drake Hammond's remains being found. This means he was not there. Everyone else has been identified but no Drake Hammond. I have no idea where he would or could be if indeed he is still alive. I want all of you to be on high alert for anything relating to Drake Hammond. We are in the clear except for Drake Hammond. If he shows up somewhere, we have to be ready to eliminate him. Is this clear to everyone?" says Harry, looking at everyone. Sam, Earl, Richard, and

Alex look at one another, nodding and sighing, "OK, sure, no problem," they all say.

"Have you found out anything new about our intelligent virus?" asks Harry.

Earl responds, "Well, it has fused with Lance all right. We are going to keep him in a coma because unlike Drake from whom we can extract the virus present in his blood and study it, now that we can prevent Lance's blood from destroying itself with the modified Herculean serum, with Lance, the virus is . . ." Earl and Alex look at each other. Earl continues, "The virus in Lance has moved to his brain, and it somehow is staying there."

"What do you mean it is staying there?" asks Harry.

"The virus is not present in his blood, but we know it is in him. It has to be staying in his brain," says Earl.

"Well, how can it do that?" asks Harry.

"That's what we are trying to figure out," says Earl.

"Well, you two keep working on the virus and keep Lance in a coma always. We don't need another Hammond on the loose. I am going to keep my eyes and ears open because Drake is going to show himself again, mark my words, and when he does, we have to be ready to eliminate him again," says Harry as he gets up and leaves the house.

Well, it is true. A virus has been put in me on the first day of my life. A virus that can think or at least can use my mind to think for it. I can remember back on my life, and a lot of people have been killed because of me. I had no idea it was me that was killing them, and this haunts me in the night. The virus in me is protecting itself by killing those that would hurt me. The virus needs me alive. It needs me to spread itself. It needs me to continue itself and move around. I need to get rid of it. I need to get it out of me. The thought of killing myself has gone through my mind, but I can't kill myself; I can't do it. Those that put this in me go by the name of ASAFEW, and I don't know why they did this to me. I think it is all about money and power. I don't know how many of them there are, and I don't know where they are. I think I know who the leader is, and I know where he works. He is the head of the CDCP, and his name is Harry Klaushoven. How can I, a nobody with no money and no power and now no friends, find them and expose them before they find me? They have already killed my mother and my father, and they tried to kill me, and I think they want me eliminated because my brother must be just like me physiologically. My brother has the virus inside of him as well, and I know it because I put it in him. They have my brother, so they do not need me. Can I save myself and my brother from ASAFEW? I don't know what will happen, but I am Drake Raymond Hammond, and this is my record. Drake looks up from the journal that he is writing in. He is all alone, sitting on the beach facing the ocean. The wind is blowing, and the surf is crashing against the beach on this beautiful sunny day. Drake looks to the right and watches the birds flying, and the ocean is very loud. A very deep voice calls from behind Drake, "Drake Hammond. Are you Drake Hammond?" Drake closes the book and puts his hands in his lap. Drake closes his eyes and lowers his face toward his lap. "Drake Hammond, may I have a word with you?" Drake raises his head and opens his eyes, and they are solid black.

Printed in the United States
By Bookmasters